CELESTIAL MAGIC

MYRTLEWOOD MYSTERIES BOOK 4

IRIS BEAGLEHOLE

CHAPTER
ONE

The heady scent of flowers drifted through the hot summer air. Music pumped, vibrating through the earth.

Rosemary moved in a fever, dancing as if possessed, under the lights in the crowd. She swayed and jumped and turned and flipped her hair from side to side as she danced, surrounded by people she didn't know and didn't care to know, losing herself in the movement of her own body.

Just then, she caught sight of him standing at the side of the crowd, wearing a suit as he normally would, but this time without a tie. The top shirt buttons, undone and hanging loose, his eyes burning with desire, his hair swept back.

Rosemary felt her mouth water as he moved towards her through the crowd.

She continued dancing, keeping her eyes on him until he got to her, reaching out for her, touching her shoulder.

"Come away with me," he said. "You know you want this. We both do..."

He took her hand and led her away from the crowd, through a

dense patch of forest. They moved at vampire speed, as Burk lifted her up and carried her to a hilltop. He set her down, soft grass beneath their feet. He laid her down and kissed her.

Rosemary relaxed, surrendering to all kinds of pleasure.

She jerked awake in her bed, mildly alarmed and shaking herself. The dream had been so vivid and intense and pleasurable.

Even though Rosemary hated to admit it, she wanted to go back there and be with a certain sexy, if ancient, vampire.

"No, no, no," Rosemary muttered, pulling herself out of bed.

Of course, it had been far too long. And she would be the first to admit it. She hadn't been intimate with anyone for some years, not properly, and she hadn't wanted to be.

Rosemary relished her independence. Besides, her priorities were already overloaded with looking after her teenage fae-slash-human and adjusting to a new town and a new magical way of life. Not to mention starting her own business, learning all about how to become a chocolatier and how to run the admin and financial side of things.

She started making her way out of her room, but the dream kept lingering seductively in the air, as if trying to lure her back into sleep. "Not going to happen," Rosemary said to herself.

"What's not going to happen?" Athena asked from the hallway landing.

"Nothing," said Rosemary. "I just had a weird dream, that's all."

She followed her daughter downstairs and began their usual morning routine of making toast and tea.

"I really wish I learned about all of this business stuff earlier on," said Rosemary. "I already missed the big chocolate seasons — Valentine's Day and Easter. Not to mention Mother's Day. By the time my business is fully up and running, well...who knows when that will be. We're heading into the heat of summer when chocolate melts and makes a big mess."

"Oh, stop your moaning," said Athena. "It's your own fault you didn't set it up earlier."

"It wasn't my fault," said Rosemary. "I was artfully putting it off. It was whatever component of my brain likes to self-sabotage that's behind it all. Not me as a whole person."

"Whatever helps you sleep at night," said Athena. "And speaking of that, what was your dream about?" she asked with a teasing lilt to her voice.

"I'm not telling you," said Rosemary glumly. "It was a private and adult matter."

"You basically just gave it away! Now what? Which of the three stooges was it?"

"Athena!" Rosemary said with a tone of mock outrage.

"Well, I think it would be going a bit far to call them The Three Musketeers, don't you, Mum? And you hate it when I call them your suitors."

"That's a good point," said Rosemary. "Why don't you just call them by their names and finally come to terms with the fact that your mother does not have a romantic life whatsoever?"

"Well, somebody's got to," said Athena. "I need something to entertain myself with."

"It's not natural for you to be obsessed with my love life."

"Mum! That's gross. I just want to play matchmaker. You never give me a chance."

Rosemary sighed. "Look, we've got bigger fish to fry. Off to school with you."

"Fine," said Athena, picking up her plate of toast and sculling back her mug of tea.

"Finish your breakfast first," said Rosemary.

"What's the point? It's not like I have to go far." She opened the door to the east wing of the house. "I'll see you later." She waved to her mother and toddled off down the hallway to the makeshift school.

After the official Myrtlewood campus had been largely scorched by a magical fire, not too long before, Thorn Manor had performed the admirable task of adjusting itself to suit the purposes of housing all forty-eight students of the old magical school. Fortunately, it wasn't an enormous student body to house.

Rosemary had wondered why a town of such a small size even had a school of its own. Although, of course, they needed a magical school for such a magical town. It would have been almost impossible to disguise the shifters and other fantastic creatures among the normal mundane children of an ordinary school.

Things had gone relatively smoothly since the temporary relocation, although Ms Twigg frequently complained that the new library wasn't large enough and that she'd have to 'spell' it to make it bigger.

Rosemary thought it was almost exactly the same as the one on Myrtlewood campus, but Ms Twigg kept complaining as if she was hoping that Rosemary would give her some kind of upgrade. She didn't seem convinced by the explanation that the house had a mind of its own.

Rosemary had never been a landlord before. She found it quite odd to meet with the school principal every Friday, especially since the school didn't believe in having a fixed principal due to the well-established fact that power corrupts. Therefore, the teachers all took turns in the role, meaning that Rosemary would meet with a different teacher every week.

Despite the hassles, the benefit of all of this was that Athena could continue her education and so could her classmates, despite the fact that their school wasn't going to be operational for at least until after the summer.

Thankfully, there were only a few more weeks until the summer holidays started.

Rosemary made her way to the car and drove slowly towards the centre of Myrtlewood to Marjie's tea shop.

The soon-to-be chocolate shop that she'd leased from grumpy old Covvey was still undergoing renovations and wouldn't be ready for quite some time. And since Rosemary didn't really want to be cooped up in the house, especially not when it was also functioning as a magical school with children running around the yard, she'd been camping out at a table in Marjie's tea shop. She referred to it as her makeshift office.

She carried in the usual stack of papers and started organising them on the table. On one side, she put her business notes and other things relating to the course she'd been taking. In the middle, she set down a stack of forms and other bits and pieces that she had to fill out. It was all paperwork relating to setting up her business. On the other side of the table she put the pile that she hardly had time for but wistfully glanced at occasionally. It contained all the details and the instructions and the coursework for her chocolatier course.

She hadn't had enough time to practice making, given all the business related stuff, and the kitchen in Thorn Manor was hardly fit for commercial use. Though she did try to do the practical exercises at home in the afternoons and sometimes in the evenings.

She also had her first in-person training as part of the course coming up in a few weeks, where she got to go to London and learn from the real experts.

She was quite looking forward to it, if only she could finish all of the preparatory exercises and assignments in time.

Marjie brought Rosemary out a cup of tea and a cheese scone. She'd given up trying to bring out a whole tea tray complete with tea pot after Rosemary complained that she didn't have enough room on the table.

"Have you got any surprises for me this morning?" Marjie asked.

Rosemary pushed a brown paper bag towards her friend, who was now much more like family.

"Here are yesterday's chocolates," said Rosemary.

"Oh, these look marvellous!" said Marjie, peering into the bag. She took them behind the counter and arranged them on a dainty little plate. "Now tell me what they all are," she said, tottering back towards Rosemary's table. "And then I'll leave you alone in peace to get your work done."

Rosemary pointed to the pink truffles at the front. "These ones are raspberry and rosewater. I added the rosewater myself, although Athena says it tastes like soap."

"She always says that," said Marjie. "But you and I know better."

"I just thought the raspberry alone wouldn't have quite the full flavour notes that I was looking for. I hope I don't get in trouble for all my improvisations."

"If they don't appreciate your culinary genius and your fine sense of taste, they're not worth their salt," said Marjie, making her spare hand into a fist up on her hip. "And what are the others?"

Rosemary pointed to the other chocolates in turn. "These are dark chocolate truffles. These ones are Earl Grey flavour, and the long ones are cardamom and apricot."

"Oh, that sounds just divine," Marjie exclaimed. "I can't wait to sample them all. And then I'll do my usual trick and offer them around as tasters for the townspeople. Stir up a bit of interest in your shop."

Rosemary smiled. "They're not really perfect yet."

"You might say that, my dear," said Marjie. "But I think they're just divine. And I know that once everyone's had a little taste of what you're capable of, they'll all be queuing up as soon as your wonderful shop opens."

"I'm going to leave the marketing department to you then, Marjie," said Rosemary. It was the part of her coursework that Rosemary was least enjoying. She didn't really like blowing her own horn, so to speak.

"You're going to be so popular!" Marjie crowed. "Oh, come to think of it, have you thought about looking into a stall at the Summer Festival?"

"Festival?" Rosemary asked. The word brought back memories of the dream she'd just had. She had to shake her head vigorously, just to bring herself back to the present moment. "Is it like all the other seasonal rituals?" Rosemary asked.

"Oh no," said Marjie. "The Summer Festival is a proper affair. I mean, not proper in the hoity toity way. I mean, it's a big festival that draws in thousands of attendees. Haven't you heard of it?"

"I suppose people may have been muttering about it," said Rosemary. "But I didn't realise it was a big deal."

"Oh, it's the biggest deal of all," said Marjie. "Myrtlewood town makes most of our additional money for the year over the summer, and the festival is the crowning jewel. Big bands come, you know? And DJs."

"Really?" Rosemary said. "I didn't think this was a raving kind of place."

She felt a whiff of concern in relation to the dream she just had and hoped it was just a coincidence.

"Oh yes," said Marjie. "People come from all around the country, and even from abroad, to celebrate the festival. It all starts with an opening ritual in the town square and then everyone matches up and parades all the way to the top of the tor and the stone circle there where the druids have their annual sacred rite."

"What tor?" said Rosemary. "I thought Glastonbury was the one with the tor. Isn't a tor just a big hill, anyway?"

"Bother Glastonbury," said Marjie. "They think so highly of themselves."

Rosemary could tell she'd struck a nerve.

"Myrtlewood is just as important in terms of sacred sites and places," Marjie insisted.

"Why have I never heard of the standing stones on the tor and the druids that come here?" said Rosemary.

"Don't be silly," said Marjie. "You must have."

"I don't think so," said Rosemary, crossing her arms.

"Well, you are still a little bit new here," said Marjie. "But let me tell you they're quite a big deal. Nobody goes up there except on the solstice. People say it's because it's sacred, you know. And an important protected historic site, but really, everyone knows it's much more than that. It's dangerous."

"No, not more danger!" said Rosemary. "I think I'll steer clear of that after the last couple of months."

"No, dear," said Marjie. "On the solstice. It's when we cast *away* the bad spirits."

"Bad spirits? Do you mean like poor quality bourbon?" Rosemary joked.

"Of course not. Now you're just pulling my chain," said Marjie. "It's a serious matter. People have been hiking up to the top of the hill and performing the druid rite in the stone circle for hundreds of years, perhaps thousands. It drives the bad spirits away from these lands."

"Well, I wish they'd remembered that last Beltane," said Rosemary.

"That was sprites, dear," said Marjie. "Spirits rarely light fires."

"I feel like there's so much I still need to learn," said Rosemary. "What are these spirits? Are they ghosts?"

Rosemary's mind wandered to thoughts of her grandmother. Granny Thorn had been absent for some time after haunting Thorn Manor, occasionally being incredibly helpful and oftentimes being a pain in the neck.

"Not exactly ghosts, dear," said Marjie. "It's hard to explain."

"Never mind," said Rosemary. "I'm sure we'll be just fine, although I am getting suspicious of all the seasonal rituals now, after everything we've been through. I think I might try and give this one a miss."

"You absolutely will not," said Marjie.

"Is this another case of the town needing my family magic?" Rosemary asked. She took another sip of tea and felt a lot better. "Did you dose this with your magic formula? You did, didn't you?"

"Of course I did," said Marjie. "We need to have you in as good a mood as possible so that you can make the best possible chocolates for us!"

Rosemary smiled. "You are a sweetheart, Marjie," she said. "And I'll think about having a stall at the Summer Festival, if it's possible between my coursework and setting up the business and everything else."

"Perfectly understandable," said Marjie. "But it would be a great way to help establish your name as a chocolatier with all the visitors coming through. You'll have people from all around the country ordering from your shop in no time at all. Plus, you've already missed Easter and Valentine's Day and even Mother's Day."

Rosemary groaned. "That's what I was saying to Athena this morning."

"Exactly," said Marjie. "So there's no time to lose. Hop to it, quick smart!"

Rosemary smiled and gulped down the rest of her tea. Despite all the drama in Myrtlewood, there was no place on earth she'd rather be.

CHAPTER
TWO

Athena made her way down to folklore and history. It had been a strange experience over the past few weeks, going to school in her own house. It wasn't without its benefits, when she could take her breakfast with her.

Classes had been starting a little bit earlier than usual, as part of Rosemary's agreement with the teachers to host the temporary campus. Athena had not been impressed with this arrangement.

Rosemary had insisted that it was in everyone's best interests, purely because it suited her to send Athena off to be occupied by something else early in the morning, keeping her out of trouble.

Despite the early mornings, and the utter embarrassment of having her mother so close by, there were some perks.

Athena walked into class, carrying her plate of toast, and smiled broadly at Beryl across the classroom, who, as usual, glared at her. Priceless.

Athena smiled as she took a seat next to Elise and Sam, and Beryl's glare only intensified.

"Toast?" she offered from across the classroom.

Beryl narrowed her eyes. "You think you're so smart, Athena Thorn," she said. "Just because the school happens to be in your ridiculous house, it doesn't give you any more power than anyone else. And it certainly doesn't make you better than me. It's not fair that you're trying to make a fool out of me like this."

Athena laughed. "I don't think it would be necessary," she said. "You're quite capable of making a fool out of yourself."

"Now, now," said Ms Twigg. "Settle down, students. I have two announcements to make."

The class stilled.

"The first announcement is on the dates for your upcoming exams. They will be in the second week of June."

The class groaned and Ms Twigg tutted them. "In more invigo-rating news, a new pupil will be joining this class."

Athena was only half paying attention as Elise scrawled a note next to her so that she could read it, asking if she wanted to catch up after school for some ice cream.

Athena wrote back, *yes*.

"May I introduce Finnigan."

Athena's expression hardened. She kept looking down into Elise's notebook as her blood ran cold. *It can't be*, she thought. *Not him.*

She slowly raised her gaze to see a very familiar boy, one who had been playing on her mind quite infuriatingly for some time. One she never wanted to see again.

"What's the matter?" Elise whispered.

"Nothing," said Athena. "I'll tell you later."

She couldn't believe it. How dare he turn up here after every-thing he'd done.

Athena had been so terribly deceived by Finnigan, who she'd thought she could trust, who she'd thought was a friend, a good friend, and quite a lot more besides.

Her friends had never met him before, and Athena hadn't told them much about the fae boy who'd led her into their realm and handed her over to the foul Countess of West Eloria.

She tried to squish it down. She refused to meet his gaze, even as he paused in front of her desk on his way to take his own seat.

Instead of paying attention for the rest of the lesson, she went over and over it in her mind...how he'd won over her trust. How he'd convinced her to go with him to the fae realm to learn about her powers. How he'd tricked her and trapped her and betrayed her, and then disappeared.

She hadn't seen him since she'd left the fae realm, but she'd worried about his return. Occasionally, she wondered if he thought of her. Or perhaps spied on her. Being of human and fae heritage as well, he had the rare ability to navigate between the two realms, like Athena herself could, only he was much more proficient at it.

And now, he'd shown up in her very house. Not just in her school and in her classroom. It added insult to injury. She would not allow herself to meet his gaze.

She didn't owe him anything. And if she had any feelings for him, they mostly were not the good kind. She wasn't going to allow herself to give in to any whims or fancies.

She might have forgiven her father for everything he'd done, all the terrible behaviour when she was younger, but that had been a long time ago. And Dain had hardly known how to control himself because of his upbringing and his addiction to cream, which Rosemary and Athena had fortunately resolved, at least for the time being.

Finnigan had no such excuse. He'd wilfully betrayed her. There was no way she was going to let that slide, even though there was a very annoying part of her that hoped he'd returned just for her.

She was determined that this was not going to go on. He couldn't stay here. She couldn't stand to be in a classroom with him.

She needed to get rid of him, out of the school and out of her life. Only, that probably meant telling her mother.

There was a small possibility that Finnigan would listen and she could solve the whole sorry conversation without telling Rosemary. There was nothing for it. She'd have to tell him in no uncertain terms that he was not welcome.

One thing was certain. He had to go away and never return.

By the end of the class, Athena had learned nothing of the history of the famous Summer Solstice festival of Myrtlewood. She'd been far too occupied with her thoughts.

She got up to leave the classroom, hoping she could just ignore Finnigan for now, because as much as she wanted to tell him to leave, she'd suddenly lost her nerve. The lead weight in her gut was making it too hard to say anything. She wasn't ready. She was angry that he'd shown up like this. The best course of action was, clearly, to ignore him and hope that he'd go away.

"Athena," he said, following behind her down the hallway. "Athena!" he called out again.

Athena stopped, allowing her classmates to file past. She raised her head and looked Finnigan in the eye. "What the hell do you think you're doing here?" she asked.

"I'm going to school," said Finnigan. "Only I didn't realise it was going to be at your house."

"An unlikely story," she said. "Why are you even in this realm? You don't belong here."

Finnigan looked as if he'd been stung by her words.

"Look, Athena, I know that you're probably angry at me."

"Angry doesn't begin to describe it," Athena said. "I'd be angry at you if you did something simple, like fail to return my phone call or spill hot chocolate on my favourite top. What I feel is much worse than that."

She was glad everyone had disappeared from the hallway,

leaving them alone. But still, she spoke fairly quietly so as not to cause a scene.

"Why are you here?" she asked. "I want the truth."

"Athena," said Finnigan. "I'm finally free. I didn't have the chance to explain it to you in the fae realm, but I needed to earn my freedom from the Countess. I was shackled to her because of an old pact that my mother had made. And the only way for me to be free was..."

"Was to hand over my father and me?!"

Finnigan looked down at the floor. "I needed to earn a certain amount of favour with her so that I could have my life back."

"And you didn't think you could do the dishes or something?"

"I would have been doing dishes for a thousand years," said Finnigan.

"That would have been preferable," said Athena. "Given you don't even age over there it would have hardly mattered."

"It's not how it works," said Finnigan. "I mean, I do age in the realm, just more slowly. My human side doesn't seem to, but my fae side does."

"I don't want to hear about this," said Athena. "You betrayed me."

"I know, and I'm sorry."

"That's not okay. You do not get to turn up now and say 'Oh, sorry'. You do not get to come to my house or to my school or even my town. I don't want to see you again."

Finnigan looked crestfallen and Athena almost felt sorry him, except that there was no way on earth she would allow herself to do that.

"I want you out of here," she said.

"I understand why you'd say that," he replied. "And I probably deserve it."

"Of course you do."

"I just want to try and live in the human world for a while. And...people my age go to school."

"People your age are well past retirement," said Athena. "You don't belong in this time and you don't belong in this world."

"Ouch. That hurt," said Finnigan.

"Well, you deserve it."

"I probably do."

"Please just leave," said Athena. "Or I'm going to have to make you."

There was a kind of gleam in Finnigan's eyes. "Oh, yes?" he said. "And you have the power to do that, do you?"

"Not personally," said Athena, "But this is my house, after all. If I were you, I'd leave before you get kicked out. It'll be less embarrassing that way."

Finnigan raised his hands. "After the life I've lived, embarrassment is the least of my concerns."

Athena bowled past him, rage flaring again.

She thought about going to her next class, but her emotions were running too high. So instead, she walked all the way to the end of the wing, out the door, and around to the front of the house again. She made her way upstairs to her bedroom, got into bed, and cried.

It didn't sound like Finnigan was going to leave of his own accord. Athena realised she had to do something truly dreadful.

Telling Rosemary was the last thing she wanted to do. Not only would it bring back bad memories of how she'd stupidly run off with the boy she hardly knew to the fae realm only to be betrayed by him. This whole situation could also open her up to having her life scrutinised by her mother again, removing her precious little privacy.

She had promised Rosemary that she would be more open from now on, provided Rosemary upheld her end of the deal. Meaning that Athena would have reasonable and appropriate freedoms without Rosemary becoming insanely overprotective again. Athena felt a sinking realisation that perhaps the only way to get Finnigan out of her life and gain back some control was with her mother's help, but still, she resisted making the phone call.

Athena fell asleep after shedding a few tears. They weren't for Finnigan, she told herself. They were for herself having to see him again, and the distressing nature of that situation. When she woke up from her nap it was midday already.

She decided she couldn't very well go back to school given that Finnigan was most likely still there. Red hot anger rose up again in her chest.

How dare he not only turn up, but flatly refuse to listen to her when she told him to leave? It would have been bad enough if they were at the regular Myrtlewood campus, but in her house?! She felt violated that her own home was being invaded by someone she could not stand. There was nothing for it. She had to call Rosemary.

It was time to start putting into practice what she'd reluctantly agreed to, and being more open with her mother. She only hoped that Rosemary would uphold her side of the bargain.

CHAPTER

THREE

Rosemary looked around the tea shop, took a sip of her cold tea, and sighed. As she set the cup down abruptly, she accidentally dipped her sleeve in the cream from the scones Marjie had brought over to her.

"Blast," she muttered.

"Here you go, love," said Marjie, handing Rosemary a napkin. She sighed. "I'd better go and wash a load of dishes. It's not the same without Lamorna."

Rosemary squinted at her friend. "She was evil."

"Yes, but she was also a dab hand in the kitchen."

Rosemary shook her head and started getting up from the table. "Let me help."

"No, no. You've got plenty to be getting on with. I'd hire someone new, but it won't be long before business slows down for the year."

Marjie bustled off and Rosemary looked around. The tea shop was quiet in a mid-afternoon lull. Her tea had gone cold, but she didn't want to bother Marjie and couldn't be bothered getting up to make herself a fresh pot.

She was midway through setting up a very frustrating spreadsheet on her new laptop that she'd purchased for study. She cursed under her breath at the formulas, attracting furtive looks from the other few customers. The stupid numbers weren't working the way they were supposed to. Just then, her phone rang. It was Athena.

"Hello, love," said Rosemary. "What's going on? Shouldn't you be at school?"

"I went to school this morning," said Athena. "But I had to leave and go home."

"Why? What's wrong? Are you sick?"

"Not exactly," said Athena.

"Oh no," said Rosemary. "Bad cramps?"

"No! Mum!" Athena groaned.

"What? What is it?"

"Finnigan showed up."

Rosemary was silent for a moment. In fact, she could barely speak as her vision darkened and her emotions closed in on her at the news.

"Mum?"

"No!" Rosemary said. "The nerve! Are you alright? Did he attack you?"

"It's worse," said Athena. "He's a student. He enrolled in Myrtlewood Academy."

"The little twerp!" said Rosemary, outraged. "What made him think he could just enrol in school and show up at our house like that? Do you think he's doing it just to try and kidnap you again?"

"Fat chance," said Athena. "He says he's finally earned his freedom and now he wants to live a normal life in the earth realm."

"Can he not go and do that literally anywhere else?" said Rosemary.

"Apparently not," said Athena. "He thinks he's entitled to be here."

"We'll see about that," Rosemary said. "Hang tight. I'll be home in a little while. But first, before I see you, I'm going to have to make a little detour to the principal's office."

"Okay, Mum," said Athena, sounding resigned to the inevitability that Rosemary was heading straight to the school. "Just don't do anything too embarrassing."

"Me? Embarrassing?" said Rosemary. "I wouldn't dream of it."

"Mum," said Athena, with a warning note in her voice.

"Okay, I'll try and be on my best behaviour," said Rosemary.

"Also," Athena added, "remember what you promised. You wanted me to be more open with you. And in exchange you were going to stop being all protective and weird."

Rosemary sighed. "I remember," she said. "Forgive me while I struggle against my own urges to wrap you in cotton wool and try and protect you from that dip-wad."

"Consider yourself forgiven in advance," said Athena. "Just don't stop me from seeing my friends or anything."

"As long as your friends don't happen to include him, you're totally fine," said Rosemary.

"Wow. That's never going to happen," said Athena. "There's no way I could ever trust Finnigan again."

"Glad to hear it. Now make sure you're looking after yourself. Have a nice cup of tea and I'll see you soon."

She hung up the phone and hastily shoved her various piles of paper back into her bag.

"Is everything okay?" Marjie called from behind the counter.

"It will be," said Rosemary. "I just have something urgent that I'm going to attend to."

"I know that look, Rosemary Thorn," said Marjie. "Just be

careful not to set anyone on fire...who doesn't deserve it." She winked.

"Don't worry," said Rosemary. "He definitely does."

She strode out of the shop before Marjie could delay her with any more questions and drove quickly back to Thorn Manor, making her way as fast as she could towards the principal's office. This week Mr Spruce was behind the desk. Rosemary smiled as she caught sight of the enormous man with his bushy white beard and decidedly good nature. She was pleased it wasn't Ms Twigg anymore, who had been a little bit of a pain, considering her endless requests for a bigger library and the fact that she was a stickler for annoying details.

"Rosemary! Come in! Come in! How can I help you?" Mr Spruce bellowed.

"It seems we have a problem with a certain new pupil at the school," said Rosemary. "Assuming he really is a pupil and he wasn't just lying about it."

"Ah, you're referring to young Finnigan," said Mr Spruce.

"I'm afraid so," said Rosemary.

"What seems to be the problem?" Mr Spruce asked. "Has he already caused mischief this morning?"

"In a manner of speaking," said Rosemary. "I can't possibly have him in the house. I don't even want him in this realm. And I don't want him at school with Athena. Not after what he did."

She explained a little bit about what went on with the fae realm, Finnigan's abduction of Athena, as Rosemary saw it anyway, and the way that he'd betrayed her, handing her over to the countess who was keeping her father captive.

"Are you saying he took her against her will?" said Mr Spruce. "Because that would be quite a serious matter."

"Not exactly," said Rosemary. "She...she was willing to go at the time, but it was obviously under false pretences, so I think it hardly counts."

"I see," said Mr Spruce.

"Not to mention the fact that he abducted her father against his will and cast an illusion to make us think the house was on fire."

Mr Spruce frowned in concentration. "He does seem to be a young troublemaker. We'll have to keep an eye on him."

"No," said Rosemary. "I don't want you keeping an eye on him. I don't want him anywhere near any of our eyes at all."

"You're saying you want him expelled?" he asked. "I'll have to discuss this with the other teachers. In fact, let me just check in with Ms Twigg. She's a stickler for the rules and she'll know what can be done."

He picked up a small green bell from a tray of bells with different colours and sizes, and rang it. A moment later, Ms Twigg opened the door.

"You called, sir?" she said.

"You call him sir?" Rosemary asked. "Aren't you all on the same level?"

"When he's principal, we address him more formally. The rest of the time I'll call him Aventurine. Occasionally, Mr Spruce."

"Okay, whatever," said Rosemary. She and Mr Spruce filled Ms Twigg in on the situation.

Rosemary was feeling more and more anxious. She knew what Ms Twigg was like in terms of following protocols, and the more they went through the details, the more it seemed like Rosemary didn't have a leg to stand on.

"While it might be a matter to refer to the magical authorities," said Mr Spruce, "it seems he hasn't done anything wrong since being a student at the school, and therefore, we have no jurisdiction to punish him or dismiss him."

"That's ridiculous," said Rosemary.

"He clearly needs some guidance," Mr Spruce continued.

"I'm not sure if guidance is going to help him," said Ms Twigg.

"At least that's one thing we agree on," Rosemary muttered.

"I'm sorry, Ms Thorn," said Ms Twigg. "The problem is, we don't have any rules specifically for expelling students who did something terrible before they were enrolled at the school. I do suggest you take this up with the authorities if you have further complaints."

"But he's in our house now!" said Rosemary. "This is totally unacceptable."

"The school is in your house," said Mr Spruce. "And though it hasn't been without its teething issues, things are going relatively well."

"Up until now," said Rosemary, flaring with rage. "I can't believe you're going to let him keep coming. If you do that, you might have to find another place for the school to run."

"We have an agreement," said Ms Twigg. "You wanted Myrtlewood Academy to carry on just as much as we all did. You've signed the contract, just as we all have. The school will continue to be run from Thorn Manor until the campus can be repaired. It shouldn't be too much longer. I hear they're having some difficulties considering the magical nature of the fire. But for now—"

"No," said Rosemary. "You don't understand. It's torture for Athena after what she's been through. She cannot be around that boy."

"Are you saying you're withholding her from classes?" Mr Spruce asked.

"That hardly seems fair," said Rosemary. "She hasn't done anything wrong. And she likes school. Though I'm starting to wonder why, with your attitudes!"

Ms Twigg glared at Rosemary from above her horn-rimmed

spectacles. "Now, now, Ms Thorn. That's enough of that kind of sentiment."

Rosemary felt like she was a teenager being reprimanded by a teacher again, and it didn't bring back very pleasant memories.

"Surely we can make some kind of compromise," said Mr Spruce.

Rosemary crossed her arms and harrumphed.

"It seems we can't expel Finnigan from the school since he's legitimately enrolled as a student, and everything he did wrong was a while ago."

"Not that long ago," said Rosemary. "It's really only a month or so."

"Be that as it may," said Ms Twigg. "The rules say..." She raised her finger.

"We've been over the rules," said Mr Spruce, cutting her off. "Rosemary is well aware."

"This conversation has gone on for too long already," said Rosemary.

"I was saying," said Mr Spruce, "we cannot forcibly remove any student from the campus even though it is in your house. And I apologise for that."

Rosemary shook her head, very unimpressed with his so-called apology.

"However," he continued, "we can forbid him from interacting with your daughter. We can even look into whether he might be able to go into a different class, though he tested to be at the level of the class that Athena happens to be in."

"Well, that would be something," said Rosemary. "That would at least give Athena some peace of mind. She wouldn't have to talk to him. It's not really good enough..."

"I understand your concerns," Mr Spruce said. "However, given the predicament we find ourselves in, we're just going to have to reach some kind of compromise that works for all parties."

"It's harassment," said Rosemary. "I'm sure the only reason he chose to enrol at the school was to taunt Athena and maybe try to trick her into going back to the fae realm or kidnap her again...or even worse."

"If that's the case," said Ms Twigg primly, "then his lack of being permitted to interact with her might send him packing. If the whole purpose of him being at school is your daughter, he may well choose to leave of his own accord."

"One can only hope," said Rosemary.

"Thank you for bringing this to our attention," Mr Spruce said. "We will do everything we can to protect our students. Rest assured that no harm will come to Athena via any of the other students while she's in our care."

"If only there was some way that you could guarantee that," said Rosemary. "Anyway, I've heard enough. I'm leaving, but this conversation is not over."

She stood up, stomped out of the principal's office, and slammed the door behind her, still furious.

She walked around the house three times before going inside to see Athena, knowing very well that her daughter was not going to be happy about the situation. And the fact that the school's hands were tied.

Rosemary had a right mind to go in to find Finnigan herself, and grill him until he agreed to leave of his own volition...and that was the milder version of the thoughts that passed through her head, some of which included enormous fireballs being lobbed his way.

However, being an adult, and a witch much more in control of her magic than she used to be, she turned her attention to her daughter. She had to go and make sure Athena was okay. That was the most important thing.

"First, I'm going to burn off a little bit of this rage," she muttered to herself, stalking towards the old dishevelled green-house as her anger flared.

She began lobbing huge balls of magic fire and lightning at the greenhouse until all the glass windows burst and the structure became a smouldering base. Rosemary was panting a little. "That'll do for now," she said as magic continued to sizzle through her. "I think it's time for some tea...or maybe something a little bit stronger."

FOUR

"You've got to be joking," said Athena.

Rosemary had just knocked gently on her door and quietly explained the situation with the school and Finnigan.

"There's no way I can go to school with him. The school's in my house, and I don't even want to be *here* if he's going to be around."

"I know. I know, love," said Rosemary. "I'm sorry. Also, I might have accidentally blown up the greenhouse...perhaps not so accidentally, I was just so mad. I can't believe it either."

"So he's just going to be allowed to harass me?"

"Not quite," said Rosemary. "They can't kick him out because he hasn't directly broken any school rules since he's been enrolled, but they can forbid him from talking to you, especially considering that the conversation you had earlier sounded like some sort of harassment. It was him harassing you, wasn't it?"

"Of course it was," said Athena. "He insisted on talking to me. I wouldn't have bothered otherwise."

"That's right," said Rosemary. "He's not worth the ground you walk on."

"I don't know if that's the right saying, Mum, but anyway. Never mind that. I guess I'll have to cope. I'd better get out of bed. I'm going to go into town and meet Elise soon."

"Are you sure?" Rosemary asked.

"Mum, do not start with me. You promised you weren't going to be overprotective."

"I'm not trying to stop you," Rosemary insisted. "I just want to make sure that you're feeling up to it, emotionally."

"I'm fine," said Athena. "I've dealt with a lot worse. Now, if you'll give me some privacy, I'm going to get changed."

Rosemary reached over and gave Athena's shoulder a little reassuring squeeze before leaving.

Athena exhaled slowly and got up. The situation was hopeless. Sure, what she'd said to Rosemary was true. She would cope. She had dealt with a lot worse. But it was never quite like this...having to see someone, day after day, in her own school and her own house after he'd done something so unforgivable.

"Never mind," she muttered to herself. "I'm not going to let him have any more power over me."

She changed into some more fashionable and slightly less crumpled clothing so that she could go and meet Elise. Then she walked the relatively short distance to the centre of town to Mervyn's ice cream parlour.

It had been a little while since she'd been there, but Athena felt reassured that everything looked much the same. Mervyn was helping another customer when she arrived, and Elise hadn't gotten there yet, so Athena perused the ice cream varieties to see a few new flavours like mango and wild mint and peach and honeysuckle. Those sounded delightful to Athena.

"Hey," said a voice from behind her.

Athena turned to see her friend, her hair coloured with a slight reddish tinge rather than the usual blue, making Athena feel slightly jealous that Elise had hair that changed colour with her moods.

"How are you feeling?" Athena asked.

"Is it that obvious?" said Elise, blushing. "I feel quite confused actually."

Athena nodded. "It's been a funny sort of day. I'm dreading those exams..."

"Tell me about it," said Elise.

"And what do you young 'uns feel like?" Mervyn asked.

"I'll have the usual," Elise replied, looking into the cabinet. "Actually...I might try the peach and honeysuckle. I feel like a change."

"That one does sound really good." Athena chose to sample it, but then opted for a classic strawberry ripple.

They took one of the booths by the door. There were a few other customers in the ice cream parlour that day, but they all seemed to be busy having their own conversations and so it felt relatively private.

"Are you okay?" Elise asked.

"I guess so," said Athena. "I mean..."

"I guessed who it was..." said Elise. "That guy who arrived today. That was him, wasn't it?"

"I forget you've never met him," said Athena. "By the time you all arrived and met up with us in the fae realm, he'd ditched me already. That was after handing me in to her highness the awful fae Countess."

"I definitely remember *her*," said Elise. "Anyway, you've told me enough about Finnigan and I assumed it was far too much of a coincidence that a guy matching that description had arrived as the new kid at school. It just took a moment for it to sink in. Seeing the way that you reacted confirmed it for me."

Athena groaned. "You didn't hear our conversation, did you?"

"No," said Elise quietly.

"Thank the goddesses knickers for that," said Athena.

Elise laughed. "What did he say? You can tell me. I won't tell anyone."

Athena gave Elise an abridged version of the conversation.

"That's outrageous!" said Elise. "What makes him think he can get away with that?"

"I don't know," said Athena. "But if he thinks he's gotten off scot free, he's got another thing coming. My mum already blew up the greenhouse in anger."

"I'm not surprised," said Elise with a laugh. "My mum would probably do the same in that situation. What are you going to do about it?"

"No idea," said Athena. "Is Sam coming to join us?"

"No," said Elise, her hair turning slightly pink. "I...actually...I wanted to talk to you alone."

"I don't mind Sam hearing about all that stuff," said Athena.

Elise looked around and then lowered her voice. "Not about that."

Athena noticed her friend was staring determinedly at her ice cream.

"What is it? You can tell me," said Athena. "After all, I just blurted out a whole lot of embarrassing stuff."

"It's just..." said Elise. "It's just that...Do you remember the last time we came here?"

"Vaguely," said Athena.

"So...maybe you don't remember this," said Elise. "And it's probably stupid for me to say it, but I feel bad not keeping a promise."

"You made me a promise?" Athena asked.

"Yeah," said Elise with a sigh. "Look, we were talking about crushes and..."

"Oh, that's right," said Athena. "You thought Felix liked me. Is that what this is about?"

"Not exactly," said Elise. "Do you remember how I said I didn't like anyone and promised to tell you if I did?"

"No!" said Athena in shock. "Not Finnigan. You only just met him!"

"Oh no, not him." Elise sighed again, more deeply this time. "Okay, so I probably should have told you this a while ago because it's been building for some time. I kind of hoped that it was just the Beltane spirit, getting in the way and making things confusing but..."

"What is it?" Athena asked.

There was a long pause, in which Athena worried whether Elise was going to say anything at all, or whether she'd already regretted bringing up the topic.

"Athena," Elise said, looking her in the eye. "It's you."

"Me?" Athena asked. "What have I done?"

"No, silly," said Elise. "It's you that I have..." Her words fell away.

"Oh," said Athena. "Oh, I see."

"I'm sorry," Elise said. "I shouldn't have said anything, I just felt bad because I told you that I would, and then I felt awkward, because I'm pretty sure that's not what you were expecting. And you're probably not even...you know...into girls."

"Oh," said Athena. She took a big spoonful of her strawberry ripple ice cream. "You know what's funny?" she said.

"This whole conversation?" Elise asked in a very awkward tone.

"No," said Athena. "I mean, it's funny, I've always kind of thought that I was interested in people for themselves regardless of their gender, it's just everyone kind of assumes that...you know."

"Everyone assumes you're heterosexual," said Elise. "Yep. Tell me about it. It's called heteronormativity, and I'm very familiar.

Anyway, there's no expectation at all. I just felt like it was time that I came clean, and I really hope it doesn't mess up our friendship because I do feel really close to you."

"I feel really close to you, too," said Athena, feeling her stomach drop. A strange sensation came over her that had very little to do with magic and everything to do with a whole world of possibilities opening up in her mind. "Oh, wow..." A wave of feeling washed over her. It tangled in her mind and she wondered whether this was just her hormones, doing funny teenage things. She let out a long slow breath and looked at Elise.

"It's a lot. I know," said Elise. "I shouldn't have said anything."

"No, you should have," said Athena. "It's just I've been so busy trying to avoid relationships. I mean, Mum and me both. I feel like we're a little bit cursed or something with our taste in men or boys."

"I'm not men or boys," said Elise.

"Exactly," said Athena. "Maybe it's a sign." She grinned.

"A sign?" Elise asked.

"You know, a sign that I'm not supposed to be with boys." She reached out to where Elise's hand lay sitting at the side of her paper cup of ice cream, allowing her fingers to rest gently over Elise's.

"Oh, wow," said Elise. "I feel something. Is it magic?"

"I don't think so," said Athena. "And that's definitely a good thing."

CHAPTER
FIVE

The next morning, Rosemary awoke early from another seductive dream involving Burk. A part of her mind was still dancing to the pumping music, arms wrapped around the attractive vampire. As she drifted to wakefulness, she realised the dreams she'd been having must somehow be connected to the festival, although she was sure she hadn't heard of it before the first dream.

It was somewhat unnerving.

She lay in bed listening to the dawn chorus, still half awake, soaking in the wonderful, glorious feelings of the dream.

Of course, it wasn't something she should be indulging in, not with everything else on her plate. She felt like a naughty teenager sneaking out of the house. But then that realisation only reminded her of Athena and the current predicament with Finnigan.

Rosemary was determined that the little blighter wasn't going to cause any more trouble for Athena, nor anyone else they cared about.

Her thoughts circled around plotting and planning various schemes that could put Finnigan off. In the end, she settled for a direct approach. She got dressed into whatever clothes she could find and had a quick piece of toast and a cup of tea downstairs, knowing that Athena would still be asleep. Then she dragged a chair from the kitchen table outside and around the corner to avoid being spotted from the main part of the house.

The students of Myrtlewood Academy entered for their lessons via the East doorway of Thorn Manor, skirting around the side of the building. This had been arranged for Rosemary's convenience. She didn't particularly want a whole bunch of kids traipsing through the house every day.

She found a nice sunny spot near a cluster of trees and nestled there with another cup of tea and the tea pot on a tray with the rest of her breakfast, waiting and watching as the children began to arrive.

It did cross her mind that it was a rather suspicious thing to be doing, watching a whole bunch of schoolchildren. But she was just sitting in her own backyard in a way. She did attract a few furtive and curious glances. But most of the kids either wilfully ignored her or didn't see her because they were so wrapped up in their own teenage minds.

Rosemary caught sight of Finnigan a few moments before he saw her. His dark hair flopped over his pale face with those high cheekbones that she firmly believed were utterly wasted on such a scummy being. She got up and blocked his pathway to the house before he had a chance for any evasive manoeuvring.

Finnigan groaned. "Hello, Missus Thorn."

"That's Ms Thorn," said Rosemary.

"How did you recognise me?" Finnigan asked. It was true Rosemary hadn't actually seen Finnigan very often, but he'd made quite an impression.

"I remember you from the pub," said Rosemary. "That night you whisked Athena outside when I wasn't looking. You know...the first time that you made her disappear. Not to mention those other times you came to the house."

"Oh yes. That," said Finnigan. "Now I remember."

"And I'm sure you recognised me from all the time you spent stalking our house, plotting to cast illusions on us and so on."

"Something like that." He smiled mischievously at Rosemary, making her rage flare.

"How dare you!" Rosemary's voice rose. "How dare you show up at our house and Athena's school like this? It's totally inappropriate after the havoc you caused. I should turn you over to the authorities."

In truth she had already told Neve, but frustratingly the magical powers that be were not interested in sorting out the affairs of teenagers and neither did they want to risk meddling in anything related to fae politics.

"There's no evidence against me," said Finnigan with a cocky grin.

"Athena heard you confess to kidnapping Dain, among other things, such as leading an underage girl into a different world!"

"That's just hearsay. Besides, she came willingly. She wanted to go to the Fae realm."

He was taunting her now and Rosemary grimaced, feeling her magic flare.

It was all she could do to hold herself back from throwing an enormous fireball at his smug face. That incredibly infuriating teenager! She had to remind herself that he was just a kid. Although she didn't know if being a kid from the 1950s still counted, or if he was more like the ancient vampire, Geneviève.

Athena had tried to explain to her that Finnigan actually was quite young, because he hadn't experienced all that many years of life. Time moved differently in the fae realm depending on which kind of temporal currents you happened to find yourself in at the

time. But it was all a little bit much for Rosemary's brain to understand, especially in the wake of all of the dramas they'd experienced
recently.

"Please don't hurt me," Finnigan said, clearly sensing the
dangerous magic that was brewing. "I'm sorry. I didn't mean to
cause you so much harm, I..."

"'I'm sorry' is not good enough," said Rosemary. "In fact,
nothing you say is."

"Well then, what is it I can do?"

"You. Can. Stay. Away. From. Us," she said, emphasising every
word. "Stay the blazes away from Athena. Get out of our house and
out of our lives, and preferably out of this town, out of this realm
even!"

"I can't do that," said Finnigan. "Now that I'm free, it would be
foolish to go back to the fae realm. I might be captured again by the
Countess and her forces. And who knows how long it would take
me to earn back my freedom for a second time."

"That's not my concern," said Rosemary. "Get out of here before
I do something that we'll both regret."

Finnigan cowered as Rosemary's magic sent flames sizzling up
into the air around her.

"I can't," he said. "I've got to go to school. I need to have a
normal life for a change."

"Not. Good. Enough."

Flames burst out of Rosemary's hands and Finnigan trembled.

"Please stop," he cried.

Something stilled the air and the scent of lilacs wafted over
Rosemary, making her feel slightly faint. She looked around, as if in
a daze. Everything felt lighter. Cloudy and sweet.

"What's going on?" she asked.

"I'm sorry," Finnigan said. "I was just apologising. I didn't mean
to cause you any harm."

Rosemary felt slightly lost in her own mind as a pleasant sensation overcame her. "Oh," she said. "Of course, you didn't mean to. Never mind." She wandered off in a daze, leaving her tea things on the tray in the backyard.

Rosemary wandered all the way back around the other side of the house into the kitchen and found Athena, sitting at the table, eating beans on toast.

"Where have you been?" Athena asked, narrowing her eyes.

"I was outside," said Rosemary, still feeling dazed. "What a funny morning."

"What were you doing outside, Mum? You look all weird, like you've seen a ghost, but maybe in a good way. Does that even make sense?"

"Perfect sense," said Rosemary. "The most sensible thing I've ever heard."

"Even your voice is sounding as if you're drifting, far away. What kind of trouble have you gotten yourself into this time?"

"There's no trouble," said Rosemary. "Nothing's the matter."

"Mum! Who did you just talk to? Tell me exactly what happened."

Rosemary giggled. "I went outside and talked to Finnigan," she said, her voice still light and floaty.

"Mum!" Athena cried. "Why did you go and do that? I thought we were just going to leave him alone and hope he goes away."

"I wanted him to go away," said Rosemary, squinting in confusion. "That's why I went to talk to him, but he apologised, and you know...I don't think he's that bad."

"Mum, how can you say something like that? What has he done to you?"

"Done to me?" Rosemary asked. "He didn't do anything."

"I beg to differ," said Athena. "You're all weird and fluffy brained. Snap out of it."

She snapped her fingers and Rosemary felt as if she was waking from a dream.

"Aphrodite's knickers! What just happened?" Rosemary shook herself. "I feel like I just woke up."

"Well, you kind of did," said Athena. "You came in here all dopey and said you just talked to Finnigan. I think he must have put some sort of enchantment over you."

"That little brat!" Rosemary clenched her fists. "Now I remember. I went outside to send him packing so he didn't trouble you anymore. He refused to leave school, or town, or the realm."

"And then?"

"And then...he kind of apologised. I can't remember what happened next. I do recall feeling an uncontrollable urge to explode him right there on the spot, which probably wouldn't have looked very good and would most certainly breach my contract with the school."

"But it would eliminate some of our problems," said Athena, shrugging.

"Exactly," said Rosemary. "Although I don't intend to become a murderer anytime soon, so I'm kind of glad that I stopped."

"What's a bit of light murder between friends and family?" Athena muttered darkly. "How did he mess with your head? Was he holding any kind of magical item or anything?"

"Not that I could tell," said Rosemary. "He was standing there. One moment I was practically on fire with rage and he was cowering in fear..."

"I'd like to have seen that."

"Yes, well, in the next moment I felt all weird and wonderful. It was quite a nice sensation, actually. Much stronger than Marjie's tea. I wish I could bottle it."

Athena frowned. "Mum!"

"But now I'm even madder at him. I can't believe, after all that, he would enchant me, even in self-defence."

"He's a nasty little toe fungus," said Athena. "I can't believe I'm going to have to see him at school."

"You could just stay home," said Rosemary. "I would understand. I'm sure your teachers could just give you the work to do alone, kind of by correspondence, only instead of long distance it's an incredibly short distance."

"No, it's okay," said Athena. "I want to go to school. I want to see my friends. I'm not going to let him have any more effect on my life."

"Fair enough," said Rosemary. "I'm proud of you and terribly ashamed of myself for being overcome by the little scum bucket's magic like that."

"That's okay, Mum. I forgive you. Especially if you make me a nice chocolate pudding tonight."

"Consider it done," said Rosemary. "We could both do with some chocolate therapy. Now off you go to school before you're late."

She gave Athena a hug and waved her out the door to the hallway, hoping against hope that Finnigan wasn't going to cause any more trouble.

CHAPTER
SIX

"The nerve of that boy!" Marjie cried after Rosemary had explained the situation to her. They were sitting with Nesta around Rosemary's usual makeshift office table, drinking tea.

Marjie, of course, had been able to tell something wasn't right and had insisted Rosemary tell her all about it, and Nesta had joined the conversation part way through, unable to resist the pull of drama.

"Surely there's something Neve can do," said Nesta. "Finnigan is most certainly a criminal."

"I tried that," said Rosemary. "I called her this morning, but in a way, he's right. There's no evidence against him. Athena went with him of her own free will. Dain didn't want to press charges after he came back from the fae realm, and I don't even know what that means in the magical world, because kidnapping a fairy and taking them to fairy land is not against any human laws, I'm pretty sure."

"That's the problem," said Marjie, crossing her arms. "The witching parliament and their cronies won't generally take an interest in magical problems unless someone is getting on their nerves or breaking a handful of old laws that hardly make sense these days, anyway. I mean, who would use werewolf blood for a spell when it's so dangerous? Hen's bane will do in a pinch as a substitute for most recipes."

Rosemary felt a pang of anxiety at the mention of werewolf blood. "I wish I knew that."

Marjie gave her an odd look. "Why is that, dear?"

"Oh…just an argument I had with my stupid cousin, is all," said Rosemary, still fuming that her snobby and relatively evil cousin had caused so much mayhem at Beltane and then gotten away with it, all because of a small matter of werewolf blood that Rosemary had secretly used in a spell. In order to conceal this, as well as Liam's identity as the werewolf blood donor, Rosemary had infuriatingly had to let Elamina's crime go unnoticed by the authorities and it still annoyed her to no end.

Detective Neve chose that moment to arrive, and Rosemary blushed. She'd been rather cross when they'd spoken earlier.

"Don't worry," said Neve. "Shouting 'Poseidon's-dangly-bits' at me over the phone was more funny than offensive, though you might not want to say that when any gods are present."

"We actually have some news," said Nesta, reaching for Neve's hand. "It's kind of a miracle, really." She put her other hand on her belly.

Rosemary's eyes boggled. "No! Really?" she exclaimed.

"We don't know how it happened," said Neve, her expression darker. "We don't even know if it's human."

"Don't be silly, love," said Nesta. She looked at the others. "Neve's worried, just worried."

"About what?"

Nesta sighed. "Worried it might be some kind of magical abomination growing inside me."

Neve grimaced.

"But I'm fairly sure that it's just a healthy baby," said Nesta.

"That's amazing," Rosemary said. "Also, kind of creepy on multiple levels. Sorry."

Nesta's jaw dropped.

"I mean, it's miraculous conception, right?" Rosemary continued, wondering how she could extricate her foot from her mouth. "Sure, it sounds amazing and kind of biblical, but is it like...a child of Belamus?"

Rosemary covered her mouth with her hand and bit down, trying to stop herself from saying anything else.

"Maybe it's Bridget's," said Neve, shrugging. "Who knows what the magic of the gods can do."

"Maybe it's even Neve's somehow," Nesta suggested.

"I find that highly unlikely," said Neve.

"Why couldn't it be?" said Nesta. "Beltane fires are supposed to be able to imbue fertility between beloveds, and you're my beloved."

"That's very sweet and way too happy for something you say in front of other people," said Neve jokingly. "I think the pregnancy hormones are already going to your head, love."

"I keep telling her there's nothing to worry about," said Nesta. "I've been to the doctor, who says everything's perfectly normal. They're running more tests to check on the baby's DNA. Obviously it's only early days yet. You're not really supposed to tell people this early, but I figure why not? It's not like anyone was expecting this."

"You've got that right," said Neve. "We've already got one child in the house. And now...who knows what's coming?"

"A *baby!*" said Nesta. "This is a very good thing. Don't worry, love, everything will be fine."

"How *are* things going at your place?" Rosemary asked. "How's your aunt?"

"Surprisingly well," said Neve. "It seems like the more time she spends here with us, the more her faculties seem to recover. Of course, Una and Ashwyn have given us a lot of tonics too, including the one that clears away fae memory loss. I think that's helped."

"That's wonderful," said Rosemary, clearing some space at the table so her friends could properly join her. "It's unusual for people to recover from dementia. Though I guess it was magically-induced, at least partially."

"That's what I figured too," said Neve, sitting down and idly thumbing through a pile of Rosemary's course papers.

"It's quite nice, really," Nesta added. "Meng is able to spend good quality time with her daughter. She gets Mei ready for school. We don't really have to do all that much."

"Which is just as well," said Neve. "Because I have my hands full with work at the moment."

"Why? What's going on?" Rosemary asked.

"There have been lots of strange occurrences lately. I wondered if it was your friends the Bloodstones, actually. There have even been a couple of sightings of Despina."

"I'm not surprised," said Rosemary. "Wherever she is, she's up to no good." Her hands began to prickle even with the thought. Rosemary hoped her allergy to estate agents didn't flare up again.

"That is a worry," said Marjie, bustling over with a tray of fresh tea. "But I'm sure things will work out. And I overheard everything. I'm so absolutely chuffed for you, Neve and Nesta. A miraculous baby! How wonderful!"

A warm ray of sunshine was shining through the window, making it a very pleasant place to be. Rosemary figured her course-work could wait. It was time to just enjoy the moment, though Neve's serious expression remained.

"What else is up?" Rosemary asked.

Neve reached into her bag. "You might as well take a look at these." She handed a parchment envelope to Rosemary. It contained pictures of a familiar woman, wearing dark sunglasses. She was petite, with luminescent skin and long blonde hair.

"Lamorna," Rosemary whispered.

Neve nodded. "She's been spotted in several locations around Cornwall, but we haven't managed to catch her yet."

AFTER NEVE AND NESTA LEFT, Rosemary got out her laptop and started working again, but her mind drifted back to worries about Lamorna, wondering what she was up to, and also to Athena, hoping school was going alright. It was hard to focus.

Marjie interrupted her, bringing her cream and jam scones and a fresh pot of tea.

"Have you thought any more about what I said?" Marjie asked.

"Which thing in particular?"

"You know, about the Summer Festival? Having a booth there? I'm sure it would help kickstart your business. Athena could help. It would give her something to do to take her mind off things."

"That's a good point," said Rosemary. "What are the dates of the festival?"

"It's right around the solstice," said Marjie.

"Oh, it's not very far away from the practicum part of my course where I have to go to London for a couple of weeks...leaving Athena alone for that amount of time."

"I tell you what," said Marjie. "I'll make you a deal. You sign up for the festival and I can come and stay at your house while you're away to look after Athena."

"Why are you so invested in this?" Rosemary asked with a smile.

"I'm invested in you," said Marjie. "You and Athena are family to me. And I want to see you happy. Something like this will be a good learning experience and help you focus, you know, towards building your business. You can really make a name for yourself with all the people coming from out of town. I just think it's a marvellous opportunity."

"Okay," Rosemary said. "You've convinced me. Where do I sign up?"

"Talk to Ferg," said Marjie.

"Of course."

Marjie directed Rosemary to the municipal buildings, the collection of offices surrounding the town hall that were right next to Burk's legal office, diagonally across the town square from the tea shop.

She found Ferg standing behind the desk, wearing a full suit in dark purple with a lavender waist coat, even though the weather was warm.

"I hear you work for the council, as well," said Rosemary. "How do you juggle all these different jobs?"

Ferg smiled, his grin stretching genuinely over his face. "It's easy," he said. "I work at the spa on the weekends. Taxi driving at night. And this is my new job. I'm here four days out of the week. I've had to cut back on gardening jobs since I started here."

"Four days?" Rosemary asked. "So you only have Friday off. Is that all?"

"Of course it is. On Friday, I have my own little holiday when everyone else is still at work."

"That's great, lovely, really, fair enough," said Rosemary. "Anyway, I hear you're the person to talk to regarding registering a booth for the Summer Festival."

"A booth?"

"Yes, that's right," said Rosemary.

He held up a finger and yelled. "Juniper! Juniper!"

Rosemary jumped as a woman appeared in a puff of steamy air right next to the desk. She had long, dark hair with purple streaks, and wore a matching plum coloured jacket dress.

"You called?" she said.

"Yes. Ms Thorn would like to register a booth for the festival."

"Very well," said Juniper.

"Well, this is a surprise," said Rosemary.

"I don't think we've met. My name is Juniper."

"I caught that. I'm Rosemary Thorn."

"Ah, I've heard about you."

"And you..." Rosemary was enormously curious about the eccentric woman who had just materialised in front of her but wasn't sure how to politely ask her to explain herself. Fortunately, Juniper took the cue.

"I'm a contractor. I pick up work here and there. Freelance. The mayor hired me to help organise the Summer Festival. It's nice to meet you." Juniper held out her hand.

"Yes, rather," said Rosemary.

Juniper had an odd expression on her face. "What kind of festival booth do you want to have?"

"Chocolate," said Rosemary.

Juniper's eyes lit up.

"I'm starting a chocolate business," Rosemary explained.

"Magical chocolates?" the woman asked.

"I'm hoping so," said Rosemary. "At least that's the plan. I'm starting with the regular ones."

"All righty. How quaint."

Rosemary was rather taken aback. "Anyway, how do I sign up?"

"These chocolates," said Ferg. "Are they quite safe?"

"Well, I'd certainly hope so," said Rosemary.

Ferg frowned. "They're not going to have any unintended consequences? No love spells."

"No," said Rosemary. "The town has had quite enough of that carry on."

"I'm with you on that front," said Ferg.

"You certainly don't have to worry about me when it comes to love spells. No, I've been considering very minor enchantments. You know, things like helping people focus on studying or maybe some sort of relaxing truffles."

"Mood altering," said Juniper.

"Like drugs?" Ferg raised his eyebrows.

"Not exactly," said Rosemary. "I mean, if it's against the rules, I can always just serve totally normal chocolates."

"Nonsense!" said Ferg. "The Summer Festival's a big party. I'd much rather people enjoy more controlled substances rather than taking illegal pills regardless of whether they're mundane or magical. At least if somebody has one of your chocolates we can track you down and hold you accountable."

"Yeah, that sounds great," said Rosemary flatly. "Maybe I will just stick to regular old mundane chocolates and nice flavours."

"I hope not," said Juniper. "I could do with a little chocolate pick me up."

"Chocolate is its own kind of magic," said Rosemary.

"I like the way you think." Juniper beamed at her. "Here." She held out her hand and a stack of forms materialised.

"Thanks...Umm, how did you do that thing before where you appeared out of thin air?"

Juniper shrugged. "It's a family thing. Not many magicians have this particular gift."

"A magician?"

Juniper nodded. "And I take it you're some kind of witch. The Thorn name is famous."

Rosemary smiled. "I suppose I am."

"Anyway, it was nice to meet you. You can return the forms here when you're finished with them."

"Within business hours!" Ferg added.

"Will do," said Rosemary. "Oh, and Ferg?"

"Yes, Ms Thorn?"

"You look nice today."

"I aim to serve," said Ferg, and he bowed elaborately.

Rosemary giggled and turned to leave. But on her way out she got the sense she was being watched. She turned to see Juniper following her out of the building.

"Can I have a word?" the woman asked.

"Sure," said Rosemary. "What is it?"

"I don't want to alarm you," said Juniper. "I...just being a contractor, I hear all sorts of things. You know, about various types of work that are going on in the magical community."

Rosemary gave her a questioning look.

"I've heard your name mentioned," Juniper continued. "A few times, actually, with regard to some particularly dodgy-sounding jobs."

"That sounds great," said Rosemary flatly. "I'm pretty sure I know who would be behind such a thing."

Then she realised multiple different parties could be responsible. "Actually," said Rosemary, "you wouldn't happen to be able to tell me anything more?"

Juniper grimaced. "These kinds of jobs tend to disguise who the actual request is from. I can't give you any more than a vague rumour. Besides, I need to be careful not to put my professional reputation at risk."

"Well, thanks anyway," said Rosemary. After all, Juniper had given her a heads up, even though the main effect of that information for Rosemary was just to make her feel on edge, as though something terribly violent was likely to happen at any moment.

"I'm on the way to the pub," said Juniper. "Care to join me for a drink?"

"Actually," said Rosemary, "now that you mention it, I could do with an afternoon pick me up, even if it's just to ease the sense of impending doom."

"That's the spirit," said Juniper. "Let's go."

Juniper disappeared in a puff of air, leaving Rosemary feeling slightly jealous. "I want to be able to do that trick!" she said aloud to no one in particular.

"What trick?" said Ferg, who had clearly followed them outside.

"That puff of air teleporting thing."

"Oh, that," he said. "It's overrated."

"You mean, you can do that?" Rosemary asked.

"If I tried I probably could," said Ferg.

Rosemary raised her eyebrows at him questioningly, but he remained silent. "Why did you come out here?" Rosemary asked. "Have I forgotten something, or are you on your way out anyway?"

"Just eavesdropping," said Ferg.

"That's rude, you know. You shouldn't do that," Rosemary scolded.

"So I've been told," said Ferg. "But if people insist on having loud conversations in public, then who am I to ignore them?"

"Or to at least avoid following them to listen."

"Exactly!" said Ferg. "I'm glad you understand."

Rosemary sighed and turned to go.

"Don't you think it's strange?" Ferg continued as she walked away.

"What's strange?" said Rosemary over her shoulder.

"Strange that you just met Juniper and now you're suddenly chums who go for a drink at the pub together?"

Rosemary paused, pondering this. "No, I don't think it's particularly strange."

"Oh," said Ferg. "Just checking."

Rosemary turned, with half a mind to continue the conversation, but Ferg had already disappeared back into the municipal buildings, leaving her alone and slightly perturbed.

CHAPTER
SEVEN

Athena had practically glided into school that morning. She was relieved that Rosemary hadn't noticed anything different about her or interrogated her good mood. There was a risk of it looking like Athena had been enchanted the way that her mother had been by Finnigan. She felt all light and floaty. It was a welcome change from the intense foreboding doom she had become quite used to.

As soon as she saw Elise she butterflies in her tummy.

Their interaction yesterday was most definitely responsible for Athena's happy mood, but she felt confused about how to act or what to do. Elise was already seated in Ms Twigg's class, so Athena took a seat next to her and gave her a quick smile, trying to act normal.

For a moment Athena was worried that Elise had reconsidered or had a change of heart after the day before. Athena felt a creeping sense of dread, then Elise smiled shyly back at her, and all else was forgotten.

Athena barely noticed when Finnigan walked into the classroom. And when she did realise he was there, he suddenly felt unimportant. She had much better things in life to think about, and he seemed to be doing what the school had promised and avoiding her.

Beryl, however, seemed to have taken an interest in Finnigan and had engaged him in some sort of intensive whispered conversation.

Ms Twigg entered the classroom and put a stop to all that. With a wave of her hand, she sent Beryl and Finnigan careening back into bolt-upright positions in their seats.

"Enough of that," said Ms Twigg. "Time for the lesson to begin. You'd do well to take notes, as I promise you this will be relevant for your exams."

"She says that every class," Felix whispered.

"And I'm right, young Mr Lancaster."

"Are we going to talk about the Summer Solstice?" said Felix with a cheeky grin. He'd been asking about the solstice since Beltane, as he'd evidently found the whole fiery debacle thrilling and was hoping for more action at the next seasonal festival.

"No disruptions, Mr Lancaster," said Ms Twigg.

"No, I was just going to thank you," said Felix.

"Thank me?" said Ms Twigg.

Athena could tell she was trying to tame the smile that curled up her lips.

"Yes," said Felix.

"*I* should be thanking you, really," Athena said to the teacher. "The assignment you gave us for Beltane really helped to turn things in the right direction, gave us a heads up about what kind of dangers might have been causing those fires...So, if you *do* have any ideas for anything else that might be particularly useful..."

"The Summer Solstice is coming up," said Felix. "Things are gonna get steamy!"

"They couldn't possibly get any steamier then Beltane, surely?" said Elise, blushing. "Those fires were quite something."

"They were disturbing indeed," said Ms Twigg. "And I daresay the town should be thanking you, Miss Thorn, and your mother."

Beryl stared daggers at her, prompting Athena to grin. "The mayor already did thank us."

Ms Twigg gave a dismissive laugh. "I think our fine magistrate would much rather thank himself."

"It was a team effort, really," Athena continued, somewhat enjoying Beryl's particularly sour expression. "But Felix has a point. Maybe we should be learning about the next festival. Is there any lore on the Summer Solstice that you think would be useful to know about?"

Ms Twigg regarded her cautiously. "Now...the Summer Solstice is otherwise known as Litha. For many hundreds of years it has been a time of banishing evil spirits."

"Why would the summer relate to evil?" Elise asked. "It seems like such a nice relaxed time, compared to some of the other seasons at least."

"Exactly," said Ms Twigg. "Make hay while the sun shines! Summer solstice is when the solar energy is at its highest point. The sun is the most powerful magical and physical force that we work with, as human beings and as magical beings. At its peak, the solar energy can be harnessed, and that is why, for such a long time, people have used the important culmination of energy at the solstice to chase away any evil spirits that might be lingering. As you probably all know, in Myrtlewood, we celebrate Summer Solstice at the top of the tor."

"I didn't know that," said Athena. "Why isn't it celebrated in the town square, like everything else?"

Ms Twigg raised her finger to quiet the class down. "Let me continue. The Summer Solstice in Myrtlewood has long been a shared celebration with the druids of Cornwall. Several hundred years ago, Myrtlewood was struggling with a great many evil spirits. They were drawn here by the magical nature of the town. Some of your families were probably involved at the time. However, if you remember or value history—" She sounded rather bitter. "—an accord was struck with the nine druid clans of Cornwall, sending some of the most powerful druids to support and work with the Myrtlewood townsfolk to cast out the spirits which had been wreaking havoc, not only in our village, but across the entire region. It used to be that all of the important seasonal festivals were celebrated at the top of the tor...back in the old days. But after that fateful summer, and the powerful ritual performed then, it was decided that only the solstices would be carried out there – winter and summer. And the others would be conducted from the relative safety of the town circle."

"How peculiar," Athena muttered to Elise.

Ms Twigg shot her sharp look. "Are you quite finished?"

"Yes," said Athena. "Go on."

Ashwagandha raised her hand. "I have a question."

"Yes, Miss Rashad?"

"Why is it that everything bad seems to happen when we need to do some kind of traditional seasonal ritual? Shouldn't we stop celebrating them if they're causing so much mayhem?"

"Don't be silly," said Beryl. "It's tradition!"

"Actually," said Ms Twigg. "It's a good question. We all have our theories, but the predominant hypothesis is that the magical energy of Myrtlewood grows stronger near the eight traditional sabbats whether we like it or not. Of course they don't necessarily cause any mayhem themselves, but other things seem to magnetise to them. The reason that we have to keep celebrating them is because that energy would build regardless of whether we were planning a ritual or not. The rituals themselves help to release that energy – they are an outlet. And they also then bind the energy back into the earth, where it can do more good than harm."

"It's a nice theory," said Athena.

"It's more than a theory," said Beryl in a haughty voice. "It's been true for generations. Some families might not pay attention to the history of Myrtlewood, but mine does."

"Yes, thank you Ms Flarguan," said Ms Twigg.

"Not everyone has the privilege to grow up here, or know much about magic," said Felix defensively. "It's not like that makes you any better than anyone else."

Beryl turned her nose up at him and shot Finnigan a smile so charming it made Athena feel nauseous. She looked away from the two of them, focusing back on Ms Twigg.

It was a shame, in some ways, that the classroom was set out so that all of the chairs and desks were in a semicircle, meaning that they could all see each other. She would have preferred for Finnigan to be out of her line of vision, and Beryl too, for that matter. She could do without either of them in her life.

Beryl might have helped, at some point in Rosemary's attempts to get through to the fae realm to rescue Athena, but the endeavour certainly hadn't improved her character.

"Have you thought about what might happen at the Summer Solstice?" Felix asked.

It was the most Athena had ever seen him engage in Ms Twigg's class, as he was usually too terrified to speak in front of the tiny reptile-like teacher aside from occasional cheeky outbursts.

Ms Twigg seemed to be glowing with the unusual amount of attention she was receiving from the students.

"I'm pleased you're all so interested in our history and what it can teach us about our present and future," she said. "Well, let me see. There is a possibility that something will happen in relation to those evil spirits I mentioned...I suppose."

"But shouldn't they be weaker at the solstice?" Sam asked. They were sitting next to Elise and had been so quiet that Athena had barely registered them.

"In theory, the spirits should be weaker at that time. That's right," said Ms Twigg. "But we have seen an unusual amount of energy building in town. The number of attacks and other unusual magical occurrences have dramatically increased since the old Thorn family magic was released."

Beryl glared at Athena. "It's hardly fair that the rest of us have to suffer just because Athena and her ditzy mother can't wield their own magic."

"Enough!" said Ms Twigg. "That was highly inappropriate. Another outburst like that, Beryl, and you'll be looking forward to your first ever detention."

Beryl blanched and looked down at her desk.

"There's more magic to go around," Ms Twigg continued. "In theory, evil spirits shouldn't have a chance. But there's also the unfortunate syndrome that when something is weakened or cornered, it can become more dangerous."

"Have things like that happened in the past around the solstice?" Athena asked.

"Oh, there have been various incidents over the years," said Ms Twigg. "The energy of high summer also seems to bring out some of our more unusual magical beings."

"As long as it's not more fire sprites," said Elise.

"Actually, the fire sprites are my favourites." Felix beamed.

Elise threw her pen at him.

"Settle down, class," said Ms Twigg. "Now turn to page eighty-five of your books and begin to read. I don't want to hear another word spoken out of turn for the rest of the class."

Despite Ms Twigg's reluctance to go into any depth on the Summer Solstice festival, to Athena's surprise, their following class was themed on that very topic.

Astrology and Ovations was usually a reasonably quiet but interesting subject focusing on topics like drafting natal charts and the theory behind tarot card reading and other forms of divination. Athena enjoyed the classes, finding astrology particularly interesting. She also seemed to have a natural talent for it, which helped her feel better about not growing up in the magical world.

The class was taught by Dr Stella Ceres, a quiet but amusing teacher with round thick-rimmed glasses, who usually styled her bright pink hair in plaits. She also had a tendency to wear bright robes that clashed spectacularly with her hair. Athena was still confused about whether this made her very cool or the total opposite, but either way, she liked Dr Ceres for her clever wit and dry humour.

On this particular day, the teacher wore tangerine robes and had pinned her plaits up onto her head. Combined with the glasses, this gave her a rather owlish resemblance.

She began the class by clearing her throat. "Alright, class. Today we will be charting—"

Felix sighed. "Not another birth chart."

"I'm afraid not, Felix. Though I appreciate your enthusiasm."

Athena smiled as Felix opened his mouth and closed it a few times but couldn't seem to find a clever retort.

Dr Ceres paced the room as she continued. "Charting the sky for significant events is one of the most ancient forms of astrology. People across the ancient world believed that the placement and movements of the planets could give them an insight into war strategy and other significant things. The planets, as you know, are associated with and named after gods. This varies between cultures, but interestingly, their meanings are often similar."

"What event are we charting?" Beryl asked, clearly keen to get into the work and prove she could still be top of the class in every subject.

"The Summer Solstice," said Dr Ceres. "As you will be aware, our recent seasonal festivals have been somewhat heightened. I have been following the astrological correspondences, naturally. I was going to encourage the class to analyse them, but then I thought more of a future focus could be a more practical application."

Athena felt her brain light up at the possibility. This could definitely come in handy, considering the high likelihood that she and her mother would be embroiled in any future festival chaos.

Dr Ceres tapped the large glass panel she used to display things for the class, which was clearly some kind of magically-induced projector.

A chart appeared. Athena stared at the familiar round wheel, divided into twelve segments dotted with glyphs of planets that the class had been trying to memorise for several months. These were connected to each other with red and blue lines in a way that always looked web-like to Athena.

"See here, we have the chart for Beltane." Dr Ceres picked up her wand. It was a pale colour and she'd explained to the class it was made from a particularly thick mugwort plant. She pointed it at the glyph at the top of the chart. "Mars on the midheaven, in Aries, making strong aspects to Jupiter and Uranus – talk about a fiery combination!"

She talked them through the other two previous seasonal festival charts before circling back to the upcoming solstice.

"So you want us to chart something that hasn't happened yet?" Felix asked, sounding unimpressed.

Dr Ceres nodded. "You'll find this is the very class for focusing on things that haven't happened yet, as is the ovate tradition. Your astrological ephemeris goes all the way up to five hundred years in the future and you'll find it's no different from making a past chart."

In a burst of excitement, Athena raised her hand.

Dr Ceres nodded in her direction.

"Is there anything in particular you want us to look at for these charts?" she asked. "I mean...you must have looked at the Summer Solstice already..."

Dr Ceres smiled. "Cheeky of you to ask, but since you're so enthusiastic, I suggest paying particular attention to the alignments of Neptune and Venus in a T square to Saturn, Mars, and Jupiter – potent astrological energy."

Athena gulped. "That sounds like it could be bad."

"Not necessarily bad," Dr Ceres explained. "But not easy, either. If any of you are going to the Summer Festival or celebrating the solstice, take care. The energy will be particularly strong at sacred sites, and especially so with all those people there..."

"Thanks for telling us all this," said Athena. "Is there anything else you think we should know?"

Dr Ceres stood in silence for a moment, and then she lifted her wand and pointed to the planet that looked a lot like a trident. "Neptune is significant in the chart you'll be making."

She pointed to the stereo in the corner of the room and it began playing a lulling and captivating tune. "This is one of the songs by Stellium for Neptune."

"It sounds so different to the Saturn one she played last week," Elise muttered.

Athena nodded. Dr Ceres liked to talk about this particular astrology-themed band in class and occasionally played their songs, and the Saturn album was basically death metal. This was quite different, soft and trance-like. Indeed, Athena noticed that Ash, Sam, and Deron were all swaying gently to the music, whether they knew it or not.

Dr Ceres cut the sound with a wave of her wand. "Remember, Astrology is a mirror – it shows us the patterns in the universe. Wherever the planet of the mystic is, it will be spellbinding, captivating...but there will also be distortion and delusion."

"Sounds like my kind of party," said Felix with a smug grin.

CHAPTER
EIGHT

Rosemary walked to the pub along the streets of Myrtlewood village. It was a lovely day. Sunlight warmed her skin and birds almost seemed to harmonise with the other usual sounds. She couldn't help but replay the conversation she'd just had with Ferg, wondering if it was strange to be having a drink with a person she'd just met.

Perhaps it is, thought Rosemary. *But I'm hardly normal anyway.* And Ferg was one to talk. He was a particularly odd personality as far as Rosemary could see.

There were plenty of good reasons to go to the pub. Juniper was intriguing and had some interesting and potentially dangerous information that Rosemary needed to know to keep herself and Athena safe. And anyway, she wanted to talk to Sherry.

Despite all this, part of her mind wondered if she was making excuses. Was she under some kind of enchantment again, like with Finnigan? It certainly didn't seem that way, but with Juniper clearly being so powerful, was it possible that she could influence Rosemary without her ever noticing?

For a moment, Rosemary warred with herself, trying to decide if she should just go home, instead. She turned back in the direction of the car, then meandered on the main street, checking the progress on her new shop through the window. Everything seemed to be in order.

After all this, Rosemary didn't feel as if she needed to have a drink with Juniper or anything and that convinced her that she wasn't under any kind of magical compulsion. She turned back, and headed towards the pub after all, hoping that she wasn't going to come across as rude for being so late.

Seeing as it was only early afternoon and the lunch rush was over, the pub was rather empty. Rosemary made her way over to Juniper, who was sitting on a bar stool, sipping a pink drink out of a martini glass.

"That looks good," said Rosemary.

"It's a cosmopolitan," said Juniper. "I think it's cranberry and something."

"Sounds divine," said Rosemary.

"And what will you have, love?" Sherry asked. Her greying sandy hair was pulled into two plaits and she looked tired.

"I think I'll have the same," said Rosemary.

Sherry smiled. "Not too early in the day for cocktails then?"

"Never," said Juniper with a wink.

Sherry pulled out the cocktail shaker and began preparing the drink while Juniper excused herself and headed towards the restrooms.

"How are you going?" Rosemary asked Sherry.

Sherry and Rosemary hadn't talked very much, not since their escapade into the fae realm where Sherry had admitted to stealing Rosemary's necklace.

Though they'd had numerous interactions since then, their friendship had been strained and awkward.

"As well as can be expected," Sherry replied. "Considering how weird things were for a while. I was so embarrassed after how I'd acted. I could barely face you. I'm sorry. I didn't mean to cause you any trouble at all. And I certainly didn't mean to steal from you. The whole situation with the fae realm just had me out of my mind for a while."

"Yeah, I get it," said Rosemary. "I wasn't really myself either. Not with Athena missing."

"It's so good to have Mei back," said Sherry.

"Have you seen her lately?" Rosemary asked.

"Oh yes, we have play dates every Thursday afternoon. Neve lets me pick her up from school, and we go to the park for a while. I mean, it's a little bit strange that my best friend is still an eight-year-old girl. Now I'm an adult...at least I'm supposed to be. The fae realm does such weird things to your mind."

"It must be strange for her too," said Rosemary. "I hear her mother's doing a lot better."

"Oh yes, Meng's wonderful. It's so good she's recovered from her memory issues. Did you hear about Neve and Nesta?"

"Isn't that exciting?!" said Rosemary. "I was thinking about throwing them a surprise dinner, and that was actually one of the reasons I wanted to talk to you. I thought it would be great if you could come."

"Of course," said Sherry.

"Thank you."

"Is it sort of a baby shower thing?"

"I don't know," said Rosemary. "Just an excuse to get together and celebrate. I thought I'd invite them around and surprise them with a whole lot of good friends and nice food."

"Maybe a few chocolates," Sherry suggested.

"Maybe," said Rosemary.

"Excellent!" said Sherry. "Count me in."

She shook up the cocktail, poured it into another sugar-rimmed martini glass, and handed it over to Rosemary, then she went to attend to another customer at the other end of the bar.

Juniper returned and leaned against the bar. "Tell me more about these chocolates."

Rosemary wasn't sure how much she should be sharing with this woman she hardly knew. She took a sip of the drink, finding it deliciously tart and fruity. "Yum. This flavour would make an excellent soft centred filling, don't you think?"

"I do like the idea of cocktail chocolates," said Juniper. "So this is your business, is it? Fancy and possibly magical chocolates?"

"Yes," said Rosemary. "Well, that's the idea. It's something that I dreamed about but never thought was possible. And now that I've got a little bit of money from an inheritance, I don't really have an excuse not to do it."

"Do you have a shop?" Juniper asked.

"Yes, in fact it's being renovated right now. I'm just trying to learn how to be in business, and how to be a bit more professional with regard to chocolate making, too. I did a little bit of chef school, years ago, before I had Athena."

"Your daughter?"

"Yes, but everything's fallen by the wayside, I'm afraid. I can do the basics myself, but I'm a far cry from being a proper chocolatier."

"I'm sure you'll master it quickly," said Juniper.

"How do you know? You only just met me."

"But I'm an excellent judge of character," said Juniper.

Her words reminded Rosemary of Athena.

Juniper continued. "You seem like a person who goes after what she wants with stubborn determination, a woman after my own heart. Besides, the Thorn family magic is supposed to be incredibly powerful."

"So everyone tells me," said Rosemary. "Although, I'm afraid I'm a bit of a novice."

"To magic?" Juniper asked, and Rosemary got the distinct feeling that she was digging for information.

"Something like that," said Rosemary, trying not to give away too much. "Why was it you asked me to have a drink?"

"You seemed intriguing," said Juniper. "And I'm always looking forward to making new friends. You know, I don't have normal colleagues, because I don't work in an office or anything, so I just have to meet people wherever I find them. More to the point, why did you agree to have a drink with me?"

"I don't think that's more to the point," Rosemary argued jokingly. "But anyway, I have to admit, I was curious. Based on what you said before, it sounds like there's a whole lot of dodgy dealings going on that you know about. I felt like you might be a good person to know."

"So you're trying to get some more information out of me?" said Juniper.

"I'm just trying to keep myself and my daughter safe," said Rosemary, taking another swig of the delicious beverage.

"Admirable cause," said Juniper. "I'll drink to that."

Rosemary raised her glass to clink Juniper's. Her intuition was telling her Juniper was alright.

After several more cocktails and a shared bowl of chips between them, Rosemary asked Juniper about how she was able to travel by apparition or teleportation.

"Oh yes," said Juniper. "I'm told it's quite a rare gift."

"Can you take other people with you?" Rosemary asked.

"I can, but it's not very pleasant for them," said Juniper.

"That's a shame," said Rosemary.

"But I'm game if you are," said Juniper. She reached out and touched Rosemary's arm.

"Go on then," said Rosemary, feeling slightly silly.

The room swirled around, and motion sickness rose up. She didn't know which way was up or down. It was as if she'd spun around in a circle fast many times.

Something hard hit the side of her body and she opened her eyes to see the ocean on a funny angle. She was lying sideways.

Rosemary picked herself up, realising from the salty air and gritty sand beneath her that she was on the beach.

Juniper giggled. "Sorry. I told you it was unpleasant."

"It certainly was interesting," said Rosemary, trying not to give away the strong urge she had to throw up the contents of her guts.

"It should pass in a little while...the nausea, I mean," said Juniper.

"The beach..." said Rosemary. "It's funny. We've lived in Myrtlewood for months, but we've hardly spent any time here."

"It's not so nice in the colder seasons," said Juniper. "Plus it's very windy in spring."

"Not too bad today, though," said Rosemary.

The sun was shining and there was only a slight breeze.

"No, we picked a good day for it."

Rosemary propped herself up but remained lying down because she wasn't sure she could deal with standing yet.

"We should have brought a picnic," said Juniper.

"I don't think I could stomach it."

"I did warn you."

"True," said Rosemary. "I should probably head home soon. Athena will be finishing school for the day."

"Do you need to pick her up?"

"Oh no. School is kind of in our house at the moment."

"That's right, I heard something about that," said Juniper.

"So you're from Myrtlewood?" Rosemary asked. There was so

little that she knew about this new friend, and yet, they had already somehow gone on two excursions together.

"I'm from here and there," said Juniper. "I did spend a little time in Myrtlewood, growing up. I went to high school here, and it's the closest place to a home that I've ever really had. My family are kind of mercenaries of the magical world."

Rosemary raised her eyebrows.

"Not in a murderous way," said Juniper. "We just go wherever we're needed. Do whatever job needs doing. That's how I was raised."

"Sounds quite adventurous," said Rosemary.

"You could say that. When I was younger I just yearned for stability, but I guess it's not really in my blood. I can't seem to stay still or in any one place for very long."

"I'm finding it quite nice to finally have a home," said Rosemary. "We moved around a lot as well. And finally, I'm somewhere I don't really want to leave."

Juniper smiled. "It does sound nice, in a way. I mean, I'm sure I'd get bored and restless if I tried it, but the sentiment is nice."

"It is," said Rosemary. She pushed herself up to sitting. And then dropped back down. "I might need a few more minutes."

"Take your time," said Juniper. "We're not too far from Myrtle-wood town, so it won't take long to get back."

She looked around at the stunning horizon. "Why do you think they built the village a little distance from the sea, and not directly by it?"

"I don't know," said Juniper. "There's no natural port here, so it's not really important for Myrtlewood. I suppose the beach was always just for holidaymakers, people taking in the airs or whatever they used to do back in history...going to the seaside to eat well or something."

"That sounds about right," said Rosemary.

"Myrtlewood town is quite distant from everywhere else," Juniper continued. "You know, being a magical village, there's a little bit of tourism but it's carefully managed. We have a few public events. And of course there's the Summer Festival."

"I've been hearing more and more about that," said Rosemary. "But I'd love to know more."

"It's just a festival," said Juniper. "It may be magically enhanced in some ways. People come from all over the country, some even come from abroad. It brings in some good income for the town, keeps everything flowing, builds some energy too, which I understand is captured."

"Captured?" Rosemary asked.

"In a matter of speaking," said Juniper. "The Summer Solstice ritual is said to capture the bountiful energy of the sun. Anyway, it kind of helps to clear the air, having a big party in the summer. There's some magic at play and I think the witching authorities have a way of collecting the energy. It's supposed to help in the smooth running of the town."

"Intriguing," said Rosemary. "Is it in the small print on the tickets?"

Juniper chuckled. "I'm not sure the non-magical attendants would be quite comfortable with that."

"No one reads the small print, anyway," said Rosemary. "I bet they'd never notice."

Juniper laughed mischievously. "Maybe we'll put a few things on the tickets just to test that theory. How about we go for a quick walk if you're feeling better?"

"I don't know," said Rosemary. "I should be getting back, soon."

"Oh well, we'll walk back then."

"That would be for the best," said Rosemary. "I don't think I could manage travelling back in your usual mode. I've had quite enough teleportation for one lifetime."

"Don't speak too soon," said Juniper. "Who knows, with the strength of the full Thorn family magic you might be able to master it, yourself."

"I find that very hard to believe," said Rosemary. "Although I am getting rather good at lightning balls."

"Intriguing," said Juniper. "Come on." She held out her arm to pull Rosemary up.

They walked back along the seaside. About halfway along the beach, there was an outcrop of rocks.

A woman stood there, and at first Rosemary thought nothing of it. But as they drew nearer, she realised there seemed to be blood on her face.

"What's going on?" Rosemary asked Juniper.

"I don't know. Do you think she needs our help?"

They approached. The woman had a dazed look. She appeared to be in her early fifties and was wearing a t-shirt and blue jeans.

"Hi there, are you alright?" Rosemary asked.

The woman looked at her, confused. "I don't know. Where am I?"

"You're on the beach in Myrtlewood," said Juniper.

"Myrtlewood," the woman said blankly.

Rosemary tried to give her a reassuring look. "What's your name?"

"Name?" the woman repeated, stumbling and then sitting down on one of the rocks.

"Yes. What's your name, dear?" said Juniper.

"I don't know."

"You don't?" Rosemary was becoming more concerned.

"I don't...know my name."

"Oh dear," said Juniper. "We'd better get you back to town. Come on."

Rosemary took the woman's arm, noticing that her clothes were wet. "She's shivering."

"You think she went for a swim? Did you go for a swim and hit your head?" Juniper asked.

"Swim?" the woman repeated. "Oh, I don't know. It's cold...too cold to swim."

"She obviously remembers how to talk, at least," said Juniper.

"Talk," the woman repeated.

Rosemary shot Juniper a concerned look. She took off her jacket and wrapped it around the woman. "Let's get her to town."

The woman didn't budge as Rosemary tried to pull her up. "I hate to ask, especially because I didn't really enjoy it the first time, but I don't know how else we're going to move her..."

"We could call an ambulance," Juniper suggested.

"We could," said Rosemary. "Or you could just zip us back to town with magic. I'm hoping Neve might know what to do."

"Oh...Neve," said Juniper with a slight edge to her voice.

"Do you know her?" Rosemary asked.

"We go way back," said Juniper with a somewhat awkward smile.

"Oh yes?" said Rosemary, feeling slightly uneasy. "Well, if you don't mind, please take us back to town now and hopefully we'll be able to sort things out for this woman. I don't know how long it would take an ambulance to get out here, and besides, it looks like I've got no phone reception." She waved her phone around.

"If you think that's the best approach," said Juniper. She reached out, touching both Rosemary's and the woman's shoulders.

Rosemary gritted her teeth. She felt her nausea rising again as the world spun around her. Everything went grey and white and blue and purple. And then she found herself lying on the soft grass of the Myrtlewood town square that was actually a circle.

"Ugh...Thanks," said Rosemary. "I guess."

It didn't take her quite so long to adjust this time, but by the time she pulled herself up and checked to see if the confused woman from the beach was okay, she looked around to see that Juniper had gone.

"What a strange woman," Rosemary muttered to herself.

"Woman," said Rosemary's confused new friend.

"Yes, that's right, dear," she said, pulling out her cell phone.

It wasn't long before detective Neve arrived in the town square.

"Where did you find her?" she asked Rosemary, after checking to see if the woman was okay.

"On that big outcropping of rocks at the beach."

Neve and Rosemary helped the woman to her feet and began walking towards the station, reassuring their bewildered new acquaintance that everything would be alright, although Rosemary wished she felt more confident.

"So you were out on the beach alone?" Neve asked as they crossed the town circle. "Was anyone else there?"

"I was there with Juniper."

"Juniper?" said Neve, her eyes bulging in surprise.

"It seems that you two know each other."

"I wish we didn't," said Neve. "We went to school together. Juniper's bad news."

"She's a troublemaker?"

"Something like that," said Neve. "Her family are all kinds of mercenaries."

"Yes, she told me that," said Rosemary.

"Are you best buddies now?" said Neve, sounding slightly jealous.

"No, I only just met her. Although we did then go out for cocktails and go to the beach."

"It sounds like you really hit it off," said Neve, guiding them across the road.

"We seem to get along pretty well."

"Well, watch your back. I don't know too much about her these days, but I know she's not trustworthy. She is some kind of magical freelancer, but she never gives the police any good information, even though I'm sure she has plenty."

"She did tell me a few things," said Rosemary as they entered the station. "That's partly why I went for a drink with her. It seems there are a few people out to get me. Perhaps it's not just the Blood-stones, after all."

"That's terrible!" said Neve. "But take anything she says with a big pinch of salt...or even a whole salt circle, since you are a witch."

Rosemary smiled. "Anyway, enough about me. How are we going to help her?" She gestured to the woman.

"I'll call the medics."

"We have medics?" said Rosemary.

"Of course, with all the magical injuries around here we definitely need medics."

Rosemary glared at Neve. "Next you'll tell me we have a whole hospital!"

"We do," said Neve. "Though it's not in town, it's further up north."

"Why doesn't anyone tell me any of this?" said Rosemary.

"Be thankful that you've never needed it," said Neve.

"That's a good point, in a way, especially given all the trouble we've been through," said Rosemary. "Problem is, if I did need it I wouldn't have known."

"Perhaps you don't ask the right questions." There was an edge to Neve's voice and Rosemary couldn't help but think that it was something to do with bringing up Juniper earlier. She went off to make a cup of tea, returning moments later with a large blue mug which she handed gently to the confused woman.

"Tea?" said Neve.

"Tea," the woman repeated with a nod. She took a sip.

Rosemary sighed in relief. If the woman could drink tea then maybe there was hope for her recovery. "Hey, I'm sorry if you feel weird about the situation with Juniper. We're really not great buddies or anything. I barely know her."

"It's alright," said Neve. "You can be friends with whoever you want." A genuine smile spread across her face.

"How about I make it up to you? You and Nesta should come over to dinner on Thursday. Bring Mei and Meng as well."

"Okay then," said Neve. "That sounds lovely."

"I'll make something special," said Rosemary. "Be there at seven."

"Will do...and Rosemary?"

"What?"

"Thank you."

Rosemary laughed. "For creating more work for you?"

"No."

"For finding a strange woman on the beach?"

"No," said Neve. "Though that actually was good. I would hate to think what would have happened to her if she'd stayed out there much longer. She looks like she's already caught a chill."

"What are you thanking me for, then?"

"For being a good friend," said Neve. "I haven't had that many close friends in my life. First of all, because everyone else around me was magical, and I never fit in at school. And that's probably why I resented Juniper as well, because she's so powerful. And then, you know, being queer, sometimes it feels like people judge you. Anyway, it makes for a bit of an isolated existence. I'm lucky I have Nesta, but it's also good to have you and Athena, and it feels like you've brought a whole bunch of other people into our lives too. It feels like a real community."

"Well, it takes a village to raise a child," said Rosemary.

Neve gave her an uneasy look. "Exactly."

CHAPTER
NINE

Rosemary was slightly dishevelled by the time she returned home. She entered Thorn Manor to find Athena sitting at the kitchen table, eating a crumpet from the stash that Marjie had brought over.

"These are really good," said Athena. "Marjie should figure out how to package up her baking and sell it to rich people for five times the usual price. She'd make a fortune."

"Don't give her any ideas," said Rosemary. "She's already on an entrepreneurial bent, trying to get me to sign up for all kinds of things."

"Oh yes?" said Athena.

"Long story," said Rosemary. "How are you? How was your day?"

"I'm more interested to know how your day was," Athena said. "You look a right wreck."

"Thanks, darling," said Rosemary. "I can always count on you for your absolute blistering honesty, at least."

"I do my best," said Athena.

"Was it okay being at school today?" Rosemary asked.

"School was fun. We learnt more about the celestial alignment at the solstice. I've almost finished my chart."

"Oh good," said Rosemary. She'd been trying to ask about the Finnigan situation but was happy Athena had other things to interest her.

Athena frowned. "It's also worrying. There's a lot going on astrologically on the Summer Solstice. It could get messy, especially with so much Neptune energy."

Rosemary shrugged. "Maybe it's best not to think too much about that stuff."

Athena crossed her arms. "You're not taking me seriously. Listen to this." She flicked through a playlist on her phone, with quite different songs all coming from the same band, Stellium, the one Athena had been raving about recently.

"And what does all this have to do with the solstice?" Rosemary asked as she began toasting crumpets for herself and put the kettle on for tea.

"The songs are based on the energy of planets," said Athena curtly. "I'm just educating you."

"Not really my thing," said Rosemary. The Jupiter song was too grand and there were trumpets – a bit much for Rosemary. The Uranus song was too chaotic.

"I wish you'd take an interest," said Athena.

"I can't help it if I'm a bit put off by the woo-woo. Besides, I don't like how astrology makes me a ditz."

"Mum, you were already a ditz, it's just your Gemini Ascendant, not your whole personality."

"Still, it's not particularly fair, as I didn't choose to be born at that particular time."

"A lot of magical scholars would argue that you did, and anyway, it's not a terrible thing, just a tendency. It's a pattern – a mirror of the universe. You get to choose if you work with it or against it."

Rosemary swallowed a bite of her crumpet. "Stop that."

"What?"

"Stop sounding wise when you're disagreeing with me. I don't enjoy it."

They both laughed, but Athena still seemed grumpy at Rosemary's lack of trust in astrology. Just then, Serpentine, Rosemary's fuzzy black kitten familiar wandered over with a serious expression. "What is it, little creature?"

Rosemary patted the kitten and scratched his chin. She flinched as something black protruded from his mouth. "Ahh. Cat – gross!"

"What is it?" Athena craned her neck to look over the table as the object clattered to the floor.

"Looks like one of Granny's crystals," said Athena.

"Naughty fuzzball," said Rosemary. "You should know that isn't food."

The cat looked at her imploringly.

"What's going on with her?" Athena asked. "Hey, that stone is onyx."

Rosemary stared at the kitten who continued to give her a meaningful look and then touched the stone with the tip of her paw and walked off.

"Well, that was weird and creepy."

"Maybe not," said Athena. "Onyx is a Saturn stone. Maybe you need it."

She picked up the stone, cleaned it, and popped it into her mother's handbag.

Rosemary sighed and looked at her daughter. "Back to the subject of school, was *he* there?"

"He was," said Athena. "But I didn't really talk to him. He seemed to avoid me completely. And I think it was fine."

"He didn't just enchant you to think that?" Rosemary asked.

"I'm not that silly, Mum. That's your trick."

Rosemary frowned. "It is kind of embarrassing, though. I'm supposed to be a powerful witch. And yet, this young upstart keeps making a fool of me."

"I just had to put up with Beryl giving me nasty looks and giving Finnigan an awful lot of attention."

"Is she trying to make you jealous?" said Rosemary.

"Possibly?" said Athena. "I mean, it's not like Finnigan's from a fancy magical family or anything. I'd figured he wouldn't be in her league."

"Maybe she's got a thing for fae," said Rosemary, pouring tea for them both.

"You're one to talk."

Rosemary glared at her. "I guess neither of us are on that count."

"I don't know what you're talking about," said Athena. "I am perfectly innocent. Finnigan and I might have been friends, but it certainly didn't develop into much more than that. And now, well now...we're nothing."

"I'm glad to hear about both of those things," said Rosemary. "And I'm trying my best not to pry."

"That's good," said Athena. "Respect my privacy. Now tell me about your day."

"Well, I wish it had been as peaceful as yours," said Rosemary, taking a sip of her tea.

"Oh no, what happened?"

"Everything was fine, at first. I was at Marjie's. She convinced me to sign up for this big solstice festival thing."

"Sign up?'

"She wants me to sell chocolates. You know, like, have some sort of sales booth there. She thinks it'll be great for business. This is what I was meaning about her being on an entrepreneurial bent."

"Why not?" said Athena. "It sounds like the festival's a big deal. There'll be loads of people from all around the country. It's a great opportunity."

"Not you, too," said Rosemary. "And of course I had to go and see Ferg for that."

"Ferg does everything," said Athena. "Where would the town be without him?"

"I'm not sure. Anyway, I went to sign up and met this interesting character..."

"Oh no," said Athena. "Not another interesting character. I'm afraid we know far too many of them already."

"You're probably right. Anyway, I kind of made friends with her."

Rosemary opened the fridge, wondering what to have for dinner.

"Look at you making even more friends. Who is this person? What's she like? Do I need to investigate her history and check that she's safe for you to be friends with?"

"I'm the parent here," said Rosemary, crossing her arms. "I should be the one doing that kind of thing. Her name is Juniper. She's apparently some sort of magical freelancer or contractor."

"Does she build houses?" Athena asked. "Maybe repair schools?"

"Not that I'm aware of," said Rosemary. "She's been brought in to help organise the Summer Festival, and she's super powerful. She can even teleport herself."

"Teleport?!" said Athena. "That's amazing. I need to learn that trick."

"I'm afraid it's quite a rare gift, apparently," said Rosemary.

"Figures." Athena frowned.

"Hey, you can do cool magic now, don't complain."

"That's true. Plus, I've got my mind reading under control, more or less."

"Exactly, you're doing brilliantly. And I'm making a curry. Help me with dinner by chopping these onions?"

Athena smiled and came around to the counter to help. "Anyway, tell me what happened. Why did you come back looking like you just weathered a tornado?"

"Where was I? I met Juniper. We had a great chat, sort of, well, she told me some things that sounded interesting and invited me to go for a drink at the pub."

"You went for a drink with a total stranger? Don't you think that's dangerous? Especially considering the Bloodstone society is, by all accounts, still after us."

"Well, exactly," said Rosemary. "That's why I went. She told me she'd heard about us, being a freelancer. There are a few people after us, not just the Bloodstones. And I wanted to find out more."

"Okay, so you recklessly went and got drunk with a total stranger."

"We didn't get drunk, we just went to the pub for a drink...or two. I had to talk to Sherry anyway. I wanted to invite her to...Oh, wait a minute, that's another thing I forgot to tell you."

"What?" Athena asked, clearly tearing up from the onion juice.

Rosemary poured oil into a cast iron pan to heat up and passed Athena more vegetables to chop up. "You remember how Nesta has been feeling rather sick lately?"

"That's right. She missed the last Sunday brunch because she thought she had some sort of tummy bug."

"Turns out she's pregnant."

"No way!" said Athena. "Who's the dad?"

"That's where it gets a little bit hairy. Neve seems quite concerned."

"What do you mean?" said Athena. "Do they not know? Surely, you'd know something like that."

"Apparently, the fertility magic on the night of Beltane was a little bit more potent than anticipated."

"Get out!" said Athena. "You're telling me it was a magical conception? God-spawn?"

Rosemary grimaced. "Maybe, but that's a really gross way of putting it."

"Heh, heh. God-spawn." said Athena. "Imagine putting that on your CV! Is Belamus the father?"

"Who knows," said Rosemary. "For all we know, it could be Brigid. She might have that kind of power, being a fertility goddess and so on."

"She only came in right at the end to sort out her grandfather, though. It's a sticky situation, isn't it?" said Athena. "Sounds really disgusting. I mean, not the fact that Nesta could have babies. I just...eww, fertility and stuff."

"Yeah. I'm glad you think so," said Rosemary. "And I'm also glad that it didn't affect me."

Athena laughed. "Me too! Anyway, you haven't told me the rest of the story. What did Juniper do?"

"Well, after a few drinks she sort of gave me a lift to the beach."

"You mean you teleported? Awesome!" said Athena.

"Not exactly awesome. It made me feel violently ill."

"And is that what messed up your hair?"

"That's probably part of it. On our way back towards town there was a missing person incident."

"Oh, not another one. It can't be the fae again, can it?"

Rosemary shook her head. "No, it's more the reverse."

"What do you mean?"

"Instead of children going missing, it was a middle-aged woman being found."

The smell of the spices intensified and Rosemary gave them a good stir.

Athena passed her the chopping board of neatly diced onions and vegetables. "You found a woman on the beach, what's so remarkable about that?"

"Nothing, usually," said Rosemary, carefully scooping just the onions into the pan so they could brown. "Except that her face was all bloodied and she didn't seem to know who she was."

"Now, what a mystery," said Athena. "I bet it's connected to the Summer Solstice."

"What makes you so sure?" said Rosemary.

"Well, you know how we're so suspicious that the festivals normally coincide with chaos? Ms Twigg says the prevailing theory is that they're a culmination of energy."

"Then we should get out of town, stop celebrating them," said Rosemary, her mind darting ahead to possible places they could go. "Problem solved. We'll just book eight holidays a year to go to Bath or something."

Athena smirked. "Sounds kind of nice, actually. The problem is that the town *needs* to celebrate them to anchor the energy. It's like letting the cork out of a bottle to relieve the pressure. Apparently it helps to keep things functioning and return the balance back to normal."

Rosemary frowned. "I suppose this is another one of those situations where they're going to insist they need our magic."

"I don't know," said Athena. "They might be better off without us. Apparently our magic is part of the problem. Things weren't quite so intense until we came back and unbound the Thorn magic. But yeah, I bet as soon as we tried to get out of here, the mayhem would find a way of following us, anyway. That's how these things tend to work."

"You sound wise beyond your years," said Rosemary as she added the other ingredients to the pan and covered it so it could simmer away.

"I am," said Athena. "And you'd best remember that."

Rosemary went to the fridge and poured herself a glass of wine.

"Carrying on with the drinking then?" said Athena.

Rosemary sighed. "Maybe I don't need this. It just feels like so much has happened today."

"Was the woman okay?"

"She seemed sort of fine, if amnesiac."

"I don't think that's how you're supposed to say it, Mum."

"You know what I mean. Anyway, Neve is going to call the medics."

"We have medics?"

"Apparently we have a whole hospital slightly further north, and they didn't think to tell us about that earlier."

"Just like how I only recently found out that there are not one but two universities for magic in London," Athena grumbled.

"There are?" said Rosemary. "That's brilliant!"

She leaned back in her chair, inhaling the delicious scent from her cooking.

Athena groaned. "I forgot that I was trying not to tell you about that."

"Why not?"

"I don't want you pressuring me to study."

"I'll do no such thing," said Rosemary. "I'm not going to bully you into going to university. That's completely up to you."

"Really?"

"Really. You need to figure out that stuff yourself. I will be here to gently support."

Athena raised her eyebrows as if she didn't quite believe her mother.

"The other thing I forgot to tell you," said Rosemary, deliberately changing the subject, "is that Neve's got some sort of history with Juniper and doesn't like her. They went to school together.

Juniper's whole family are magical mercenaries, or something like that."

Athena balked. "So you've made friends with a dangerous troublemaker on the wrong side of the law just to see what they know?"

Rosemary got up to put some rice on to go with dinner. "I guess so. Although I don't know that we are friends. We only just met. And maybe I should stay away from her if Neve doesn't think she's any good."

"I don't know," said Athena. "Maybe Neve just has old baggage with her."

Rosemary poured her wine back into the bottle and decided to put the jug on for tea instead. "You're probably right, I don't need any more to drink after all. Oh...that was the other thing."

"More things?"

"Yes. I've invited people around for dinner on Thursday night. It's a kind of surprise celebration for Neve and Nesta."

"Are you sure that's wise? After all, it sounds like Neve's not exactly overjoyed about being a new parent."

"I think it's more that she's just worried about Nesta. Neve thinks the baby might be some kind of demon."

"Is that all?" Athena said flatly.

"I thought a nice social gathering might ease her mind."

"That does sound nice," said Athena. "And I suppose it won't hurt to have dinner. If a demon baby pops out there's strength in numbers."

"That's the spirit! You can bring someone, if you want."

"Oh," said Athena, sounding surprised. "I don't think..."

"What about Elise?" Rosemary suggested.

Athena gave her mother an awkward look. "Uhh, I don't think so, Mum. Elise doesn't really know Neve or Nesta all that well."

"That doesn't matter," said Rosemary, but she detected a chill in Athena's voice and felt a little bit suspicious. Had something gone wrong with Athena and Elise's friendship? Rosemary really hoped not because Elise seemed like such a good kid and it was important for Athena to have quality friends.

"Is Dad coming?" Athena asked.

"I thought I'd invite him," said Rosemary. Dain had moved out a few weeks earlier, into a small apartment in the centre of Myrtle-wood, and had some kind of job, though he hadn't told them exactly what it was. Rosemary and Athena had been guessing to no avail, though he had been wearing flashy suits lately, so they assumed it paid well.

Rosemary rubbed her chin thoughtfully. "I'm not sure what a runaway fae prince who got caught up in the foster system and is recovering from a terrible addiction to cream can do for work, now that he's finally trying to get his life together."

"He's dating, you know," said Athena.

"What?" said Rosemary. "How do you know that?"

"He told me. Not that I want to know those kinds of things."

"Then stop hassling me about my non-existent love life!"

Athena laughed. "Everyone needs a hobby. I think Dad was wondering if I was going to be upset about it. He was checking to see if it was okay."

"He didn't tell me," said Rosemary.

"Wouldn't that be awkward? You don't have to tell your ex that kind of thing. Besides, he probably thought you'd get jealous."

Rosemary put her hands on her hips and frowned. "I'm not going to get jealous! Any idea who?"

Athena giggled. "I think it's actually multiple people."

"He's sowing his wild oats?"

"Ew! Disgusting! Not like that. I think he's just, you know, going out for a drink with people to see if he likes them."

"Okay," said Rosemary. "I'll protect your innocence by not elab-orating on what that means."

Athena glared at her.

"Is he still coming over for family dinners?" Rosemary asked.

They'd been holding family dinners every second Sunday, alternating with the Sunday brunches, where they invited more of their Myrtlewood friends over. Marjie insisted on catering those.

Athena gave her mother a quizzical look. "I don't see why he'd stop being part of the family, just because he's starting to hang out with more people."

Rosemary grumbled under her breath. "Hanging out, yeah right."

"Mum! It's ridiculous of you to be so childish about this."

"I'm not being childish," said Rosemary. "You're just misunderstanding my Gemini ascendant."

"I thought you didn't like Astrology."

"I don't like how it tells me I'm supposed to be a certain way. I don't like rules."

Athena laughed. "Figures – Uranus is strong in your chart."

"Speak for yourself!"

"Dad's just trying to get on with his life. You've made it perfectly clear that you don't want to be involved with him, or anyone else for that matter."

"See! That's the real truth of the matter," said Rosemary. "So stop teasing me."

Athena raised her hands in surrender. "Fine. I just think Dad's being more mature about it. That's all. Eventually, you might want to think about whether you want to have – I don't know – more people in your life."

"No, we're not going to talk about this."

"Actually, I changed my mind," said Athena. "You do you."

"Thank you," said Rosemary. "By the way, it's your turn to cook dinner next."

CHAPTER
TEN

Two days later, the timer on the oven dinged and Rosemary rushed to the kitchen, throwing an apron over her evening dress. She'd tried to make an effort because it was a special occasion.

"Is dinner ready?" Athena called out, coming down the stairs and entering the kitchen.

"Almost." Rosemary pulled the tray with two roast chickens and assorted vegetables out of the oven. She turned the vegetables over and sprinkled some additional seasoning. Then she applied another coating of her sundried tomato and thyme glaze to the chickens before returning them to the oven.

"It smells so good," said Athena. "I'm starving. Can I have a little bit now?"

"No," said Rosemary. "You can wait until everyone else is here."

"Speaking of everyone else," said Athena. "Where are they all?"

As if in answer to her question, the doorbell rang.

Rosemary took off her apron and went to answer it.

Marjie was standing on the doorstep with a box of something

that Rosemary was sure was going to be delicious. Behind her stood Una and Ashwyn, the two apothecary sisters, with the three foundling children they were fostering in tow.

Rosemary greeted and hugged them all, then ushered them in.

"We arrived at the same time!" said Marjie.

"Good timing," said Rosemary. "Dinner is almost done."

"Wait," said Marjie. "I need to set up some decorations."

She held up her index finger and pointed it at the four corners of the room. Balloons and streamers burst forth from the ceiling in a rainbow of pastel tones.

The children squealed in delight.

"Now isn't that cheerful?" said Marjie.

"Lovely," said Rosemary. "As long as it doesn't leave a mess. Also, this is the kitchen and not the dining room where we're eating. Why are you decorating in here?"

"Plenty more where that came from," said Marjie. "Now come with me, children. What do you think we should do next?"

Little Harry, Thea, and Clio followed her out.

Una sighed. "It's a relief to have someone else to entertain them for a little while."

"Has it been a struggle, then?" Rosemary asked. "You're not thinking of handing them back?"

"Oh, absolutely not," said Ashwyn. "We love them dearly. We're hoping they'll be able to stay with us permanently."

"Well, as far as I know, Neve hasn't been able to track down any more suitable people," said Rosemary. "Though I can understand that it must be tiring."

"They're good kids," said Una. "So kind and sweet."

"Yes," said Rosemary. "But even the most placid fae realm foundlings are still a lot of work."

"They just...need us all the time," said Una. "They need us to answer their questions and help them tie their shoes."

Ashwyn nodded. "Even though they don't fuss a lot, we still need to be constantly vigilant, making sure they're safe and meeting all their needs."

"Surely there are some spells for that," said Rosemary with a giggle.

"If you come up with any, let me know," said Ashwyn. "Who else is coming tonight?"

Just then, the doorbell rang again.

"Let's see," said Rosemary over her shoulder on her way to answer it. "I invited a few people."

Burk was standing on the doorstep with a bouquet of purple wisteria and yellow roses.

"These are lovely," said Rosemary. "Err, they're for Neve and Nesta, aren't they?"

"These are for you," said Burk. He pulled another bouquet of equal beauty from behind his back, this time with red and white tulips. "These ones are for the soon-to-be new parents."

"Oh, how kind." Rosemary felt slightly awkward, and more awkward, still, when she noticed Liam's car pulling up the driveway. "Come inside," she said to Burk, ushering him in. "Here, hang up your coat. I'm just going to greet Liam."

Rosemary turned back outside to see Liam approaching. "Flowers from vampires," he said with a grin.

"I suppose you didn't bring me any foliage."

"Can't say I'm that way inclined," said Liam. "And, as I recall, when you were younger you always thought it was hilarious that people gave each other plant genitals as a romantic gesture."

Rosemary giggled. "That's true and I also thought it was morbid that they were all really dead plant bits."

"See, I know you well," said Liam with a wink.

She gave him a hug. "You did back then. Come in."

"Who else is coming?" Athena asked.

"Well, obviously Neve and Nesta, but they won't be here for a little bit longer. I wanted it to be a surprise so everyone was here when they arrived."

"Okay," said Athena, sounding unsure.

"And Sherry's coming. At least, she said she was."

"And Dad?"

"Yes. He doesn't have the best track record."

"He's been pretty reliable lately though," said Athena. "I hear he turns up on time for all his dates."

"That's enough information," said Rosemary.

"Sherry sends her apologies, actually," said Liam, hanging up his coat. "She's not feeling too well. I don't know what's wrong."

"Do you think it could be the fae realm again?" Athena asked. "We're not close to an equinox. Surely the solstices don't do that too."

"No, I think it's something else. Who knows, it might even be a normal virus." Liam shrugged.

"That's a shame," said Rosemary. "I was hoping to try and make things more normal again between us."

"You'll get there," said Liam. "Things just take time with Sherry."

Rosemary busied herself, attending to the cooking, while Athena wrangled the children into helping set the dining table. As they weren't entirely sure who else was coming, due to Rosemary's habit of throwing out careless invitations and not following up, they just set up for the maximum number of seats that fitted around the table, which grew, several times, to accommodate the extra plates the children set down.

The doorbell rang again and Rosemary was still busy in the kitchen.

"Don't worry, dear. I'll get it," said Marjie. She bustled off towards the door and returned a few moments later with a slightly concerned look on her face.

"What is it?" Rosemary asked.

"Dain's here."

"That's okay, Marjie. I invited him."

"No, that's not all," she replied. "He's brought a guest."

"A guest?" Rosemary asked. "Do you mean a date?"

"I assume so," said Marjie. "Look, we can send them away if you like."

"Don't be ridiculous, Marjie. Dain and I are old news, ancient history. There's no point in me getting silly and childish over him bringing a date, even though the social appropriateness is obviously not quite right there. I'm afraid that Dain's mixed upbringing means that he's never quite gotten his head around social graces."

"If you're sure, dear," Marjie said. "Wait till you see who it is."

Rosemary walked cautiously out of the kitchen. Dain was already approaching in a deep emerald suit with a matching paisley silk shirt. On his arm, in a deep aubergine dress, was none other than Juniper.

"Aphrodite's knickers," Rosemary muttered under her breath.

"What was that?" Dain said.

"Nothing...erm...Welcome."

Juniper blushed. "I'm sorry, Rosemary, I didn't realise this is where we were going. Dain said he just wanted to take me to a party with some friends. I didn't know it was at your house."

"No doubt you didn't realise that Dain is Rosemary's ex either then," said Marjie, bemused.

"Oh no, really?!" Juniper said. "This is a pickle."

"That's not what I'm most worried about," said Rosemary.

The door opened and Neve stepped through, followed by Nesta.

"Surprise!" Marjie called out.

Nesta's eyes lit up in excitement while Neve looked startled and raised her arms as if to protect herself from an attack. "What's all this?" she said.

"Just a little surprise celebration for you," said Rosemary awkwardly. "I made a special dinner and invited friends." Neve's eyes locked on Juniper.

"Friends," she said.

"Come with me." Rosemary led Neve promptly to the kitchen. "I'm so sorry. I had no idea Juniper was going to come."

"Then how did she end up at your house?"

Rosemary gave her friend an unimpressed look. "Dain brought a date."

"No!"

"Yes."

"Sorry," said Neve. "What a kick in the guts for you."

"No, it's not," said Rosemary. "I'm perfectly fine. I'm an adult."

Neve gave her a questioning look. "Rosemary, I know your stance on relationships, and I admire and respect you as a person, but no one is going to be happy with their ex bringing an unexpected date to a party at their house. That's just not normal."

"Well, Dain's not normal, is he? None of us are. In fact, I think it's high time I stopped trying to be normal."

Rosemary was fine. Totally fine. She was just trying to ignore the pinching sensation in her chest. She tried to breathe through it and focus on Neve. "I'm more worried about you. I mean, you don't like Juniper. You don't trust her. I don't want to spoil your night – this dinner is supposed to be about you and Nesta."

"I'll be fine," said Neve. "I've been through a lot worse."

Rosemary gritted her teeth. "That's not really the effect I was hoping to have in throwing you a surprise party."

"What can I say?" Neve said apologetically. "I don't really like surprises."

"I didn't realise...I bet that's a terrible occupational hazard if you're a detective."

"That's the thing," said Neve. "Most of the surprises in my life have been rather unpleasant and grim. The idea of a surprise party is not really in my list of good things."

"I should have thought of that," said Rosemary.

"Hey, it's not really about me. Nesta seems delighted. So thank you. I might be feeling a little bit out-of-sorts, but it's nice to see her beaming."

They looked back through the door towards where Nesta was standing surrounded by doting friends.

"Look how happy she is," said Neve. "I love her so much. Obviously, I want what's best for her and I really hope that everything works out with the baby. I'm just terrified."

"That's understandable." Rosemary patted Neve on the shoulder. "Where's Mei?"

"Oh, she should be here any minute. She was just showing Meng around the garden."

"It's all so heart-warming and fuzzy isn't it?" Rosemary said. "You know you told me how isolated you were not so long ago? Athena and I were much the same. We didn't really have any proper friends and we weren't close to most of the family."

"Now it's like one big happy family," said Neve.

Rosemary raised her eyebrows. "Though not entirely happy?"

"Okay, I can put up with Juniper if she's important to Dain," said Neve.

"I wouldn't go that far," said Rosemary. "Athena said he's been shopping around."

Neve scrunched up her face. "It's a bit distasteful, isn't it? Telling a teen about that."

"Well, I'm not known for having the best taste in men now, am I?" said Rosemary.

Neve shook her head. "It's not a curse, you know, and I'm sure you don't want to hear this, but you could take a leaf out of Dain's book."

Rosemary laughed. "Ask Juniper out on a date?"

"No," said Neve. "She's not in your league."

"I'd say she's way above my league. Have you seen what she can do?"

"Oh yes, I know all about the teleportation." Neve rolled her eyes.

"Right, sorry," said Rosemary.

Neve looked Rosemary in the eye. "Think about it this way, you've got your whole life to live. You've got only a certain amount of time, and pretty soon Athena is going to be growing up and out of here. Isn't she almost seventeen?"

A shiver ran down Rosemary's spine. "When you put it that way..."

"She could be out of the house in the next couple of years," Neve continued. "I mean, what will you be doing?"

"Making chocolates," said Rosemary.

"Making chocolates in a big house all by yourself?"

"I'll have you and Marjie and everyone."

"That's true," Neve said. "You're not getting rid of us that easily. But think about it. Think about what you want."

"I already did that and decided I wanted a chocolate shop, and look at the mess that's got me into."

"Your shop's going to be brilliant," said Neve. "I've tried your chocolates. Outstanding. And you deserve to be loved."

"Look at you – gushing romantic!" said Rosemary, giving Neve a quick hug. "All right, now let's put our big girl pants on and go and join the others."

Neve shot Rosemary a nervous smile. "Wish me luck while I try not to insult Juniper."

CHAPTER
ELEVEN

"This is awkward," Athena muttered to Nesta, who giggled as they sat next to each other at the dinner table.

"It's a lovely sentiment, isn't it?" said Nesta.

"Yeah, Mum just wanted to do something nice for you to celebrate."

She looked around at the others seated around the large dining table.

Athena had found it hilarious when her dad showed up with a date, although then she'd wondered whether it would stress her mother out too much.

However, Rosemary seemed to be taking it all in her stride. It was even more surprising that the date in question happened to be the woman that Athena had heard about yesterday from her mother. Who, apparently, Neve couldn't stand.

"Do you know anything about Juniper?" Athena whispered to Nesta, aware that everyone else was talking so loudly that nobody would be able to hear.

"Oh yes, there's a long term rivalry between her and Neve. I imagine the poor woman is finding it just as awkward to be here. Imagine being brought on a date only to find that you're at a dysfunctional family dinner with a few people who have reason not to like you."

"That does sound unpleasant," Athena said. "How are you, anyway?"

"I'm brilliant," said Nesta, returning to speaking at a normal volume.

"That's so good to hear," said Rosemary from across the table. She lifted her glass – filled with the non-alcoholic punch she'd made so as not to leave Nesta out. Athena was sure her mother was wishing she had something stronger in her cup, given the events of the evening. She could tell that Rosemary had her I'm-on-my-best-behaviour-face firmly intact.

Athena's thoughts drifted away from the dinner entirely to Elise, who'd seemed slightly distant recently. She hadn't even attempted to invite Elise to the dinner party, as she'd felt confused. Athena wasn't sure if she'd done something wrong, or maybe Elise had changed her mind and didn't like her after all.

The thought made her feel slightly queasy. Almost as much as the thought of telling her parents that she might have a girlfriend. She didn't think her Dad would mind, for some reason. And although Rosemary was very open minded, Athena didn't want to give up any more of her privacy.

She noticed that Rosemary was keeping her distance from Burk over dinner and wondered if that meant anything. Despite Athena's amused teasing, she didn't really want to know about her mother's personal life and she absolutely wanted to avoid her parents knowing about hers.

The thought of talking about the situation with Elise made her feel strange, but she had promised to fill Rosemary in on what was going on with her, and this seemed rather significant.

She didn't want to risk going back to the emotional tug-of-war that they'd had before. If Rosemary found out she'd been hiding something like this it could set them back to square one as far as trust was concerned.

She took a bite of Rosemary's delicious roast chicken but barely tasted it as she was so lost in her own thoughts.

From across the table, Neve raised her glass and tapped it a few times with her spoon, making a tingling sound. "I just wanted to say an enormous thank-you to Rosemary, for everything you've brought into our lives. And for throwing us this lovely dinner party. Now I know I'm not always the most fun person to have around—"

"Don't be ridiculous," said Nesta.

"You're a bag of laughs," said Dain.

"I know I have a serious disposition," said Neve. "And I have been worried about the baby given how surprising the whole situation is." She laughed nervously. "Anyway, putting all that aside, I'm just grateful that I know for sure whatever happens, you're all here to support us and look after us. It makes me feel reassured for our future, and for Nesta, and hopefully for this baby too."

Everyone cheered and Nesta smiled warmly.

"Since we're doing formal toasts," Rosemary said after the cheering had subsided, "I'll raise a glass to our honoured guests, Nesta and Neve. To their wonderful family. And many good things to come."

"Here, here," said Marjie.

After the toasts, people around the table broke into separate conversations again.

Juniper and Dain seem to be wrapped up in their own discussion. Marjie and Liam were entertaining the children. Rosemary had a slightly strange look on her face, and Athena couldn't help but listen in on her conversation across the table with Neve.

"So what's going on then?" said Rosemary. "Did you find anything else out about our new friend?"

Neve gave her an odd look, and her eyes swivelled to Juniper.

"No, not her," said Rosemary. "The woman we found on the beach."

"Nothing yet," said Neve. "She's been taken to the hospital and has been murmuring about a magical island and bears. That's all we can get out of her."

"Do you think she was on an island?" Rosemary asked.

"Well, she could have been on one of the little ones around here, though there aren't any bears as far as I know."

"Perhaps she had a run in with a shifter," Athena suggested.

"Maybe," said Neve. "I take it your mother filled you in on the situation."

"Was I not supposed to?" Rosemary asked.

Neve shrugged. "As far as I can see, you're a civilian and you happened to be there at the time, so you can tell people whatever you want, as long as it's not compromising our investigation."

"Surely not," said Rosemary. "There's hardly anything to investigate at this point is there?"

"Exactly," said Neve.

"I only know one bear shifter," said Athena. "And he's quite a cuddly guy, really. I wouldn't imagine he'd be too terrifying to run into. You'd probably just pinch yourself, thinking you're in a dream if you came across him."

"Our wee Deron is a lovely lad," said Marjie, joining in the conversation. "This food is superb, Rosemary. How did you get the chicken to have so much flavour?"

"Sundried tomato glaze," Rosemary said.

"Brilliant! I just know your chocolate business is going to take off with your knack for combining delicious flavours together to make them really pop."

"Yes, I can't wait to eat more of your chocolates," said Neve as she finished up her plate of dinner.

"That's good news," said Rosemary. "Because I've made a huge bowl of truffles for dessert!"

"And I brought cake," Marjie added.

The children cheered and were all too happy to help clear away the dinner dishes, stacking them on the bench so that Athena could use her automancy to do the washing up. At first, Rosemary had insisted on Athena washing the dishes manually in order to atone for running off to the fae realm, but after a while she caved, persuaded by Athena's argument that this way was helping her with her magical mastery and her schoolwork – which had included learning automancy. It was the one area of her education where Athena was truly excelling. She was even better than most of the teachers, thanks to the generations of Thorn witches who had mastered the magical specialisation of automancy and passed this down into her genes.

By the time Athena got back to the table, dessert was being served. She helped to slice up the chocolate cake and plated it with cream and a few truffles.

Dain was staring at the bowl of cream with a slightly nauseated look.

Athena smiled.

"I'm glad the spells are working," said Una, clearly noticing Dain's expression.

"It's getting to the point where I can stand to be around it, at least," said Dain. "Barely."

"I'm glad it's faded somewhat."

"It would be nice if I could just enjoy high fat dairy products, like the rest of you can."

"In a perfect world," said Una. "But you can't have everything you want." She looked longingly at the cream.

"These truffles are amazing," said Neve. "What's in them?"

"The lighter ones are strawberry and rose, and the darker ones are orange and cardamom," said Rosemary.

"Oh, I can't wait for your stall at the Summer Festival," said Marjie, giving Rosemary a knowing look.

Rosemary smiled. "Yes, I've been practising, but I'm afraid our kitchen is just not really equipped for commercial use."

"I insist on you coming to my shop in the late afternoons," said Marjie. "Once the kitchen's closed and we've cleaned up for the day, it's all yours. As long as you don't make a terrible mess."

"I can't promise that, but I can promise to clean it up," said Rosemary. "Especially if I'm going to start practising using my magic as part of the process."

"Surely that's not part of your course, Mum," said Athena.

"No, not exactly," said Rosemary. "And I suppose there are no chocolatier majors at the magical universities."

"Highly unlikely," said Marjie. "Or I'd have already pointed you in that direction."

"Oh well, my magic will definitely come in handy when I've only got a week between the in person component of my chocolate making course and the festival. I'm going to have to get moving very quickly if I'm going to prepare enough truffles to meet Marjie's expectations."

She grinned.

"Aren't you going to add little charms to your truffles?" Juniper asked. "That sounds marvellous!"

Everyone looked around the table slightly awkwardly.

"Juniper's helping to organise the festival," Rosemary explained. "We've already had a big long chat about my chocolates."

"I didn't realise you were such good friends," said Nesta, her voice strained.

"Alright, I think I'd better be going," said Juniper.

Dain looked at her, surprised.

"You know I have that thing later."

"You do?" Dain asked.

She gave him a tense look.

"Oh yes. Apologies. The time slipped away rather quickly. We'd better go."

The table sat in awkward silence as Rosemary got up to see Dain and Juniper out. Neve shrugged and helped herself to seconds, then Nesta giggled, which turned out to be contagious. They all chuckled quietly at the awkwardness of the situation until Rosemary returned to the table.

"I'm so sorry," she said, sitting down again. "I had no idea that was going to happen."

"Pretty bold, bringing a date to your ex's party, isn't it?" Liam said.

"I don't think Dain would consider it bold," said Rosemary. "Fae have different kinds of social graces altogether."

"Yeah," said Athena. "Dad wouldn't have thought twice about it. He probably considered it a clever way of clearing up a double booking."

"Well, they're gone now," said Neve. "We can all just relax and enjoy the rest of the evening."

"Actually, we'd better get going," said Una. "The kids need to get to bed or they'll be cranky in the morning, I expect."

The children had run off to play after getting bored of the dinner. They were in their old nursery with Meng, who had been uncharacteristically quiet over dinner.

"It's true," said Nesta. "That's the same for Mei. And tomorrow is school day."

"Of course," said Rosemary. "How's she settling in?"

"Mei is loving Myrtlewood Academy. Plus, she gets to come *here* every day, and this place is so familiar."

Rosemary smiled. "I haven't seen her around. It's funny, I hardly see the school kids at all."

"The sign of a well-run school," said Marjie. "I'm glad they're not bothering you while they're all getting educated."

Athena gave Rosemary a knowing look. They hadn't told Dain about the boy. They didn't want to have to deal with how he would react. But now that he'd left the house she thought it might be a good time to explain the situation.

"What?! Outrageous!" said Una. "After all that you've been through."

Neve grimaced. "And there's nothing we can prosecute him on. Besides, he's too young really, isn't he? Teenagers are not really fit to make good decisions."

"I take offence to that," said Athena. "Though I don't have the best track record, do I?"

"That's very self-aware of you," said Nesta with a smile. "Though, I think you're doing all right."

"Do you think the other kids will be okay?" Ashwyn asked. "Is it safe to have Harry at school? He's not going to be in danger?"

"I don't think so," said Athena. "I mean, the younger classes don't really mix with us. And besides, Finnigan hasn't shown any interest in anyone outside of our class."

"But he's harassed you," said Nesta with concern.

"He tried to talk to me at first," Athena admitted. "But then the school's obviously come down on him. He's been told he has to avoid me."

"They can't expel him?" Neve asked. "After everything he'd done?"

"I tried that," said Rosemary. "He hasn't behaved badly at the school and they don't really have any grounds to expel him yet. But if he puts one toe out of line, he'd better watch his back."

"Does Dain know?" Marjie asked.

"Not yet," said Rosemary. "I thought I might try and tell him tonight before he left, but it wasn't exactly the perfect situation, was it? We've got a family dinner on Sunday night, so hopefully he doesn't bring a date to that."

"We can tell him then," Athena said. "He does have a right to know, I guess. Since Finnigan abducted him."

Rosemary grimaced. "Finnigan better watch out. I don't think Dain's going to take too well to knowing the boy who kidnapped him, deceived his daughter, and endangered her life is hanging around the house."

CHAPTER
TWELVE

Earlier that evening, as Rosemary had gone to get Juniper's coat, the woman had handed her something. It was a crumped piece of paper.

"I thought you might find this interesting," said Juniper with a gleam of concern in her eyes. "I snuck it out of a contract that has been floating around."

"A contract? Oh–"

Juniper looked apologetic. "Unfortunately there are still people after you, though they are careful about disguising their identity. I told my agency I'd take a look, to see if I could give you any more help – off the record, of course. The contract was standard and involved "relocating" you. But reading between the lines anyone could tell it was a front for kidnapping."

"And you–"

"I don't tend to take that kind of work. Anyway, this was inside."

Rosemary opened up the loose scrap of slightly crumpled paper to reveal some kind of glyphs.

"What does it mean?" Rosemary asked.

"Something planetary, at a guess," said Juniper. "I was never strong on Astrology at school."

"I suppose I should ask Athena," said Rosemary. "Though she's already too obsessed with planets for my liking."

Juniper shrugged. "It happens."

"But this is hardly reassuring," said Rosemary.

"Don't worry too much," said Juniper. "As far as I know, no one from the agency has taken the jobs relating to you and Athena. Word is you're too powerful to mess with." She winked. "I might have spread a few extra rumours to put the fear of Cerridwen into anyone who thinks twice about messing with you."

"That's something," said Rosemary. "Thank you."

She stuffed the piece of paper into her pocket until she had more time to think about it and returned to the dinner party.

ROSEMARY LAY in bed that night feeling anxious about her conversation with Juniper and the new danger-of-the-month. She kept circling between those worries and her conflicted feelings regarding her conversation with Neve, the one that had stemmed around her romantic life or lack thereof. Neve's words repeated on her like a bad meal.

On the one hand, they were in potential danger again, despite Juniper's clever rumours. On the other hand, she felt as if she'd been neglecting her own personal life because there always seemed to be imminent danger around!

It was true that Athena was growing up. Within a few short years, she'd probably be off to university or flatting with friends or even moving in with a boyfriend. And what would Rosemary be left with but an enormous, and hopefully empty, house?

She was definitely counting on at least the school being out of Thorn Manor by then. Part of her regretted letting all the fae realm children go. She'd enjoyed having them around. But she knew they had much more to gain from living with Una and Ashwyn, who doted on them.

Rosemary didn't want any more children. Something that she'd long known. Athena was wonderful. And Athena was enough. But that didn't mean she didn't want company.

Of course, she could look at renting out some of the rooms. The house was big enough to run a large inn, but she didn't really want to have to manage all the work of that. And though Myrtlewood had a lovely environment and she had a vibrant community around her, she wasn't sure that would be enough.

She did occasionally miss the intimacy of being in a romantic relationship. Mostly the cuddles. She wrapped her big blanket tightly around her shoulders. And a part of her mind wished that it was Burk's arms wrapping around her. Although...perhaps the vampire would be too cold.

That was part of the problem, of course. At first, when Liam had asked her out, she thought he was a nice normal man, even though she was definitely not ready to date back then. Now, she was aware that Liam was not entirely normal and had quite a big wolfy chip on his shoulder. Burk was an ancient vampire, and Dain...well, he was old news, really. There was too much water under that bridge and a few big blistering logs of baggage to go with it.

Athena had heckled Rosemary endlessly about all this, especially when she'd overheard a certain conversation with Elamina revealing Liam's secret werewolf identity. They'd begun using the code word "Virgo" so that no one else caught on, which was working well, even though Liam had overheard them once. It turned out he was actually a Virgo, so it had all worked out without him stressing about his secret getting out.

Of course she had feelings — very confusing feelings — conflicting and twisting and frustrating feelings. And she sometimes got jealous, which was even more annoying.

She liked Liam. And she had some rather complex feelings for Dain. But if she was going to be completely honest with herself, of the group of men Athena teasingly referred to as Rosemary's "suitors", Burk was the one among them who sparked the most fire in her blood.

Rosemary wasn't sure how much this view had been influenced by the steamy dreams she'd had recently, night after night. This was enough to make her cautious.

She didn't know whether the dreams were simply her unconscious mind trying to communicate with her about where her heart lay, or something more sinister. And it was certainly more than just her *heart* involved.

Rosemary felt flustered, just thinking about him. Her mind swung back and forth on the pendulum between living out her years alone and lonely with only cats for comfort, and the blistering fire of those dreams.

Eventually, she reached for her phone and texted Burk.

Hi.

But what else would she say? Why was she even resorting to sending badly thought out messages in the middle of the night she would no doubt regret?

Rosemary promptly decided to delete the text, but her thumb accidentally slipped.

She fumbled for her phone and found, to her gut wrenching dismay, that it had started calling Burk.

Oh no!

Rosemary turned it off immediately, her cheeks reddening in the dark as blood rushed to her head. Hopefully he would realise it was some kind of pocket-dial situation and not worry about it.

I'd better text him and reassure him.

She started composing the message when the phone rang again.

Oh, bother.

She decided that the safest course of action was to answer it. Knowing Burk, he could – and would – be at her house in an instant if he thought she was in trouble. And that would be a far more embarrassing situation. She pressed the green old-fashioned phone icon.

"Uhhh, hi, Burk," Rosemary said.

"I got a missed call from you," Burk said in his annoyingly silky voice.

"Yeah, sorry." Rosemary tried to sound breezy and casual. "It was a pocket dial."

"Pocket dial?" said Burk. "Are you out somewhere? I thought you'd be in bed by now."

Rosemary felt a warm sensation in her nether regions at his mention of bed.

"Well, I suppose I am in bed," Rosemary admitted. "I was actually...err, I was trying to text you."

"Do you need help with something?" Burk asked. "Is there anything wrong?"

"Not really," said Rosemary, her blush deepening.

"You can tell me," said Burk.

"To be honest, I was just feeling kind of lonely. You know, this big old house..."

"Is something scaring you? I could come over and keep watch."

Rosemary gulped. Her imagination couldn't help but picture him turning up at her window, shirtless in the moonlight.

"That's sweet of you," said Rosemary. "But it's really not that at all. I wasn't scared. I was just...oh, if you really must know, Neve and I had a conversation earlier. It was one of those moments of truth situations where I felt my whole lonely life flashing before me, with Athena going off and living her life..." Rosemary realised she was rambling. "I'm sorry, I shouldn't have said any of that. What I meant was...Well, I wondered whether I should actually start dating again."

"Really?" said Burk, barely disguising the wry tone of his voice. "I'm flattered."

"What, now?"

"You thought all that and you called me."

Rosemary blushed again. "I'm sorry. I mean, you've probably more than moved on by now."

"I thought maybe you and Dain were thinking about giving it another chance, until I saw him at the pub with a date. Was that what set you off?"

Rosemary turned over this possibility in her mind. "I don't think so. It's not really anything to do with him at all."

"Well, I'm honoured," said Burk. "I thought if there was nothing going on with Dain, then surely Liam..."

"There is Liam," said Rosemary. "I don't know, my whole situation is complicated. And as you know I haven't been dating anyone."

"Thanks for thinking of me," said Burk.

"This is the awkward part, isn't it?" Rosemary gritted her teeth. "Where you tell me you've moved on and are seeing someone else or you've taken a vow of celibacy for the next hundred years or joined the priesthood."

"It's possible that I've done all three, you know," said Burk.

Rosemary sighed, and then groaned. "This is so embarrassing. I'm not even drunk, so I can't blame the alcohol."

"No, Rosemary. There's no reason at all to be embarrassed. Like I said, I'm honoured."

"But..."

"And I would like nothing more than to take you out for dinner.

I just wanted to make sure that this wasn't just some passing whim."

"You think I'm that flaky?" Rosemary asked.

"No, that's not how I'd describe you at all," said Burk.

Rosemary lay there, feeling the richness of his voice and imagining his eyes...hazel green, giving her *that* look. She felt the infatuation sweep through her body.

"Good night, Rosemary," he said. "Sleep well, I'll be seeing you soon."

Rosemary felt a pang of anxiety. She hung up the phone. They hadn't made any particular plans. And everything seemed so up in the air.

She put the phone back on the side table next to her and wrapped herself up again in the blankets.

There was something so teenage about the whole affair: midnight texting and secret phone calls. Though she'd barely had any of that as a young person. Cell phones were relatively new when she was a teen and they wouldn't have existed at all when Burk was younger, considering he was some kind of archaic being.

Even still, she felt like a teenager as she squirmed in bed and giggled to herself.

"I'm going on a date," she said quietly and giggled again.

She hadn't even realised how much she'd been looking forward to something like this. How light and excited she would feel for a change.

Just wait till Athena hears about this.

And then realised she couldn't possibly tell her daughter. Imagine the teasing that would ensue!

CHAPTER
THIRTEEN

"Now, now, class. Settle down," said Mr Spruce. "Today I'm delighted to announce that we have official news regarding the Summer Ball."

An excited murmur went around the small classroom.

"What's that?" Athena asked Sam, who was sitting next to her.

"Some kind of fancy dance," Sam whispered. "The senior students are allowed to go."

"It can't be a very big dance," Athena muttered. "There's only us and the other small class in the final year."

Athena hadn't had much to do with any of the other years at school, since they tended to stick to their class bubbles.

She knew there weren't very many seniors and it seemed awkward to have a dance, let alone a ball, with such small numbers.

"Quite right," said Mr Spruce, and for a moment Athena thought he'd read her mind before she realised she'd been muttering out loud.

Athena blushed.

"You'll be reassured to know that the Summer Ball is held in

Glastonbury, hosted by the Grand Order of Druids, inviting magical students sixteen years and older from across the country."

"And Ireland, of course," Felix said with a cheeky grin. "Got to invite those leprechauns."

"That's enough stereotyping, young Felix," said Mr Spruce. "It is customary to bring a date to the ball. However, if you can't find a date—"

Felix burst out laughing. "If you're desperate!"

"Settle down," Mr Spruce said. "If you don't have anyone to bring to the ball with you, fear not because it is a great opportunity to mix and mingle with other magical people from all over."

Athena glanced around the room. Felix winked at her. Sam looked nervous. Elise looked down at her desk. Meanwhile, Beryl and Finnigan both studiously looked at their school books.

This was going to be interesting.

The rest of the day seemed to dissolve in a puddle of classes and magical exercises. It wasn't long before it was the end of the week.

On Fridays Athena and her friends had taken to hanging out around the house, usually in the back garden, if it was a sunny day. And so without invitation, they all strolled out to the back lawn.

Sam had brought some baking, and Athena, although she was more in the mood to be alone, ducked inside and returned with two jugs of lemonade, courteously prepared by her house, or her fridge. Athena still wasn't sure whether the parts of Thorn Manor worked independently or as part of the same greater whole.

Either way, she was grateful for its dedicated anticipation to the needs of her and her friends on a hot summer afternoon. It would have been stifling, but the breeze that drifted over from the sea nearby was gentle and cooling.

They lay on the grass, drinking lemonade and eating the lemon tarts that Sam had made, along with some crisps that Deron had brought.

It would have been a perfect afternoon with friends if Elise didn't still seem to be avoiding Athena's gaze. After a while of idle chit chat, Athena got up and wandered across the lawn, hoping that Elise would follow her so that they'd finally be able to have a conversation.

She heard footsteps behind her and turned to see Felix.

"Oh, hi," said Athena.

"Not who you're expecting?" said Felix in his usual cocky demeanour.

"Not exactly," said Athena.

"Expect the unexpected with me." He winked. "So what do you say? Will you be my date to the ball?"

"Oh." Athena gasped. "I wasn't expecting that."

"I'll make it worth your while," said Felix. "Who wouldn't want to step out on my arm? Everyone will be terribly jealous."

Athena smiled. "I'm sure that's true. But—"

"But what?" Felix asked. "Oh, you've got your eye on someone else. It's not that new fairy boy, is it?"

"No way," said Athena, remembering that Felix wasn't clued in on the entire story. He didn't know that Finnigan was the same boy who had led Athena into the fae realm, despite the fact that Felix had been part of the rescuing party. Elise, along with the school faculty, had kept that secret. Sam knew, but Athena didn't think they'd mentioned it to anyone else.

"Suit yourself, I guess." Felix shrugged and walked off towards the group.

Athena had wondered why he'd bothered to follow her over, especially as when he got back to the group he immediately called out, "Hey, Ash!"

Ashwagandha looked across at him from where she was lounging on the ground next to Elise. "What?"

"Want to go to the ball with me?"

"Okay, sure," said Ash, shrugging casually.

Athena had wished that she could have been so casual. Felix must have been less certain when it came to her, otherwise he would have been more brazen and asked in front of the group. Not that it mattered. That would have just made her feel more pressured.

Elise shot Athena a grateful look as Athena walked over.

"Elise," Athena said. "Can you help me with something for a minute?"

"Sure."

She held up her arm to help Elise up off the ground. They walked towards the house.

"What is that?" Elise asked.

"I actually just wanted to talk to you. Things have been a bit awkward."

"I'm sorry," said Elise. "I thought you would have changed your mind."

"What do you mean?" Athena asked.

"I know I came on too strong the other day, and now things are weird. It's okay. You can forget that anything ever happened and we can go back to being friends."

Athena felt a stab of disappointment in her chest. "Really? Is that what you want?"

Elise looked miserable. "No. No, it's not what I want. I...was surprised, actually. Was worried that you secretly liked Felix. I was sure he was going to ask you to be his date for the ball. And you know what he's like. He's so charming."

"He did, actually," said Athena.

"And you turned him down?" Elise turned to look at Athena, her blue eyes wide.

"Of course I bloody well did. I like you." She looked around to make sure nobody had heard. She wasn't quite ready for people to know about her most intimate feelings – and probably never would be.

"I just..." Elise looked off into the distance.

"What did you think? I would have changed my mind so quickly?"

"Well, you never texted or called," said Elise. "And I didn't want to pester you. So I just figured that you weren't really interested."

"You didn't call me," said Athena. "And you seemed so distant. So I figured you wanted space. Nothing much has changed for me. I just...I guess I'm not really sure about how to act in these situations. I've never had any kind of, you know, relationship, if that's what this is, or what this is going to be? Oh, no, I think I'm doing the thing that Mum does and rambling."

"It's okay," said Elise. "It's kind of cute, actually."

Athena felt a glow of happiness rush through her. "So what do you say?" she said, realising how nervous and timid Elise really was and knowing that she had to take the reins a little bit. "Would you like to go to the ball with me?"

"Of course, silly," said Elise. "I would be delighted to."

They strolled slowly back to the gathering of friends.

"Felix just told us how you rejected him," said Ash, rolling her eyes with a grin. "Thanks for making me second place, Felix."

"I aim to please," said Felix.

"Have you got someone else in mind then?" Ash asked Athena.

She looked at Elise, who smiled and nodded. "Actually, yes...Elise."

"But Elise is a girl," said Felix. "You're not supposed to go with a friend."

Athena cleared her throat. "Felix, you're a friend. Elise is..." She looked across to Elise, who responded by taking Athena's hand.

A look of recognition dawned on all of the faces of their friends. Athena and Elise grinned.

"No! Really?" Sam said.

"So romantic," said Ash. "You two are perfect for each other."

Athena sighed in relief. She hadn't felt sure about how her group of friends would react to finding out, but she knew they'd have to know eventually, especially if Elise and her were showing up to the ball together. It was good to know that despite the common discrimination against werewolves in the township, there wasn't so much discrimination based on relationship preferences. That was the last thing they needed to worry about. She knew that she'd either have to try and hide this from her parents, or just come out and be honest about who she was going to the ball with. And she wasn't really looking forward to either keeping more secrets or having awkward conversations.

Rosemary had been in a particularly good mood that morning, although the dinner the night before had gone in a fairly haphazard way. Athena took a sip of the delicious refreshing lemonade, hoping that Rosemary's good mood held, or telling her was going to be way too awkward.

CHAPTER
FOURTEEN

Rosemary stood in the tea shop kitchen the next evening, cleaning up. She'd just finished rolling the final peppermint crisp. It was a twist on the recipe that she'd been given in her coursework. She'd made it slightly more oval shaped and enhanced the flavours. The dark chocolate truffles were then dipped in a thin coating of white chocolate before rolling them in peppermint sugar. Every time she got a recipe she couldn't help but change it just a little bit. There was something about following instructions that didn't work for her. Sure, it was possible that whoever invented the recipe had created the most perfect possible thing, but everyone had different tastes. And surely, a little creativity couldn't hurt.

The door of Marjie's tea shop opened and Rosemary looked up to see Neve entering.

"I hope you don't mind me popping in."

Rosemary smiled. "Not at all."

"What kind of magic are you going to put in these ones?"

"These ones? Nothing," said Rosemary. "Although maybe I should be experimenting."

Neve picked up a truffle and popped it into her mouth.

"Sorry, I hope you weren't needing every one of those. I couldn't help myself. It was rude of me not to have asked first though." Neve had the look of a naughty schoolgirl on her face. "Mmm. So refreshing."

"I know," said Rosemary. "If I *was* putting little enchantments in them for the festival, this would be some sort of fresh mountain air spell. You know, clearing away the cobwebs, perfect for resolving hangovers."

"I could do with a few of those."

"You're drinking heavily at the moment then?" said Rosemary.

"Not exactly," said Neve. "Clarity sounds nice to me, especially given the day I've had."

"What's wrong?"

"That's what I wanted to come in and talk to you about. Two more people have gone missing."

Rosemary's jaw dropped. "More?"

"Well, I say more people because I assume that woman you found on the beach went missing from somewhere before she reappeared. These other two were on the same beach. They were both men who just walked into the sea, apparently, and haven't been seen since."

"Not regular drownings?" said Rosemary.

"It doesn't sound like it," said Neve. "No bodies were found, so we don't know if they actually have drowned."

"What do you mean? They walked into the sea!"

"Yes. One bystander recalls watching from up on the hill."

Rosemary frowned. "They were probably just going swimming."

"They were fully clothes... and no one knows what happened to them."

"You think it was magical?" said Rosemary.

Neve nodded. "Something sinister is going on. I'm sure of it."

"The poor families," said Rosemary. "It was bad enough when Athena disappeared into the fae realm. If I'd known she'd walked into the sea I would have clearly assumed the worst. Is there any hope that they could be alive? I mean, surely they couldn't breathe underwater."

"I don't know," said Neve. "It's possible somebody kidnapped them using some sort of cloaking spell."

"It would be a fairly mysterious way of doing it, don't you think? Were the two men connected?" Rosemary asked.

"They were friends," said Neve. "But the families can't think of any reason anyone would hurt them."

"No enemies then," said Rosemary. "I guess I should count myself lucky given the fact that I seem to have a few enemies and yet here I am perfectly dry on land."

Neve gave her a stern look.

"Sorry," said Rosemary. "This is no time to joke, I know. Why are you even telling me about all this?"

"I might need your help with this case," said Neve. "I'm sure it's magical, and the bigwigs are preoccupied with something else at the moment. I doubt they'll care about a couple of missing people."

"I'm happy to do what I can," said Rosemary. "But I'm no detective. You'd be better off asking Tamsyn to help as far as magic's concerned."

"Tamsyn has already tried, but no seeking spells seem to be working at the moment, not even with her magic."

"It might not be magic," said Rosemary. "Or at least not a spell."

"Well, let me know if you have any ideas, anyway," said Neve.

"Wait a minute. Before you go. I'm just going to try something." She put one of the peppermint truffles on a plate and then waved her fingers over it, weaving a light and intricate spell. She envisioned fresh mountain air. "Are you willing to be my test dummy?"

"Sure," said Neve. "It can't hurt..." She popped the truffle into her mouth and immediately groaned.

"What is it?"

"Oh!" said Neve. "It's like a blizzard in my mouth!"

Rosemary's eyes widened and she panicked. "I need a counter-spell."

"No, it's fine. A bit strong and unexpected, but it cleared my sinuses," she said, sniffing. "I wasn't prepared for the shock. But I am feeling a lot clearer now. Like I've had a strong coffee and a freezing dip in the ocean."

"Maybe I'll try it a little subtler next time."

"That's probably wise," said Neve. "You wouldn't want to give anyone a heart attack."

"Certainly not."

"I'll be off then."

She gave Rosemary a quick hug.

Rosemary's phone buzzed. She looked at the screen to see a message from Athena. *Dinner's almost ready.*

She picked up the rest of her truffle equipment and said a quick cleaning spell to make sure Marjie's tea shop kitchen was sparkling clean. But as she headed out the door she jumped in shock.

Another figure was standing in the doorway.

"Back, foul demon!" Rosemary cried.

Burk stepped into the light of the shop, looking bemused. "I'll have you know I recently showered."

Rosemary laughed. "Sorry. All I could see was a shady figure."

"And you thought the best course of action was to insult them?"

"Naturally."

"I'm sorry I startled you," said Burk.

"It's fine," said Rosemary. Seeing the handsome vampire after their late night phone call was more than she was mentally prepared to deal with and so, of course, she began to ramble.

"But...I'm on my way out and I should probably lock the door. Not that it's not nice to see you, and I'm not trying to lock you out, it's just that Neve was in here before and she was distracting and now I have to go and Athena has dinner ready."

"My apologies," said Burk.

He took Rosemary's hand and kissed it briefly, looking her in the eyes.

Memories of her steamy dreams drifted back into Rosemary's mind, and she forgot all about being in a rush.

"Oh, I..." said Rosemary. "Erm...Hi."

"Hi," said Burk with a smile. "I realised that during our phone call we hadn't made any specific plans. And then I also realised that you'd been in maybe not such a good place last night, and I didn't want to take advantage of that."

"Oh, no, not at all," said Rosemary. "I was fine. Really. I was just, you know..."

"Reconsidering the terms of your existence?" said Burk. "Compensating for a future empty nest syndrome?"

Rosemary sighed. "I'm sorry. Did I sound *that* desperate?"

Burk shook his head slowly. "I don't want to be the man you turn to just because you're worried about being alone."

"You think I'm pre-emptively empty nesting towards you?"

"Are you?"

"No," said Rosemary. "It's just that..." Her heart skipped a beat. "I actually do like you. The other stuff – well, the circumstances now are just clearing a path through all my resistance, that's all."

"And here I am at the end of that path?"

"Yes, if you want to be."

"As long as I'm not—"

"You take this all so seriously," said Rosemary. "I'd have thought a vampire of your age would be playing the field."

"I suppose I'm a romantic at heart. Besides, I've had many years to soak up all kinds of experiences. I'm more interested in something deeper," said Burk.

"Does that mean you don't want to go out with me?" Rosemary asked, slightly offended at what she assumed Burk was implying. "Are you calling me shallow?"

He laughed. "Not exactly."

Rosemary squinted in confusion. "So do you want to date me or not?"

"I do. Of course I do. I just want to make sure it's actually what you're wanting."

Rosemary felt a burst of fire twisting in her midsection and just below.

"Yes," she said.

"Yes?"

Her heart raced and she fought against her instinct to run away and avoid this entire excruciating situation, but she was done with all that. Rosemary was tired of running. This time in her life was for getting what she really wanted.

"It's what I'm wanting," she said. "I do want to go out with you. I've wanted to for ages. It's just...it's taken a bit of a reality check to make me prioritise my own romantic life. I had a lot of resistance and the conversation with Neve just helped me see through it all."

Burk smiled his heart-melting smile. "I suppose I should be thanking Neve then."

Rosemary shook her head with a laugh. "She's got enough to think about already without random vampires showing up at her place."

"Alright," said Burk. "Shall we go out next Friday?"

"Yes...Oh wait, no."

"No?"

"The end of the term is coming up way too quickly and I've got plans with Athena on Friday before I get ready to go away for my course."

"I take it that Saturday's not suitable, either."

"Not exactly." Rosemary frowned. "Sorry."

"It's fine."

"Thursday?" she suggested.

"That's the Law Society board meeting, and if I tried to take you along you'd be extremely bored."

Rosemary smiled. "Sounds like my cup of tea, a bunch of lawyers talking about law stuff. Okay, how about Tuesday?"

"It's a date," said Burk. He kissed her hand again. "I won't delay you any further, Rosemary Thorn."

He disappeared into the night.

Rosemary sighed, but it wasn't in exhaustion this time, it was more like the sigh of an infatuated teenager. She didn't have the magic of the Beltane fires and the sprites to blame for her sudden loss of reason. And it wasn't strictly lustful thoughts that invaded her mind, it was everything else as well.

Rosemary drove home with a smile on her face she couldn't seem to shake and didn't really want to.

"What's got you in such a good mood?" Athena asked as Rosemary entered the house and took a seat at the kitchen table where Athena was serving the homemade pizza that she'd prepared for dinner.

"Nothing," said Rosemary.

"That's not fair, Mum. I'm supposed to tell you everything."

"Supposed to?" said Rosemary, raising an eyebrow.

Athena looked away and Rosemary felt a pang of concern. She'd really hoped they'd gotten past having to conceal things from each other, though she wasn't quite ready to talk about Burk. Perhaps whatever it was Athena was hiding would be something she'd be prepared to share about in the next two days, if not immediately.

Rosemary tucked into the pizza. "This is delicious."

"I made it with herbs from the garden," said Athena proudly, picking up another slice dripping with mozzarella.

"I might have to get your help with my truffles," said Rosemary. "You've obviously got a good sense of taste."

"I inherited it from the best," said Athena with a grin.

Rosemary beamed back, not accustomed to such praise from her teenager.

As they ate, Rosemary's mind drifted back to her previous conversation with Neve that evening, and the men who'd gone missing.

"What's wrong, Mum? You came in all smiling and now you're frowning."

"Something's happened." Rosemary told Athena what the detective had explained to her earlier.

"Very odd," said Athena.

"Keep it confidential, though," said Rosemary. "I'm pretty sure that Neve only told me because she wants me to help with the investigation. Of course I'm not a cop, but she sometimes gets me to help as a consultant."

"You're a freelancer like that Juniper lady," said Athena.

"It's probably best not to compare me to her."

"What? I quite like her," said Athena.

"I do too," said Rosemary. "After all, we did end up going for a drink together and we went to the beach after only knowing each other a few minutes. But she's got some sort of reputation which is probably for a reason."

"Okay," said Athena. "Dad's not keeping girlfriends around for very long at the moment, anyway. I think he's playing the field. It's disgusting." Athena smirked. "I mean, I know I've told you he should be dating. In fact, that's my main source of teasing ammunition. But actually when it comes down to it, it's kind of gross. I don't really want to think about my parents dating at all."

Rosemary blushed. Perhaps she didn't need to work up to telling Athena about Burk after all. She could just try to keep it on the down low. She changed the subject back to the safer topic of the mysterious disappearances. "Whatever you do, stay away from the beach. At least for a little while."

Athena shrugged. "We were thinking about going there this weekend."

"Who?" Rosemary asked. "You and Elise?"

Athena gave her a funny look and Rosemary again wondered what her daughter was hiding.

Athena shrugged. "Just kids from school."

"Surely there's something else you could do."

"Yeah, there's tons to do if you're a young person in a small village," said Athena jokingly. "Don't worry. I'll let the others know that it's not safe at the moment. See what they say."

"Thanks for listening to me," said Rosemary.

"You say that as if I've never listened to you before," said Athena.

"I'd say your track record is a little bit hit and miss."

"Hey, I've been putting in a lot of effort lately."

"That's true. You have, love. You've been doing brilliantly. Keep that up." Rosemary reached over and patted Athena's hand on the table. "Please tell me if there's anything you think I need to know."

"Okay." Athena took a sharp breath. "At school today they talked about some kind of ball."

"A ball? Sounds grand. But isn't the school too small for such carry on?"

"That's what I wondered, but no, it's a big ball that's held every year in Glastonbury for magical teenagers. Apparently, it's loads of fun."

"A hoarde of magical teenagers? Sounds dangerous."

"Don't worry, it's chaperoned — by druids of all people."

"I'd love to meet some of these druids," said Rosemary. "Maybe I will at the Summer Festival. After all, they're supposed to be quite heavily involved."

"The only thing is...the ball is going to be held when you're out of town for your course, and I was hoping..."

Rosemary looked at her daughter. Her first instinct about any situation that could be dangerous was to try and wrap Athena up in cotton wool and protect her from a terrifying world. She knew that wasn't going to work."

Athena looked back anxiously, as if waiting for bad news.

"Of course," said Rosemary. "I'm sure Marjie will be happy to step in and help out, since she's already fallen over herself to volunteer to look after you."

"Really?" Athena asked, beaming.

"I see no harm in it, as long as Marjie's happy to make arrangements and take you there or you go with the trusted parent of another school friend. Somebody like Fleur — somebody I know."

"That's brilliant! Thank you, Mum." Athena grinned from ear to ear and Rosemary knew she'd made the right decision.

"Now, what are we going to do about a dress?"

CHAPTER
FIFTEEN

It was a sunny Saturday morning. Athena clenched her fists nervously as she waited for Elise in town near the ice cream parlour. Elise arrived only a few minutes late, and she kept looking at the ground shyly as they exchanged small talk and went in to order their ice cream.

Athena took a spoonful of the apricot and chocolate gelato that she'd chosen, focusing on enjoying the flavour rather than her racing heart.

"It's funny, isn't it?" said Elise. "I've had a crush on you for a while now, and I thought that telling you about it might settle things down. But now I just feel like a total idiot whenever I'm around you."

"You don't have to do that," said Athena. "I already know you're a total idiot."

Elise laughed and gently whacked Athena with the back of her hand.

"Well, you'd have to be, wouldn't you?" Athena continued, a

smile spreading across her face. "To like someone like me. I'm totally clueless."

"You can't help who you like," said Elise.

"Hey," said Athena. "Don't you know you're supposed to argue with me and tell me all the reasons why I'm a likeable person?"

Elise smiled. "You're charming, and interesting, and intelligent, and brave. And, I don't know, hanging out with you just makes me feel good."

They'd reached the end of town, away from prying eyes. They'd initially planned to go to the beach, but Athena had decided to heed Rosemary's words after all. She didn't want to endanger Elise, especially not if this was some kind of date. Though neither of them had called it that.

Instead, they took one of the well-trodden paths through the forest to the southwest of Myrtlewood, a forest that Athena suspected would eventually lead her back to Thorn Manor if she walked far enough.

Elise reached down and took Athena's hand. It was a sweet gesture which filled Athena with a nice warm feeling, making her feel particularly special.

"Are you gonna tell your Mum?" Elise asked.

"I don't really want to think about my Mum right now."

"Oh...no, it's just that I told mine."

"You did?"

Elise shrugged. "She kind of guessed actually. She knows me really well."

"That's...great," said Athena, her voice rising into a high pitch.

"Err...Isn't your Mum...Didn't you say she was going to the spa this morning?"

"Yeah, it's her usual monthly massage that she's going for," said Athena. "You think maybe she'll tell my Mum?"

"Not intentionally," said Elise, sounding stressed. "But it's the sort of thing she might reveal by accident, thinking that Rosemary already knew."

"Oh no," said Athena, her heart starting to pound. "I'm not sure if I'm ready for that."

"You sound ashamed." There was a rawness in Elise's voice that made Athena uncomfortable.

"Not ashamed," said Athena. "It's just—I don't know. I like having my privacy."

"Fair enough." Elise shrugged as if it was no big deal, though Athena suspected that she didn't really feel casual about it. Thoughts circled in her mind and her chest tighten.

There was the sound of a thud in the distance.

"Who's up there?" Elise asked, fear in her voice.

Athena snapped to attention.

Further up the path there stood a tall figure in a tan cloak, his hood pulled up. Athena could tell he had a big red scraggly beard. "Hopefully somebody minding his own business," she muttered.

"Athena Thorn!" the man's voice boomed.

"Uh oh," said Athena.

"I don't think he's minding his business, after all," Elise said. "What should we do?"

"Run?" Athena suggested.

But very quickly the man seemed to appear in front of them, as if he could move at such a lightning speed it was undetectable to the naked eye.

"Watch out!" Athena pushed Elise behind her. She flung her arms up. Magical flames burst forward towards the would-be attacker. He jolted as if startled.

Athena grabbed Elise's arm. They started to run back towards the town.

Thunderous footsteps sounded behind them. The man was right on their tail.

Athena blasted a ball of energy. It was lightning this time. It sent him spiralling off the path. "Hopefully that will do the trick."

They ran faster and faster until they were back out of the forest in the bright sunlight.

"What was that about?" Elise panted. "Who was that?"

"I don't know," said Athena. "But I'm hoping we never have to find out."

Athena was grateful that they quickly made it back into a more populated area and doubly relieved that the man didn't seem to be following them anymore.

"Maybe I should go home," said Athena. "Being out with you is putting you in danger."

"Don't you think we should report what just happened to the detective?"

"Yeah, you're probably right. I guess we'll head to the station."

They walked together towards the town square.

"This is not quite how I envisioned this day going," Athena said.

"Well, life with you is certainly eventful." Elise gave Athena a cheeky smile.

CHAPTER
SIXTEEN

Rosemary sighed blissfully as all of the tension was slowly massaged out of her shoulders and lower back. "This is the life." Her voice was muffled through the massage table.

Fleur laughed softly. "Thanks. It's good to be appreciated."

"You are most definitely appreciated."

Rosemary had previously considered regular professional massages to be frivolous luxuries, but was quickly coming to depend on them to manage her sense of wellbeing.

"I'm almost done. I'll leave you to get dressed."

Fleur left the room and Rosemary put on her clothes, wishing longingly that she'd booked a whole day at the spa rather than just a massage.

Fleur returned a few moments later.

"That was wonderful. As always," said Rosemary. "Maybe I should book in weekly rather than monthly."

"You'll keep me in business," said Fleur with a big smile.

"You're looking very happy this morning," said Rosemary.

"Oh, just excited. Elise is so looking forward to the Summer Ball."

"Athena is too," said Rosemary.

Fleur gave her a knowing look.

"Teenagers!" said Rosemary.

"What would we do without them?"

Rosemary walked out to reception. Before she could reach the desk, three tall people in beige robes blocked the hallway. It looked to be one woman and two bearded men.

"Excuse me," said Rosemary as she angled herself to squeeze past.

"Rosemary Thorn," said the ginger-bearded man in the centre. "We've come to collect you."

"You bloody well have not!" said Rosemary, feeling a jolt of adrenaline as magic tingled through her veins. The robed figures didn't move. They just stood there, holding their ground. Rosemary made the most of the pause to inspect them for any identifying details. She caught a glimpse of embroidered holly around the cuffs of their robes.

"Hardly the time for Christmas decorations," she said. Clearly her comment threw them off-guard. They looked at her, confused. "Out of my way!" said Rosemary. "Or I'm going to make you move."

"You're coming with us."

"I don't think so," Rosemary said, keeping her voice calm as a shot of adrenaline bolstered her stubborn determination.

A huge burst of light issued from her fingers. It wasn't just a ball of energy. It was a veritable stream.

It washed all the way down the hallway, and when it faded all three of her would-be assailants were passed out cold.

"Well, that was terrifying," said Fleur from behind Rosemary. "But you seemed to handle it well."

"I guess I've had quite a lot of practice now, unfortunately."

"We should call the police," said Fleur.

They stumbled over the unconscious cloaked bodies. Rosemary took a closer look at the cuffs of the robes, which were indeed embroidered with holly. Its gleaming red berries were usually a sign of hope, but Rosemary only felt dread as she headed towards reception.

"Ready to pay?" said Ferg, beaming.

"Wait a minute," said Rosemary. "I think we should call Neve first."

"But I'm here to take your payment." Ferg frowned.

"Didn't you see what happened just now?"

"Yes," said Ferg, "but that's not my job. My job is just to take your payment."

Rosemary rubbed her hands against her closed eyes and exhaled slowly.

"Now isn't really the time, Ferg," she said, rummaging in her handbag. "But fine. Just keep an eye on those guys in case they wake up."

"Which guys are you referring to now?" said Ferg.

"The guys who just tried to kidnap me," said Rosemary.

"You know, they're two men and one woman."

Rosemary narrowed her eyes at him. "I'm just going to call them guys in a gender-neutral way because anyone of any gender could have the gall to try to blow up the authorities like Guy Fawkes. And anyway, I don't know what else to call them."

"Excuse me?" Ferg raised his left eyebrow.

Rosemary shrugged. "You know... that's where the word 'guy' comes from."

"I'm not here for an etymology lesson, Ms Thorn. Besides, the hallway's empty."

Rosemary turned around to see that indeed it was.

She groaned. "Now that's just great!"

"It is?" Ferg asked. "You don't seem very happy about it."

"No, it's not," said Rosemary, with some annoyance. "I was hoping to hand them over to the police so that they could be questioned. Now I'm afraid we're going to be clueless about who they were and who sent for them, unless you have any ideas?"

"Sorry, that's not my job. I can take your money though."

"Honestly," said Rosemary. "Why do I bother explaining myself sometimes?"

Her spine tingled in awareness of a wider threat. If these guys had gone after her, then what about Athena? Would she be safe?

Rosemary quickly settled her bill and said goodbye to Fleur, who also had an equally worried look on her face.

"I'll go check on the girls," said Rosemary.

"Thank you," said Fleur. "I just texted Elise but no response."

"Teenagers! They're only really active at communicating when they want something."

"Don't worry. Everything's going to be fine."

Rosemary hoped very much that that was true. She drove home figuring that Athena should be back from her walk by then, feeling her anxiety creeping to a fever pitch.

As the car pulled up the driveway towards Thorn Manor, her heart plummeted as she recognised detective Neve's car parked outside the house.

"Oh, no. Oh, no, no, no."

Rosemary jumped out of the car and dashed inside.

She almost collapsed in relief as she saw Athena sitting around the kitchen table with Elise and Neve.

"Thank goodness you're alright!" Rosemary said. "What happened?"

"Some great big bearded bloke tried to attack us," said Athena.

"Not you, too!" said Rosemary.

Neve's eyes widened in shock. "You're saying there was another attack?"

"Yes, just now after my massage. I went to pay and these three people in tan robes appeared..."

"Sounds like it could have been the same outfit," said Neve. "Based on Athena's description."

"What were you doing?" Rosemary asked Athena, barely concealing the accusatory tone in her voice. "I told you to stay away from the beach."

"I did," said Athena. "This has nothing to do with the beach. Or, I don't think it does. We weren't at the beach at all. We were in the forest."

"The forest?" Rosemary asked. "Why would you go into the forest?"

Athena gave her a guilty look.

"You weren't trying to get through to the fae realm again, were you?"

"No, Mum," said Athena.

"Rosemary," said Neve in a conciliatory tone. "You should be praising Athena for coming straight to me. After they were attacked they went to the police station."

Rosemary sighed. "You're right. I'm glad you're sensible. Plus, it seems like they would have targeted us no matter where we were."

Athena's eyes lit up in awareness. "That's right! I checked the Astrological Ephemeris and the Moon was conjunct Mars today – so a high chance of conflict."

"I'm not happy about that," said Rosemary. "I don't like the idea that someone abducting us was written in the stars. But I do admit to feeling scratchy, despite my lovely massage...and I suppose I should have told you about this."

Rosemary rummaged in her handbag and found the crumpled piece of paper from Juniper.

Athena frowned. "I can't believe you hid this from me."

"I was going to tell you. I just didn't want to throw fuel on the fire of your obsession."

Athena, Elise, and Neve looked over the symbols, trying to decipher them.

Athena's brow furrowed in concentration. "I'm sure it's what Dr Ceres was talking about. Look, there's Neptune and Venus...you definitely should have showed me."

"And me," said Neve.

"Yes, okay," said Rosemary, trying to stifle her frustration with the whole situation. "You're right. But moving on...I'm guessing whoever attacked us today was part of the crowd that Juniper has heard of. Apparently there are a few people out to get us."

Neve nodded. "From the descriptions you gave, it sounds like it could be some druids."

"Druids?" said Rosemary. "But aren't they the ones that are supposed to help the town?"

"There are lots of different groups of druids," said Neve. "Some of them are more shady than others."

"Besides," said Athena. "They could have been in disguise. It might be nothing to do with druids at all."

"You're right," said Rosemary. "It could even be the Bloodstones or somebody they've contracted."

"So what do we do then?" Athena asked.

"I think I should check in with Juniper," said Rosemary.

"Actually, I don't think you should leave the house right now," said Neve. "Whoever is after you obviously knew that you and Athena were both out and about. They deliberately targeted you when you weren't at home. To me, that's a good sign."

"A good sign?" said Rosemary.

"Yes, it means that the protections on Thorn Manor—the strengthened ones put on when they moved the school here—must be too much for them to get through. That's a good thing. You're safe here."

"Is there some way of making us untraceable?" Athena asked. "I could look for a spell."

Neve nodded. "It's not a bad idea. I think we should talk to Tamsyn."

"Why Tamsyn?" Rosemary asked.

"Well, that's the other thing her magical specialty is good for, isn't it? Finding things and hiding things."

"That makes sense in a strange kind of way," said Athena. "It's like the reverse."

"Exactly," said Neve. "I'll call her and ask if she can drop by later."

"Thank you," said Rosemary. "I don't know what we'd do without you."

"Be stuck in the house eating beans on toast forever," said Neve with a smile.

"Sounds like a cosy sort of existence," said Rosemary. "I could get used to that."

"No, you can't," said Neve, giving her a playful shove. "You need to get out there and live your life."

Rosemary beamed at her friend. "I know. I've been listening."

Her mind drifted to the date she'd confirmed with Burk and she hoped that Tamsyn would be able to offer some sort of solution and conceal them from whoever was after them so that she'd be able to enjoy some freedoms.

"What are you smiling about?" Athena asked.

"I'm just grateful you're okay."

"Yeah, right. You're up to something and I'm going to find out what it is."

CHAPTER
SEVENTEEN

Athena opened the oven, standing back to let the steam billow out as she checked on the roasting vegetables.

"It smells good, love," said Rosemary, coming into the kitchen and inhaling the aroma of herby roasted lamb with new potatoes and garlic.

"Thanks," said Athena. She closed the oven and began tossing the salad.

It was the evening that Athena had come to refer to as 'dinner with Dad', the family meal they'd scheduled fortnightly since he'd moved out into his apartment in Myrtlewood.

Dain came over every second Sunday. The agreement had been reached when Athena realised she would actually miss her father's presence when he moved out.

Rosemary said she didn't mind since Dain had been on his best behaviour, aside from the awkward incident of him naively bringing a date to Neve and Nesta's celebratory dinner, one that Neve couldn't stand.

In fact, Rosemary and Athena both thought it was quite nice to have the company. Aside from the fact that a third of the house at least was taken up by the school, it had felt much quieter at the manor, especially during the weekends, since Una and Ashwyn had fostered the foundling children.

There were, however, a few things that Athena wasn't really looking forward to. Such as Dain finding out about Finnigan being at the school, and other aspects of her personal life she wasn't ready to share with either of her parents.

Rosemary smiled. "You've sure picked up a lot of cooking skills over the last little while."

Athena felt a warmth spread over her at the compliment. "Yes. I used to only be proficient in beans on toast, and bacon and eggs. Now I can cook for an entire tribe."

Athena had helped Nesta and Rosemary with a lot of the cooking over the weeks when there were far more people living in Thorn Manor. Dain had helped too, although he'd had a habit of wandering off halfway through a process and forgetting about the food, which resulted in a number of burnt and inedible meals.

After a while it had been decided that he was only allowed to cook if he had assistance. And so Athena had helped him out as well, keeping him on-track, a skill she'd become rather proficient at with having not one but two easily distractible parents.

Rosemary, who loved cooking, had been far too busy a lot of the time, not just with setting up her business, but also helping to solve various mysteries and other odds and ends. Besides, she was putting a lot of effort into inventing new types of truffles, taking a lot of her creative energy.

Dain arrived half an hour late, as usual. Knowing his tendencies, Rosemary and Athena had invited him half an hour earlier to suit their dinner timing preferences.

He arrived in a deep burgundy suit, without a date this time, carrying an expensive bottle of red wine and small bouquet he'd picked near the gate.

"Thanks for bringing us flowers," said Athena with a cheeky grin.

"Hey, I saved you the trouble of picking them," said Dain with a wink.

"Nice suit...When are you going to tell us what your job is?"

Dain beamed. "When the time is right."

Athena wrinkled her nose in mock-annoyance but gave her father a hug. "How have you been, Dad?"

"Excellent, how about you?"

"Up and down," said Athena.

"Why? What's going on?" He followed Athena and Rosemary into the house and towards the dining room. For these dinners they'd usually sit at the kitchen table. Since it was only the three of them, the dining room felt too formal. But this time, because of the large dishes of lamb and potatoes, Athena had opted for the bigger table. She'd lit the candles and everything.

"This is fancy," said Rosemary, coming into the room and taking a seat.

"You've outdone yourself, kid," said Dain.

Athena beamed, feeling proud of the meal she'd managed to cook all by herself to satisfaction. She began carving up the lamb and serving as Dain magically uncorked the bottle and poured the wine.

"This is very nice," said Rosemary.

Athena noticed she sounded slightly nervous.

Dain cleared his throat. "So tell me what's been happening."

"Oh, nothing much," said Athena. "Apart from the fact that we were attacked yesterday."

Dain had been taking a sip of wine which he almost spat out. "Attacked? What happened?"

There was a dangerous edge to Dain's voice. Athena knew that he was very protective of both her and her mother, despite his inconsistencies as a person.

They filled him in on the details of what had happened, carefully omitting any clues that would give away too much of who the assailants were, worried he might go after them in a vigilante way and put himself in danger. They didn't need Athena's telepathy to be on the same page about this.

After hearing the story, Dain's face became pale and his lips pressed together in a thin line. "I'm going to find out who they were. And I'm going to kill them."

"Settle down," said Rosemary. "They weren't even trying to kill us."

"How do you know, Mum?"

"I'm pretty sure the ones that came after me were trying to kidnap me."

"That's hardly much better," said Dain.

"Fair point," Rosemary said. "Being kidnapped does not sound great."

"It's not. I should know," Dain replied.

"Speaking of that," said Athena, "there's something else that we have to tell you."

Rosemary shot her a warning look.

"What?" Dain asked, rather sharply.

He's going to find out anyway, Athena communicated to her mother. *It's a small town. At least this way we can calm him down a bit before he goes all commando.*

Rosemary's expression was strained, but she nodded.

"You remember Finnigan?"

"You mean the fae boy who tricked you into going to the realm and was apparently the one who kidnapped me?"

"Yeah, that's the one," said Athena, her tone resigned.

"You haven't seen him around town, have you?" said Dain. "I've got a score to settle with him."

"Actually," said Athena. "He's now going to my school."

"What?!" Dain thundered.

Rosemary and Athena leaned back as if in response to his rage. Dain wasn't usually violent or aggressive, except perhaps occasionally when cream had been involved before they'd resolved his little addiction issue.

"It's okay, Dad," said Athena.

"It is *not* okay!" Dain yelled. "How can you say such a thing? It's not okay what he did to you."

"It's not okay that he's at your school either, actually," said Rosemary. "The problem is, there's not much we can do about it."

"He kidnapped me!" said Dain.

"But you didn't press charges," Athena pointed out.

"I didn't want to have to deal with the police...I may not have the best record with them."

"Well, there you go," said Athena. "And even if you did press charges, he's young. It's not like it'd be jail or anything. And there's so little evidence. You didn't even see him."

"He should at least be thrown out of school!"

"Not according to the school rules, unfortunately," said Rosemary. "He hasn't done anything at school to cause trouble."

"Stupid loophole," said Dain. "You okay?" He turned to Athena.

"I'm fine. It was a shock at first, but the school has basically made him ignore me. And if he does harass me, then I guess there'll be grounds for them to discipline him, and hopefully kick him out."

"You sound so calm and sensible," he said. "What happened to my girls? You're supposed to be wild and vindictive."

"We are not *your* girls," said Rosemary with a dismissive wave. "And we're not vindictive, though maybe a tad wild."

"Your hair is, at least," said Athena, her voice gently teasing.

"I can't believe it," Dain said. "I'm going to find that little blighter and I'm going to wring his stupid little—"

"Dad," said Athena. "Stop it." She rushed to change the subject in a hurry. "There's going to be a ball!"

"A ball?" Dain said.

"Yeah, the Summer Ball. Apparently it's held every year in Glastonbury."

Rosemary shook her head. "I know I said you could go but...I don't know about that now we know we're in danger again."

"Oh, Mum! Don't you think it would be safer to let me go? There will be lots of powerful magical people to protect me. You promised to let me have some freedom if I was more open with you and I told you lots of things that I would normally try to hide."

"Cold comfort," said Rosemary.

"Come on! Isn't it better that I go to the ball openly? Maybe even chaperoned with my friends rather than sneak out?"

Rosemary shot her a betrayed look. "You wouldn't."

Athena stared back, waiting for Rosemary to cede some ground.

"Okay, fair enough. I'll think about it."

"Thank you!"

"Who are you going with?" said Dain suspiciously. "I assume this is the kind of thing where you bring a date."

Athena and Rosemary looked at each other.

"Yes," said Athena. "This is an *appropriate* situation for a date."

Dain looked slightly confused. "Who is taking you to the ball? Not Finnigan."

"Of course not! I'm not stupid. I'm trying to avoid him, remember?"

"Have you got a date to the ball?" Rosemary asked, beaming.

Athena looked down at her plate. She'd lost her appetite, despite having cooked the food just perfectly so. She reached for her water glass.

"You do?" said Dain. He seemed to have forgotten his anger from moments before and his voice had become lilting and teasing instead. "Who are you going with? Who is it? Tell us!"

Athena glared at her parents, who'd become like teenagers themselves in an instant, both grinning at her.

"If you must know I'm going with Elise," said Athena.

"What?" said Rosemary, her brow furling in confusion. "As friends?"

"No, on a date...or something," said Athena.

Dain's smile brightened even more. "Now that I can live with!"

Rosemary stuttered. "You're...You're dating Elise?" She sounded shocked.

"Is that a problem?" Athena asked. "I figured I better tell you because you're going to find out one way or another."

"But..." Rosemary looked at Dain and then back to Athena. "I didn't know you were into girls."

Athena shrugged.

"Of course she is," said Dain. "All fae are bisexual."

"What?!" Rosemary's jaw dropped.

"Or maybe pansexual..."

Athena laughed. "That's so appropriate. Like Pan the god who hangs out with nymphs and dryads."

"You didn't think to tell me this?!" Rosemary glared at Dain.

"I didn't think it was particularly important," said Dain.

"All those years we were together and you didn't think to tell me about your...preferences?"

"What difference would it have made?" Athena asked, crossing her arms.

"I just think it's something I should know about."

"Are you a homophobe now, Mum? I thought you were supposed to be open-minded."

Rosemary's face grew red. "Of course I'm not!" she blustered.

"I'm not discriminating. I'm just shocked. I just... I had no idea. That's all."

Athena shrugged.

"I think it's brilliant!" said Dain. "Girls are ten times better than any boys, especially teenagers."

Athena grinned. "You're hilarious sometimes, Dad. How do you even quantify that?"

"Based on the sound science and deductions of my personal experience," said Dain. "I mean, take me, for example. As fine a specimen of a man as I am, I can't hold a candle to even a mediocre woman."

Athena burst out laughing.

Rosemary seemed to have adjusted somewhat after taking a big gulp of wine. "You know what? I think it's brilliant too. Elise seems like a good kid. I would much rather you go to the ball with her than someone like Felix. Don't get me wrong, he's a sweet boy but—"

"But he's a little devil." Dain laughed. "He reminds me of myself when I was younger."

"That's another reason not to go out with him, then," said Athena. "Not that I would, anyway."

Rosemary and Dain both gave her a knowing look that made Athena uncomfortable. Could they possibly know Felix had asked her, or were they just reading something into her tone?

"The point is, I'm going to the ball and I'm going to go with Elise."

"Fine," said Rosemary. "But I want to make sure somebody goes with you. Marjie did offer to look after you while I'm away on my course, but I haven't had a chance to ask..."

"I'll go," said Dain. "I'm happy to supervise."

"I don't know," said Athena. "I don't want you breathing down our necks."

"I can be discreet," said Dain. "I can spy on you from a distance."

"No spying."

"Okay," said Dain. "I'll go and spy on everyone else to make sure that nobody causes trouble, and there'll be no more attacks on either of my girls."

Rosemary gave him an awkward look. "I'm not one of your girls!"

Dain had been being rather possessive that evening and it was clearly bugging her.

"In fact," Rosemary blurted out, "I've got a date myself."

"What?" said Athena. "Is that what you've been hiding from me?"

"With who?!" Dain asked, his voice choked, on the verge of anger again.

"With Perseus Burk."

"Finally!" said Athena. Her mother had been flirting with that vampire for long enough.

"Perseus!" Dain crowed with laughter. "Is that his name?" He waved his arms in the air dramatically. "What a ridiculous name for a ridiculous little man."

"He's taller than you, Dad," said Athena. "And he's not really a man. He's a vampire."

"A vampire man," said Rosemary.

"He's too old for you," Dain protested. "I don't like it."

Rosemary scoffed. "While you're dating everyone in town, apparently! Besides, it's none of your business, really. I just don't like you being so possessive."

"Well, you won't date me," said Dain.

"With good reason, I think," said Rosemary, folding her arms and looking away with disdain.

"I guess I'll be going then," he said, pushing his chair out from the table and making his way towards the door before they had a chance to say goodbye.

"That went well," said Athena flatly.

"Perhaps as good as it could have," said Rosemary. "I guess now all our secrets are out in the open. Thanks for telling me, kid."

"Thanks for getting over your weirdness very quickly," said Athena.

"No problem. I accept you for whoever you are. You know that."

"I know," said Athena. "For the most part anyway, as long as I'm not making dumb life choices."

"I said for who you are, not what you do. Teenagers are always going to do dumb things."

Athena shrugged. "We didn't tell dad everything, did we?"

"You mean about the fact that it was probably druids who attacked?" said Rosemary. "I didn't want him getting the wrong idea. We don't know if it was them or just somebody pretending to be them, and judging by his reaction it's safer for everyone if he doesn't know. He could totally go off the rails and start blowing things up."

"That's true," said Athena. "His magic is powerful, even though he doesn't use it very often."

"He doesn't even think to use it most of the time," said Rosemary. She sighed. "I'm still not thrilled about the ball."

"I thought you said you accepted me," said Athena.

"It's not that," said Rosemary. "I'm not thrilled about you going at all considering people are after us."

"I'm sure there are going to be lots of things that you're not thrilled about Mum," said Athena.

"That's fair enough. Maybe I'll be able to take the afternoon off from my course and go to Glastonbury so I can be there for you."

Athena groaned. "Please don't. It's gonna be embarrassing enough with Marjie and probably Dad there as well."

"Well, I doubt we'll be able to talk either of them out of going."

"I'm sure it'll be fine," said Athena, smiling at her mother. "You go to your course and you'll be back in time for the Summer Solstice festival and I promise to help you with your store."

"Thank you. I appreciate that offer and I intend on taking you up on it. I'm going to need all the help I can get, and not just with the chocolate stall."

"You're worried about the solstice?"

Rosemary nodded. "I'm sure all of these different things are connected —the suspicious disappearances, the Druid-looking-people attacking us, the woman turning up on the beach with no memory of who she is, mumbling about bears."

"Hey," said Athena, patting her mother on the arm. "Sea bears sound pretty cool. Besides, we've probably been through a lot worse."

"That reminds me, kid, I was going to offer to help with the dishes." Rosemary smiled at Athena. "We can both do with an early night. I think we're going to need our rest, given what's coming."

"No help required," said Athena. "Our very helpful house combined with my automancy have got it covered."

CHAPTER

EIGHTEEN

"I hate to be a walking cliché," said Rosemary, entering the kitchen where Athena was making herself dinner. "But I've got nothing to wear."

"That's ridiculous, Mum," said Athena. "You have a whole new wardrobe."

"But it's not as fancy as even Burk's casual shirts." Rosemary pouted.

"It's not a competition. If he didn't trust you to make yourself presentable enough, I doubt he would have asked you out in the first place."

"This is so hard!" said Rosemary. "I've never had to do any of this before. I feel so awkward. And nervous."

"Hang on." Athena turned off the stove where her sausages were frying and walked her mother back upstairs to her room. Clothes were flung all over the bed. "This is a right mess!"

"I know," said Rosemary. "I feel ridiculous. I'm too old for this."

"Don't act like a teenager," said Athena. She rifled through the clean clothes that Rosemary had thrown on the bed. "Here. This one." She passed Rosemary a lacy black velvet top.

"It's not too revealing?" said Rosemary.

"Actually, maybe you should wear a dress."

"Something even more revealing?" Rosemary asked.

"Stop being so self-conscious," said Athena. "Look." She picked up a dark green silk cocktail dress that was lying still attached to its hanger on the bed. "This one's new. You've never worn it before." Athena held up the tag.

"It seemed a little bit posh."

"Isn't that what you're going for, since Burk is such a fancy guy?"

"You've got a point." Rosemary picked up the dress, the silk sliding through her fingers in a pleasant way.

"Plus, it'll bring out your eyes."

"You're really enjoying this, watching me so uncomfortable," Rosemary grumbled.

"I just think it's funny," said Athena. "But also good. You should be going out and hanging out with people. I just don't want to hear any details."

"You're not going to get any, trust me."

"I guess you should put on the dress. Burk is supposed to be here in a minute."

Rosemary looked at her watch. "Oh crap, you're right."

Athena laughed, then left the room. Rosemary frantically stripped off and threw on the dress. She didn't have time for makeup. She'd been pacing her room trying out outfits that had gotten more and more ridiculous for over an hour. She did put on some lipstick and some earrings. She was never any good at makeup, anyway.

She left the room and then ran back to apply lick of mascara.

The doorbell rang. All of a sudden, she was dreading the evening ahead.

"Mum!" Athena called out as Rosemary made her way downstairs.

"Maybe you can tell him I'm sick or something," she said.

"No way," said Athena, crossing her arms.

"I'm not ready," said Rosemary in a stroppy voice.

"Yes, you are." Athena grabbed her mother's arm and led her to the door and even opened it up for her before fleeing back to the kitchen.

"Rosemary." Burk was standing on the doorstep in a crisp designer shirt. Pale grey that Rosemary assumed was probably Italian. "You look ravishing."

"I hope you don't mean that literally," said Rosemary.

Burk laughed. "Do you think I invited you on a date so I could eat you?"

"Sorry," said Rosemary. "It's just...as you know, I can't control things that I say sometimes."

"I am impressed you're not rambling right now," said Burk.

"It really is impressive," said Rosemary. She took her coat off the hook and allowed Burk to take her arm in that old-fashioned way of his. He led her to a rather expensive looking car and opened the door for her. It was something she'd been expecting, but it gave her a feeling of being special.

As she got into the car she thought maybe the evening wasn't going to be a total disaster after all. Then she realised she'd spoken her thoughts aloud. Not only that, but Burk was impeccably fast and had already seated himself in the driver's seat a second after he closed her door, meaning he'd heard everything.

"Oh. Sorry," said Rosemary.

Burk laughed again. "Is that what you really think of me? So you're expecting me to take you out for a disaster?"

"No, I was expecting to *be* the disaster," said Rosemary.

"Maybe that's what I like about you," said Burk as he began driving away from Thorn Manor.

Rosemary blushed with embarrassment. "You like that I have a habit of making a fool of myself...A great thing to be known for."

"You're refreshing, Rosemary. There are a lot of things I like about you."

"Oh, yes?" Rosemary said, feeling herself begin to glow.

There was a serious expression on Burk's face. "You're strong willed and feisty and clever. Being around as long as I have, I've met quite a lot of people."

"Don't remind me how old you are," said Rosemary. "I've only just talked myself into believing this whole thing was a good idea."

Burk turned towards her. "Is it a problem for you?"

"I don't know," said Rosemary, shrugging. "I suppose it was more of a way of talking myself out of all this. But I'm done with that."

"Good," said Burk. "Because there's not much I can do about my age."

He continued driving and Rosemary noticed they were going towards the seaside.

"Isn't it dangerous down here?" she asked. "People have been going missing."

"For an ancient vampire and a powerful witch? I doubt it." Burk grinned. "We're a force to be reckoned with, Rosemary."

"That's how I used to refer to my granny. She was quite some force."

"Please don't tell me I'm so ancient I remind you of your grandmother."

Rosemary laughed. "Now that you mentioned it. No. You're nothing alike."

They carried on down the coast a fair way in silence. Burk's expression was serious, almost sombre, and Rosemary had to bite her tongue to refrain from making jokes about broody vampires in case that was inappropriate. Instead, she looked out at the inky blue sky as it darkened to night. "The sea looks so beautiful out here. Where are you taking me?"

"You'll see."

"That's no fun."

Moments later Burk pulled up outside a restaurant that Rosemary would describe as fancy masquerading as rustic. He got out of the car and instantly appeared by her door to open it. He took her hand to help her out, placing the other on the small of her back, something that made her insides squirm.

They made their way inside the restaurant which jutted out over the ocean to panoramic views. The space was dotted with elegant round tables dressed in pure white tablecloths. Clearly it was an expensive joint and Rosemary had never heard of it.

"Where are we exactly?" she asked. "There was no sign outside."

Burk smiled mysteriously. "The restaurant's called Neptune. And yes, don't worry, it is magically-inclined. You don't have to worry about what you say around here. You could even do some magic as long as it's not too destructive."

"I bet the repair bills would be astronomical," said Rosemary.

Burk smiled at her. "Probably best we don't find out."

"It's funny how we have this entire magical community living all around England, probably all around the world — even an entirely magical village — and yet, nobody knows about it."

"Magic is sometimes more powerful when it's hidden," said Burk. "Besides, can you imagine how the mainstream media would deal with finding out about this?"

Rosemary looked around the room. It seemed relatively ordinary, although there was certainly magical detail that she hadn't really noticed when she came in. For instance, the lighting in the ceiling turned out to be thousands of candles floating in the air rather than the light fixtures she assumed would be there. Similarly, on each table instead of a candle was a tiny flame hovering above a quartz crystal.

"I'm surprised they'd get enough business," said Rosemary. "It seems quiet."

Only a few tables were occupied with discreetly-dressed diners.

"We're early," said Burk. "Most of the clients come later in the evening."

"Vampires?" said Rosemary, knowing they preferred to be active outside of daylight hours, safely away from the sun.

"Quite a few of us," said Burk. "And also a lot of the same clientele as the spa gets."

"Oh yeah, it sounds like a wonderful weekend away actually," said Rosemary. "Go stay at the spa and be pampered, then pop out here for a nice dinner. I assume the food's actually good."

"You'll find out soon," said Burk, and looked out the window towards the sea view.

A waiter appeared at the side of the table, startling her. He was dressed in a silk waistcoat, with a crisp white shirt and what appeared to be rather nifty bloomers instead of trousers. Rosemary wasn't sure if he'd simply snuck up on them, or appeared out of thin air with some other kind of magic trick like Juniper.

"Mr. Burk," the waiter said with a flourish. "Welcome back. I see you have a new guest this evening."

The waiter was young and somewhat pimply faced, but he carried himself with an air of confidence that made Rosemary assume that he was a vampire and probably much older than he looked.

"Cedric," said Burk with a nod. "This is Rosemary Thorn."

"An infamous Thorn," said Cedric with a little bow. "How may I serve you this evening?"

There were no menus and Rosemary looked up at him questioningly.

"I'll have a bottle of 97 Cabernet Sauvignon from Norwood," said Burk.

"Are you ordering wine for the table or for me?" said Rosemary. "Do you intend to drink that all yourself?"

"My apologies, Rosemary. Is there something else you'd prefer to drink?"

"No, red wine sounds good. I'm not fussy. I'm just not used to being ordered for."

The waiter smiled. "Very well. And for dinner?"

"You don't have menus here?" Rosemary asked.

"My apologies, Ms Thorn. I assumed that Mr Burk would have filled you in on how the establishment works. We can make you any dish in the world that you care for. Even one from your memories." He said the word memory slowly, looking at Rosemary.

Out of nowhere, a particular Christmas dinner popped into her mind where Granny had cooked a beef roast soaked in port and served it with crispy potatoes and gravy.

"Ah," said Cedric. "I know just the thing."

He turned away and then promptly disappeared into the shadows.

"Did he just read my mind? What kind of place is this?"

Burk smiled. "Cedric has a particular gift. He can conjure food memories and then recreate the meal. He was a very famous chef at one point before he was turned."

Rosemary gave a slight nod, Burk seemed to be surreptitiously letting her in on a secret, although the fact that Cedric was a vampire had already become fairly obvious to her.

"I didn't know vampires could have psychic powers like that or do magic."

"Sometimes, if they had some sort of latent abilities as humans, those get strengthened after the turning," said Burk quietly.

"What about you? Any mysterious abilities?"

Despite having known Burk for some months now, Rosemary knew very little about him. He'd never shared with her anything about what his life was like as a human or how he became a vampire. He just occasionally gave little hints, casually in conversation. A true man of mystery. Looking at him now, she wondered how many secrets he was hiding.

"I'm exceptionally fast for a vampire, though some of that comes from age. Just like strength. I can withstand the sun fairly well. But that too is because I'm what they called an elder."

"An elder..." said Rosemary.

Burk's voice lowered to a husky whisper. "We're a lot harder to kill."

"Let's hope it will never come to that," Rosemary joked. There was an awkwardness in her voice, revealing that she really *was* hoping she didn't have to stake her date at some point in the future.

He looked her in the eye. "You're wondering if I've ever harmed a human being?"

"Have you?" Rosemary asked.

Burk's expression darkened and Rosemary wondered if that always happened when he thought about his past. "In the first few hundred years after I was turned, I was quite – shall we say – hedonistic? I did hunt people. And I did kill, but it was a different time. I enjoyed the chaos of war, and the confusion and the lack of demon hunters as well. Up until recently, many humans believed very much in the supernatural, which made it quite a lot more dangerous for us. But in wartime, people had other things on their minds."

"So you went from war to war, having fun?" Rosemary grimaced.

Burk shook his head. "I wasn't barbaric, if that's what you're implying. I've never enjoyed people's suffering. But there definitely was a time that I enjoyed the hunt."

"But you killed people."

"If I felt it was warranted."

"You mean you hunted down the bad guys like some sort of vigilante? And here I was the one worried about being clichéd."

"There's nothing clichéd about you, Rosemary Thorn. You're a true original."

"No, I get it," said Rosemary. "There are plenty of terrible people in the world. You probably made it a better place in their absence. I can understand why you could get drunk on the power of being a vampire and go after them. If anyone hurt Athena I don't know if I could stop myself from using magic to get revenge."

Burk had a wry grin on his face. "Do you need someone taken care of?"

"If you'd asked me a few weeks ago, I would have said yes," said Rosemary, and she explained about the situation at school. "But Finnigan seems to be keeping his distance. I wouldn't mind though...if he woke up in a different town or a different plane or a different planet. Just saying."

"Just say the word and at least two of those things can be arranged."

"I'll keep that in mind. I'm keeping a close eye on him. I asked Tamsyn to cast a special spell on him that would alert her if he's up to no good."

"How devious," said Burk. "I love it."

There was a tiny clinking sound and a bottle of wine appeared in front of them on the table along with two crystal glasses.

Rosemary jumped in surprise, eyes wide as the bottle proceeded to pour itself into the glasses which then moved smoothly into position in front of each of them.

A little sparkling purple light appeared above Burk's glass.

"Cedric's all about the theatrics," said Burk.

"If that's so, you'd think coming into this place would have been more dramatic. We just strolled right in."

"He's aware that patrons here appreciate the privacy. Many of them never see him at all. They just turn up, enjoy the meal and leave. He makes a special point of saying hello to me because of our history."

"That's remarkable," said Rosemary, taking a sip of the delicious wine. "What's wrong with yours? What's with the purple light?"

He gave her a look and raised an eyebrow.

"Of course," said Rosemary. "It's being blood enchanted right in front of us!"

He nodded.

As the evening proceeded, various guests appeared at the tables around them. It could have been a fairly ordinary restaurant at a glance. But on closer inspection, there was none of the usual bustle of waiters or other staff.

People just slunk in or swaggered or sidled in, or in one case, even waltzed. And there were certainly a few among the patronage who sauntered.

Rosemary watched them. The clientele were indeed a lot like the patrons at the spa. Though there were certainly more vampires, moving in at such speed that Rosemary barely noticed them until they were seated at the tables.

"Try not to stare," said Burk gently. "It's considered just as rude in the magical community as it is in the mundane one."

"Pardon me," said Rosemary. "I'm just a rather nosy person sometimes."

"Noted," said Burk.

"It's killing me that I know so little about you. When are you going to tell me about your past? All I know is you're very old and had a brother who I *might* have killed in a dramatic feat of self-defence before I knew you were related."

Burk's gaze darkened again. "Don't remind me."

"I'm sorry. Way to kill the mood – casually drop into the conversation that I murdered your brother."

"Murdered is a strong word," said Burk. A pained expression crossed his face and then quickly vanished. "I gave up trying to help my brother a long time ago. I'd say you put him out of his misery. He was never happy. Not as a human when we were growing up in the French countryside and not after we returned."

"Your name's not French."

Burk looked out towards the darkening horizon. "My human father idolised the ancient Greeks, and of course the Burk name comes from my...sire."

Rosemary gulped. "So vampires really do use those old fashioned words for their makers?"

Burk smiled enigmatically. "We often tend to be old-fashioned – those of us who have been around a long time. However, I was *sired* by an ancient vampire called Charles, and I tend to call him my father. We have been family for far longer. As for the surname Burk, it's old English for a family that lives in a fort on a hill – though I must admit the name has changed over the centuries as we've adapted to new countries and cultures."

Rosemary had a woozy feeling. "So you grew up in the French countryside? That's more information than I ever had before."

Burk nodded. "Although it was back when it was the French Empire."

"Do you remember it all?"

Burk's eyes clouded over. "As crisply as this morning. I recall sneaking into my father's study one spring morning and knocking over his favourite decanter, then racing my brother through the fields to escape his wrath."

"Tell me about your father."

Burk cleared his throat. "There's not much else to tell. We were usually kept well away from him. My brother and I were two bastard sons of the Duke of Aquitaine."

Rosemary coughed on her wine. "Do you mean like Eleanor of Aquitaine?"

"I suppose she was my great, great niece. You know of her?"

"Of course, we learned about her back in school history class – the only woman to be the queen of both France and England in her lifetime. She must have been quite a catch."

"I didn't have much to do with her," said Burk, but there was a twinkle in his eyes at the mention of the famous woman in his line, which faded again as he spoke more of his past. "My brother and I were traders. He was always getting into trouble. I followed him halfway across the continent and through several wars before I gave up and came back to France."

"It's quite some history," said Rosemary. "You must have lived through so much."

Burk shrugged, as if trying to be more casual than he actually felt. "History's a strange thing. You're there at the time, and it's all so immersive. Then it just disappears in the blink of an eye. When you've lived as long as I have you don't want life to pass you by."

He gave Rosemary a meaningful look that made her insides squirm in a pleasant way.

She took a sip of her wine. "I would have thought you would have gotten terribly bored of it by now."

"I'll admit, some things do become boring," said Burk. "Many vampires my age give up. They go dormant."

"They go to sleep and don't wake up?" Rosemary asked, looking at Burk suspiciously, as though he might nod off one day and disappear.

"It's not quite like that," said Burk. "If the mind is not kept occupied, it just slowly becomes less and less active. There's a kind of defence mechanism that sets in at some point where the vampire reverts back to a primal creature-self and buries itself deep in the earth."

Rosemary nodded. "That makes sense. I suppose that stops them from just going to sleep one day and getting burned in the sun when somebody rudely barges in on them in what they think is a deserted house."

"Indeed," said Burk.

"Is it like a virus?"

Burk gave her an odd look.

"Sorry, that did sound rude didn't it? I mean, is it like in most stories...can you make vampires? Werewolves have a kind of virus, don't they?" She said it casually, flippantly, still not wanting to give away Liam's secret.

"I'm not like your bookshop man," he said.

"You know about Liam?" Rosemary asked.

"Werewolves have a distinctive smell."

"I wonder if he knows that," said Rosemary. "He's been trying to keep it all a secret. Does he know that any vampire could out him at any moment?"

"That would be a horribly rude thing to do," said Burk with a frown. "Vampires have been persecuted in the magical community before, as well as by mundane humans, much like werewolves have been. It would be dishonourable of us to begin outing them. It's only been in the last few hundred years since blood enchantments were invented, allowing us a semblance of civility, that vampires have been able to live fairly peacefully, without fear of persecution from other magical beings."

"That's what they need for werewolves, too," said Rosemary.

"That's what you've been helping him with," said Burk. It wasn't a question.

"But I'm hardly an expert," said Rosemary. "I hardly know the first thing about how to help."

"I trust that you can find a way," said Burk,

Rosemary smiled at him. She really was enjoying herself.

Dinner appeared on plates in front of them, just as mysteriously as the wine had.

Rosemary was delighted to find the beef and potato dish brought back a lovely feeling of nostalgia of that happy Christmas when she was nine years old.

Burk's dinner had been a rather humble looking soup – blood enchanted, or course. He explained that it reminded him of something his mother used to cook in the French countryside after she'd been abandoned by their adulterer of a father. Rosemary noticed that every time he spoke of his past, he became sombre. It clearly held a lot of pain and other complex feelings, which left her wondering whether living a long time just compounded one's emotional wounds, or did it also give them more opportunities to heal? Maybe both, she decided.

"Thanks for telling me about your history," said Rosemary. "I know you don't talk about it often."

"It's a privilege being in your company like this," he replied. "I hope you're enjoying the evening."

"I'm having a great time. Thank you for all this. I'm kind of wondering why it took me so long to agree."

Burk shrugged. "When you've lived as long as I have, that kind of time is a mere blink. I could wait a lifetime for you, Rosemary Thorn. In fact, I probably already have waited several."

"More than several if you're *that* old."

Burk smiled. "Another reference to my age. It does bother you, doesn't it?"

"I suppose it's just like in the vampire books and movies," said

Rosemary. "What actually bothers me is silly, especially considering this is only one date."

"You're worried that you will age and I'll continue to stay the same?"

"That's true, isn't it?" said Rosemary. "In the blink of an eye I'll be eighty years old, and you'll still be..."

"Thirty seven, give or take a few years. They weren't the best at accounting for time back then. But I like thirty-seven. It has a nice ring to it."

"So that's the thing, isn't it?" said Rosemary. "Right now we're a similar age and yet, it won't be too long – in your sense of time anyway – before I'm the new Granny Thorn. Though I'm not ready to think about Athena having children."

"She's got great genetics."

"Thank you," said Rosemary. "Like I said, I'm not ready to think about that just yet. Anyway, this is all silly conjecture, isn't it? We should be enjoying the evening."

"You think it's silly conjecture to bring up eternity on our first date?" said Burk.

"Well, no...Yes and no. That part is more just me ridiculously worrying about everything and jumping to conclusions."

"Very well," said Burk. "What would you like to talk about? Chocolate?"

"I'm not sure if I can think about chocolate right now. I'm neck deep in it. What I really want to talk about is probably not romantic."

"The latest Myrtlewood mystery, I take it?"

Rosemary smiled sheepishly. "If you don't mind. I could do with some of your sharp wit and analysis."

They spent their rest of the evening enjoying the food as well as dessert.

Rosemary had a rich panna cotta with berries. Another one of Granny's favourite recipes.

They talked all about the different factors and the possibilities leading up to the Summer Solstice, which Burk agreed was bound to cause some sort of trouble.

After a good conversation, and rather a lot of delicious wine which did not seem to affect Burk in the slightest, he dropped Rosemary off at Thorn Manor.

He walked her to the front door with his hand on the small of her back, again giving Rosemary more squiggly feelings. She couldn't help but wonder if he'd kiss her, being such a gentleman.

He raised the hand of hers that he was holding up to his mouth, kissing her knuckles, looking at her with those steel grey eyes which contained such longing that Rosemary nearly forgot to breathe.

"Thank you for a wonderful evening, Rosemary Thorn."

Rosemary felt a slight yearning as he let go of her hand and stepped away towards his car.

"Burk?"

"What? What is it?" he asked. "Would you like to make plans for a second date?"

There was a sweet hopefulness in his voice. But Rosemary wasn't thinking that far ahead. She took a step towards him, grabbed hold of his lapels, and pulled him into a passionate and burning kiss.

Burk resisted for the briefest moment before surrendering to the fire of her lips.

It felt a little bit like the kiss they shared in front of the flames leading up to Beltane, but this time there were no magical enhancements required. Just the soft, rough, tender feel of their lips and tongues, meeting, tangling, mesmerisingly.

Rosemary eventually pulled away, breathless. "I'm sorry," she said, realising that Burk liked to do things a little more formally.

Burk's mouth twisted into a cheeky half smile. "You never have to apologise for that. I'm always going to enjoy your unpredictability, especially if it results in such a sensual interaction."

Rosemary blushed. Part of her wanted to drag him inside and upstairs, hopefully without Athena noticing, but it was only the first date, so she held back.

"I'll see you again, very soon I hope."

She nodded. "You'd better."

With that, she watched him walk away, noticing that he did so at a normal pace, which must have felt achingly slow when he was used to moving at such speed.

He got into this car and drove away.

Rosemary sighed, leaning back against the door. This time it was a sigh of pleasure and satisfaction rather than one of tiredness or frustration.

She was awash in a warm feeling, even nicer than the one she associated with her recent dreams of Burk, and she intended to enjoy it as much as possible.

CHAPTER
NINETEEN

There was a hum of excitement in the air. Rosemary watched from the window seats at Thorn Manor as Margie and Athena sifted through fabric samples and dress patterns. Rosemary smiled and sipped her tea. She was pleased her daughter's obsession with celestial patterns and her anxiety about exams had been diverted somewhat by the ball preparations.

Rosemary couldn't sew to save her life, and Athena had something quite particular in mind for her ball dress. Over the past few weeks they'd gone on several shopping trips, scouring most of the dress stores within an hour's drive, since they could now afford nice things, but it was all to no avail.

Athena had never been to a ball before and wanted a dress like a particular fairytale princess in yellow. Unfortunately, yellow was a tricky colour for most people. Athena's more tanned skin tone, according to several of the style experts in the shops, was more forgiving towards the warmer shades of yellow which made her glow, but the cooler shades that were in fashion didn't look as good and weren't what Athena was after at any rate.

Rosemary had kept Marjie updated on their progress until they'd finally relented and let her step in to help. Fortunately, Marjie was quite the expert. She had boxes of patterns that she'd used to make costumes when volunteering for various local play productions – a hobby that had eventually led to her opening a small costume shop several decades earlier in Myrtlewood, which she assured them was not a sound business move.

Upon scouring Marjie's collection of patterns, Athena had found several that caught her fancy. Margie also knew where to get the best fabric and had convinced her old supplier to send over all her satiny warm yellow-toned materials in sample form.

Rosemary supped her tea as she watched them chatter together excitedly.

"Oh, you're going to look stunning!" said Marjie. "Will you wear a tiara?"

"Don't be silly," said Athena. "It's already going to be hard enough pulling off a yellow dress with my bright red hair. I'd look like a total goofball in a tiara."

"Don't rule it out," said Marjie. "I've got some treasures at home that might do an excellent job of highlighting your eyes."

"Is that what tiaras are for?" Rosemary asked from across the room. "Highlighting the eyes?"

"Of course they are," said Marjie. "They're shining, just like you."

Rosemary smiled. She didn't quite know what Marjie was talking about, but she certainly wasn't an expert on tiaras or dresses, or anything of the sort.

"What's Elise wearing?" Rosemary said as she walked back towards the kitchen and put on the jug for more tea.

"All she'll tell me is that it's going to be blue."

"What shade of blue?" Marjie asked.

"No idea."

"We could come up with a lovely corsage for both of you!" Marjie crowed. "There are plenty of yellow and blue flowers at this time of year."

"I suspect it'll be like her usual hair colour," said Athena. "But I really have no idea."

"Of course, even if she chooses a different shade, the corsages will still match because of her hair. That's brilliant!"

Rosemary laughed warmly. "Thank you for doing all this, Marjie."

"Thank you for letting me! It's such a treat to be able to help out like this and I'm looking forward to our extended slumber party."

Marjie had taken to calling the three weeks when Rosemary was going to be away on her course an extended slumber party. She intended to stay with Athena the whole time.

"Are you sure it's not too much to ask?" Rosemary said. "Dain's happy to take part of the time."

"You make it sound like some sort of work shift or prison sentence," Athena grumbled.

"No. I want Athena all to myself!" said Marjie with a grin. "We're going to have such a great time. We'll do our nails and practice hairstyles for the ball! Dain's welcome to come over from time to time if he likes."

Rosemary smiled again, grateful to have such wonderful warm and generous friends in her life as Marjie, Neve, Nesta, Una, and Ashwyn, and even Sherry and Liam, though they'd been a little more distant recently. Sometimes the whole town felt like one big and slightly dysfunctional family. And most of the eclectic characters had grown on her, even Ferg in all of his oddness. Though there were still a few who she'd prefer not to spend time with, including the mayor who was so pompous and arrogant. She didn't much care for Constable Perkins either, who accused her left, right, and centre of all kinds of crimes that she didn't commit.

She was feeling slightly anxious about leaving Athena for so long. But she knew that at least her daughter would be in good hands.

THE WEEK before Rosemary left for her course flew by rather quickly. She'd continued to practise her chocolate making, do her course-work for both the confectioners course and the business course, and did various things to prepare for the shop. The renovations were going as planned, and though the place was still clearly a construction site whenever she popped in, the contractors, a middle-aged couple called June and Steve who were old friends of Marjie's, assured her that all would be ready in a few weeks.

Fortunately, everything seemed to be going as planned, surprisingly well in fact. Rosemary's magic was behaving itself, and she'd even extended it towards new achievements.

Liam had reported that the potions she'd made him before the full moon had significantly reduced his wolfish tendencies. He'd still gotten very hairy but stayed relatively subdued and hadn't broken out of his shackles for a change, hadn't even tried to. He'd been rather tired for a few days, and when Rosemary had checked in on him he'd been sleeping peacefully in his cage like a great big wolfy dog.

Rosemary prepared a slightly stronger potion for next time, hoping it would work even better. She really did wish that Liam could lead a normal life. He seemed rather broody sometimes. And though he'd asked her out at one point, he'd admitted, later on, that he'd lost his nerve around trying to date.

"Can you imagine?" he'd said. "The relationship would never be able to progress beyond casual dating. I can't very well disappear once a month for three days, and where would I go if we lived together? What if she came to the shop looking for me and discovered what I am?"

He remained absolutely petrified of anyone else finding out about his wolfy tendencies. The prejudices ran deep in the magical community, for some things more than others.

Fortunately, the hiding magic put in place by Tamsyn seemed to be working well. And Rosemary and Athena had been on the receiving end of no more attacks or kidnapping attempts by big, hairy, robed people.

On the evening before Rosemary was to leave for London, Neve, Marjie, and Dain all called in casually for farewells.

Marjie had brought Rosemary a care package with various cakes.

"Thank you. This is lovely," Rosemary said, inviting them all in for tea.

She hadn't seen Nesta for a while and asked how she was doing.

"Everything's fine at home," said Neve. "Fortunately, the pregnancy looks like it's progressing totally normally despite its unusual conception."

"Well, that's wonderful news!" said Marjie.

"So why are you looking so anxious then?" Dain asked.

"That's more on the work front," said Neve.

"I thought so," Dain said with a knowing look.

"What's happened?" Rosemary asked.

"They've found the body of one of the men who disappeared."

There was a moment of silence in which everyone took stock. Athena chose that moment to walk in and loudly greet the visitors, before noticing their grave faces.

"What happened?" she asked.

Neve explained and added that he was believed to be non-magical and in the area on holiday.

"Non-magical?" Athena asked.

"Yes, although his great-aunt was a witch."

"Well, I suppose the men both walked into the sea..." said Rosemary. "I mean, it's awful, but it's not entirely unexpected to find a body. Is it?"

"That's the weird thing," said Dain.

Neve frowned. "I'm not sure we should reveal the details."

"You knew about this?" Rosemary stared at Dain.

"Err...I told you I got a job. Didn't I?" Dain said.

"You didn't tell us what it was though, Dad."

"You're talking to Myrtlewood's new apprentice undertaker!" Dain announced.

Rosemary and Athena both looked at him, gobsmacked.

"I would have thought you'd be more excited," Dain mumbled. "Given how much time you spend with dead people."

Athena laughed. "I think it's kind of cool, Dad."

Neve looked unimpressed.

Rosemary cleared her throat.

"Jokes!" said Dain. "I just wanted to see your reaction. No, my real job is as a consultant."

Rosemary was even more baffled. "A consultant? On what? How to avoid dairy products?"

"Of course not," said Dain. "I'm a consultant on all things fae. I figured I might as well exploit my childhood. Isn't that what they tell you to do in therapy?"

"No, Dad," said Athena. "I think you've missed the point of therapy, entirely. Though your new job sounds cool."

"I think that's a perfect fit," said Marjie warmly. "Besides, it seems to lead to you wearing very snappy suits!"

Rosemary was speechless, trying to process all this.

Neve shook her head. "Anyway, if you're done with the pranks...yes, Dain is a consultant and he's been helpful in identifying fae influence in one or two cases. I figured with this one the memory effects could be fae, so I brought him in, but we shouldn't talk about the details because it's still under investigation."

"Well, as a detective, you might have some scruples," said Dain. "But as a consultant, I have none."

Neve sighed. "Go ahead, then. I'll pretend I wasn't listening. It's probably good for Rosemary to know anyway, given how helpful she's been in the past."

"What is it you want to tell us?" Rosemary asked Dain.

"The corpse didn't look like it had been in the sea for very long at all."

"That is odd," said Rosemary. "It was preserved somehow, after drowning?"

Dain shook his head. "We did wonder about that at first, but usually fish would eat the flesh."

"What would be putting the fish off?" Marjie asked, grimacing.

Dain shrugged. "The even weirder thing is that there was no water in his lungs either in the autopsy." He looked inexplicably excited about it.

"That's right," said Neve uncomfortably. "That's what the report showed. It seems like he hadn't died at sea at all. Dain doesn't think it was the fae."

"But you paid me, anyway!" Dain beamed.

"It could be some sort of setup," said Rosemary. "They were seen wandering into the sea, then they could take them somewhere else and kill him there. What was the motive?"

"Nobody knows," said Neve. "We've interviewed his family and close friends. He was well liked and stable."

"I bet there is a connection to that woman we found," Rosemary pondered aloud.

"In a town like Myrtlewood things are bound to be connected," said Neve.

"Did you ever find out where she was from? Or who she was?" Rosemary asked.

"Yes," said Neve. "She's been identified as Madeline Pierce, a sculptor from St Austell."

"What was she doing all the way out here then?" Rosemary asked.

"That's where our information stops. Apparently she just went missing one day. Doesn't remember anything of what happened."

"It's possible something similar happened to those men," Margie suggested.

"You mean, Madeline went for a little trip by herself to the beach, wandered off into the sea, was abducted and then returned?" Rosemary asked.

"Maybe," said Neve with a shrug. "We don't have much to go on, unfortunately."

"I take it Tamsyn's magic is no help with this one?" Athena asked.

"Right, we've tried," said Neve. "Her magic just keeps puffing up in a big cloud of dust – not going anywhere."

"That's unfortunate," said Rosemary. "I bet this is only going to get worse as we get closer to the solstice."

"Well, it sounds like there have been no disappearances for the last two weeks," said Dain. "I take that as a good sign."

"I like your confidence," said Neve. "Let's hope you're right."

THE NEXT FEW weeks passed in a blur. Rosemary went off to London and stayed in a hotel near the cheffing school where her chocolatier course was based. It was quite a treat to stay in a nice hotel. She hadn't really done that before. And it was nice to have time alone.

She did miss Athena dreadfully, though Athena didn't seem to return the favour, in particular as she was enjoying Marjie's company and was wrapped up with preparation for her exams and getting ready for the ball.

While Rosemary's accommodations were satisfactory, the coursework was gruelling. She liked the physical space of the cheffing school with its stainless steel kitchens and the near-constant smell of cocoa and vanilla. However, she struggled to follow instructions at every step, getting her in trouble almost every day with the tutors.

She often wondered in the middle of a class whether she could just take off back to Myrtlewood and forget about this whole sorry aspiration of hers, but she'd already invested so much.

The other students were all much younger, aside from an older Indian man called Papa Jack who was her only friend in the class and her only ally.

The other students were competitive. They'd found out on the first day when Rosemary had introduced herself that she'd never fully finished her chef training in the first place and they looked down on her.

Rosemary felt like it was high school all over again.

In Myrtlewood she'd been able to use magic when preparing chocolates, which allowed her to cut corners on the boring bits. But that wouldn't have worked out too well for her during the course. It would have been cheating and also raise suspicions when she was already not well-liked.

Still, every morning when she arrived, Papa Jack greeted her with a warm smile and they often took turns making hot chocolates to share during the breaks. He told her stories about raising his grandchild and he also told her all about his life. It was an interesting story of growing up in India and moving to the United Kingdom, and his various chocolate adventures along the way, which had started with importing American candy bars in New Delhi. Something that he considered to be quite hilarious now.

Rosemary shared a little of her life as well, though none of the magical details. She knew better than to let anything slip that would make people think she was totally insane.

In the evenings by herself, she spent a lot of time reading and occasionally watching TV shows — all the things she hadn't had a lot of time for recently.

Rosemary also practised imbuing truffles with magic. She'd take home a sampling of things that she'd made during the lessons, hold each one with its flavour in mind, and think about what kind of feeling would suit. Sometimes the feelings were more like images that she held in her mind, like the mango and lime leaf bonbon which reminded her of relaxing and watching a sunset in the summer on a beach, or the cracked pepper and strawberry chocolate truffle that reminded her of fireworks and Guy Fawkes night as a child and staying up late with the air of anticipation and excitement.

She was often her own guinea pig for these. She also sent little packages of them to her friends back in Myrtlewood with feedback sheets that she'd made and had printed at the photocopy shop down the street. They had tick boxes and questions so that Rosemary could see whether the truffles really did what they were intended to do, and whether they had any unintended side effects.

She was starting to feel quite confident, in her magic truffles, at least, if not in her actual coursework. She did excel at the exercises that encouraged creativity, but this seemed to earn her even more scorn from her young classmates. Whenever she did well Papa Jack gave her a standing ovation, so she felt it was only kind to return the favour for him when he did well. His reaction to her applause included bowing with elaborate gestures, making Rosemary laugh and the other students scowl.

Every evening when she lay in bed, Rosemary tried to piece together the mystery of what was happening in Myrtlewood.

According to Neve not much else had happened recently, but Rosemary could feel trouble brewing. Was it all connected to some bigger picture?

She felt there was certainly something she was missing.

"If only it was all simple," she muttered to herself. "If only I could solve the riddle of it all."

CHAPTER

TWENTY

"How are you going, love?" Rosemary asked Athena. She'd made it a habit of calling every night just to check in.

"Okay, I guess."

Usually, Athena brushed her off quickly and went back to whatever it was she was busy doing with Marjie. But today, her voice sounded heavy and Rosemary knew something was going on.

Athena began ranting about Neptune and Venus and Rosemary had to gently tell her to slow down.

"You're not taking me seriously," Athena protested.

Rosemary sighed. "Just remember you have an obsessive tendency – like when you insisted on keeping pet rocks as a kid and would scream at me if I so much as nudged one out of place."

"I was seven!"

"Yes, but you managed to cover the entire flat in your collection and had a major melt-down when we had to move. Not to mention the various other fixations you had with volcanoes, dinosaurs, and plankton."

"Most kids have special interests."

"Most kids don't forget to sleep or eat while obsessing over said interests."

Athena groaned. "You're probably right. But I'm not happy about it."

"What's really going on with you?" Rosemary asked.

"It's nothing. I'm just stressed about the exams."

"It's funny we're both going to be having exams at the same time," said Rosemary, trying to lighten the mood. "Has Marjie been helping you study?"

"Marjie has been great," said Athena. "I just can't seem to focus properly. Some things come to me totally easily, and other things are just ridiculous. The other kids grew up in this magical world and so they've got way more of an idea of what everything means, whereas a lot of the time to me it's gibberish. I feel like a toddler, trying to understand the alphabet for the first time."

"It will be okay," Rosemary said. "I'm sure your teachers will understand that you're relatively new to this and give you a break."

"I hope you're right," Athena said. "Because I don't want to be stuck repeating a year. I would be in a different class from all my friends. Plus, Beryl would skite about it endlessly. Do you know she's going to the ball with Finnigan?"

"What!?" said Rosemary. "I'm sorry, love."

"I don't care," said Athena, though she sounded as if she was reasonably resentful about it. "It's not like I want to go with him – or *her* for that matter! They deserve each other as far as I'm concerned."

"That doesn't make it any easier though, does it?" said Rosemary.

"No, unfortunately it doesn't," Athena admitted. "I don't like him anymore, but I'm still really angry."

"It takes a while to process things," said Rosemary. "I mean even normal teenage problems are hard. But what you've been through is a lot worse."

"I even tried to warn Beryl about him," Athena said. "I tried to tell her how rotten he was. She made it sound like I was jealous — which I am certainly not! I just don't trust him. Not that I trust her either."

"I wish there was something I could do to help," said Rosemary.

"Know of any charms that help people pass exams?" Athena asked. "Or maybe some kind of local gang that could kidnap Finnigan and make him disappear entirely from our lives?"

Rosemary's mind flashed to Burk's offer. She decided against saying anything, just in case Athena got the wrong idea. After all, Finnigan was just another teenager, even if he was a problem child – a fae problem child from a different time.

"I wish I could come back and be there for you," Rosemary said. "Maybe I could skip a few days of class. Things are pretty miserable here as well."

"Why, what's wrong?" Athena asked.

Rosemary had held back on most of the details of her struggles with her course, only occasionally grumbling to Athena. She sighed. "Almost everyone in my class is still being kind of mean to me and I've noticed things have gone missing. I don't know if they're playing jokes on me by stealing my bain-marie or whether it's something more malicious or even an accident. There's only one person I trust in the entire class."

"That Popa John man?" Athena asked.

"Papa Jack, yes," said Rosemary. "He's very nice. I think I'm going to miss him when the course is done. He's been a good friend."

"You're not thinking of replacing Burk with him."

Rosemary laughed. "No, I don't think so. Papa Jack's a grandfather. In fact, he's raising his granddaughter."

"That's right," said Athena. "I forgot. Though I thought you were into old dudes."

"And don't go telling me that Burk is a lot older than that, because I'm still processing the fact that I'm dating a thousand year old, or something."

Athena laughed. "All right, Mum. I'd better get going. I'm going to try and cram in a few more hours of study in tonight."

"Good girl," said Rosemary. "But don't forget to rest and look after yourself."

"You sound like Marjie, Mum."

"I'll take that as a compliment," said Rosemary. "Good night."

"Bye, Mum."

Rosemary lay back on her hotel bed, feeling exhausted. As much as she was trying not to think about her upcoming exams, she couldn't help it. She was dreading the week ahead.

CHAPTER
TWENTY-ONE

Athena watched herself in the mirror as she slowly transformed into a princess. She'd checked her ephemeris to find a nice alignment between Jupiter and the moon in Libra - perfect for a beautiful summer ball.

Ashwyn, who was an expert with skincare, makeup, and apparently hair, had offered to come over and help out with the preparations for the ball. She expertly applied Athena's makeup, and was just in the final stages of putting her hair up into a loose woven arrangement that somehow reminded Athena of the fae realm, but in a good way.

Athena handed Ashwyn the little buttercup pins she had chosen that looked almost like the real thing from a distance. She smiled as Ashwyn put the finishing touches on her hair.

"You're a magician," Athena said. She smiled at herself in the mirror. "I've never looked so good in my life."

Ashwyn grinned back at Athena in the mirror. "You always look good. This is just the more spruced up version of your beautiful self."

"I certainly don't look as good on a regular school day."

"I'm sure all of your friends will notice," said Ashwyn. "Especially Elise." She gave Athena a little wink.

"Don't tease," Athena warned her. "I'm a witch-fae and I'm dangerous."

"So is my sister. Don't forget that." She smiled. "Do you need help getting into your dress?"

"No, I think I'll be alright," said Athena.

"Okay then, I'm going to go next door and help your friends."

All of Athena's friends had decided to come over to Thorn Manor to get ready for the ball. Marjie had set up some snacks and punch downstairs. Felix had of course spiked it with a hipflask of brandy when Marjie wasn't looking. No, Athena was sure Marjie was wise enough to have cottoned on to their plan to get very mildly tipsy before the ball.

They'd all gone upstairs to get dressed. Athena could feel a very slight effect from the brandy, although she'd barely had enough to notice.

She got changed out of her jeans and hoodie into the silk stockings and the pale lacy slip that Marjie had made to fit under the yellow silky fabric of her dress. It took her a while to get into the dress itself and she momentarily wished that she hadn't let Ashwyn go so soon, but with enough wriggling and reaching she managed to zip herself up.

She stood for a moment in front of the mirror, admiring herself for a change.

A slightly wistful feeling passed over her and for a moment she wished Rosemary could be there to see her. She knew her mother had more important things to focus on. She was neck deep in preparations for her own exams.

"You look lovely dear," said a familiar voice from the mirror.

Athena jumped in surprise as Granny Thorn swam into view in front of her. "I thought you were away on business."

Granny Thorn heaved a heavy sigh. "I have been busy. Not to worry. But I also know I need to leave my girls to get on with their own lives and deal with their own catastrophes. I can't be hanging around all the time when my life on this plane is over."

Athena smiled. "Granny. You came to see me off before the ball?"

"I couldn't miss it. Seeing my stunning great-grandchild all dressed up like this! Rosemary was never into that kind of thing, you know, and neither was her father. Puritan! I always loved dances and putting on my glad rags."

"And your blue lace-up shoes," said Athena, remembering the cryptic clue Granny had given them not long after they'd first arrived back in Myrtlewood.

"That's right," said Granny with a wink. "You're clever...and you're powerful. More powerful than even you know. You don't need me hanging around like a bad smell. You've got to forge your own destiny. Your mother needs to work that out sooner or later, too."

"She's working on it, I think," said Athena.

"I'm glad to hear it. Oh, look at you! I wish I could give you a hug and a kiss. Blast this incorporeal form. I'll just have to blow one through the mirror." She kissed her hand and blew a kiss towards Athena, who mimed catching it and holding it close. She'd never really known Granny Thorn in life, but she did feel close to the old woman, even in her ghost form. Athena liked her no nonsense approach to things and she could tell that Granny Thorn loved her and her mother unconditionally. At least she trusted them to get on with their lives, which was definitely something Rosemary was still working on.

"Thank you, Granny," said Athena. "I'll tell Mum you stopped in."

"As long as it doesn't distract her," said Granny. "I know Rosemary and I have had a few troubles. And I'm sorry for it. I can't be there for every moment of your lives as much as I might want to. I love you both dearly."

"We know that," said Athena with a smile, and with a quick "goodbye" Granny Thorn disappeared back into the mirror, leaving her looking at her own reflection again.

She heard the doorbell and wondered who it could possibly be. Felix, Deron, Sam, Ash, and Elise were upstairs getting ready. Athena wasn't expecting anybody else. Since Marjie and Ashwyn were both busy helping her friends get ready, and Athena didn't have anything else to do, she figured she might as well slip downstairs to see who it was. After all, she was a powerful fae-witch who could defend herself.

She couldn't see anyone through the side windows, but when she opened the door, there was a familiar and unwanted face in front of her.

"Finnigan," she said.

He stood a head taller than her, dark hair falling over his face. He was wearing what looked to be a tailored and expensive suit. Athena assumed Beryl had something to do with that.

"What are you doing here?" she asked.

"I had to see you," said Finnigan.

"I thought I'd made it clear—"

"Clear how?"

"Err. You're going to the ball with Beryl. And considering everything else, I'd prefer not to see you at all, ever!"

She tried to close the door, but his hand got in the way. As much as Athena wanted to slam his fingers, she held herself back.

"You've got ten seconds. Otherwise I'm going to close the door whether you lose your fingers or not."

Finnigan gulped. "I just wanted to apologise."

There was sadness in his eyes, but Athena wasn't falling for it.

"This isn't the time."

"And it probably never will be." Finnigan continued her trail of thought.

"So what?" Athena asked. "You made your choice. You betrayed me. It's as simple as that."

"It wasn't within my control."

"Too bad."

"Athena...How can I make it up to you?" he asked in a pleading voice. "I'll do anything."

"There's nothing you can do or say." She pulled the door closed sharply, unsure whether she was relieved or disappointed when Finnigan flinched his hand away just in time to not be caught.

She was still roaring with anger, even if part of her felt sorry for him. But all that was forgotten as she turned back towards the stairwell just in time to see a glorious princess in a frosty blue ball gown, drifting down the stairs towards her.

Elise's hair, though relatively short, had been pinned up in a way that made it look like a similar style to Athena's.

Elise smiled. Her normal blue hair faded to a pale pink, and she blushed.

"You look gorgeous!" said Athena.

"I was about to say the same thing to you," Elise replied. "But I thought it was a bit cliché."

"We're allowed to be clichéd," said Athena. "That's what balls are all about."

Elise giggled and held her hand out for Athena to take. Their fingers interlaced.

Athena leaned in close to Elise, inhaling the fresh spring scent of her, feeling the softness of her skin as Elise pulled her into a gentle hug. Athena leaned back, and they met in a soft kiss. It was a moment that Athena wanted to savour for much longer.

However, it was rudely interrupted by Felix barrelling down the stairs.

"Time to go! Time to go!" he crowed, then gasped. "You two!"

"Mind your own business," said Athena.

Felix shrugged with a smirk on his face. "Can't blame a guy for being curious."

Elise narrowed her eyes at him and he held up his hands in a submissive gesture.

"Sorry, sorry. I promise not to fetishize your relationship and to respect you as my friends."

"That's better," said Athena.

"Felix?"

"There's my gorgeous date!" Felix said, turning towards the stairwell.

Athena looked up to see Ashwagandha walking towards them in a plum coloured silky gown that clung to her body elegantly.

"You look beautiful!" said Athena.

"So do both of you," said Ash, beaming.

"What about me?" Felix asked. "Why do the guys always get left out?"

"You look very pretty," said Elise.

Felix batted his eyelashes.

"You look dashing in your suit," said Ash in a slightly patronising voice. Felix was mollified.

"See, I'm dashing," he said.

It was true. He looked very nice in a suit, Athena thought. His jacket had maroon paisley lining. It looked second-hand and very slightly too big for him, but he did clean up pretty well.

Deron, on the other hand, came downstairs wearing a navy

suit that was at least one size too small. "This is so uncomfortable." His voice was strained from the pressure of his outfit.

"Let me fix that, dear," said Marjie, bustling downstairs towards them. With a wave of her hand, Deron's suit expanded slightly to fit his body.

"You're a miracle worker!" Deron cried, kissing Marjie on the cheek.

Marjie gave a wink and then waved her hand at Felix, whose suit shrunk, just slightly, to look as if it had been tailored to his body shape.

"Oooh, suave!" he cried, and then started dashing around, howling like a wolf, even though he was really more of a fox.

"Settle down," said Sam as they walked shyly downstairs wearing a conservative but androgynous looking suit. "I don't feel flashy like the rest of you."

"You look great," said Athena.

"A few sparkles, dear?" said Marjie.

"Oh, go on," Sam said with a grin.

Marjie rubbed her hands together, and then splayed them out in the air in front of Sam. Waves of holographic glitter sped through the air onto Sam suit's. A satin collar appeared around their neck, to match.

"That was a little bit excessive," Sam said with a giggle.

"Is it too much? I'm sorry," said Marjie.

"No, it's perfect. Now I'm ready to be a fancy ball attendee like the rest of you."

"That looks so cool!" said Athena as they all wandered towards the door. "Err..." she continued, looking at Fleur's mint green Mini. "How are we all going to fit?"

She'd assumed Fleur would have thought to borrow a bigger car for the occasion. She looked around awkwardly at her friend's amused expressions. "What? I suppose we could go in two separate cars..."

"Don't be silly!" said Elise, pulling Athena towards the Mini. "There's plenty of room."

She opened the door to reveal an interior the size of a large limousine.

"Mum has it on the biggest setting."

Athena laughed and climbed into the magically-enhanced Mini.

The other teens clambered into the back and Marjie and Fleur got into the front. They waved goodbye to Una, who had come out to see them off.

"Take care," she called. "Be safe and have fun!"

"Those things are not all compatible!" Felix yelled out the open window. Una laughed as they began to speed away towards Glastonbury and the Summer Ball.

THE GLASTONBURY HALL looked like a relatively modest old stone building on the outside, but as they entered, it was enormous. Athena was sure magic was involved, just as it must have been for the thousands of fairy lights hanging from the ceiling, which, on closer inspection were fireflies, that occasionally swooped around the room. The walls were draped in emerald velvet, and swirls of colourful smoke drifted through the air that could not have been produced by any ordinary smoke machine, especially as each colour smelled like a different kind of fruit.

Athena gasped as she took it all in.

"Gorgeous!" said Elise, squeezing Athena's arm.

The grand space was full of people, most of them teenagers, dressed rather eclectically for a ball. Some were in costumes, or had fancy masks, though Athena couldn't entirely tell costumes from real magical creatures, especially in the low light.

The band up on stage were dressed in old suits with ruffled collars, reminding Athena of vampires, though she wasn't close enough to them to tell if they had that underworld gleam to their skin that she'd become accustomed to recognizing since moving to Myrtlewood. They played a slow, almost dreary, gothic tune, led by the cello. It seemed an odd musical choice for a ball, but Athena quite liked it nonetheless, at least until she glimpsed Finnigan and Beryl slow dancing to the morbid tones, up front.

She wasn't sure what it was about the sight of them that affected her. Certainly, she didn't want to be the one to dance with that awful boy, and she couldn't stand Beryl, but seeing them together was a duplication of awful things and bad memories.

Athena's friends gathered around in a circle, taking everything in and chatting. Athena tried to push her enemies from her mind and enjoy the evening, but as she glanced around she caught sight of a woman with light blonde hair, wearing a glimmering teal masquerade outfit.

"Lamorna," Athena whispered.

Elise turned in that direction, but the woman had already disappeared into the crowd.

"Are you sure?" Elise asked.

Athena shook her head. "It could have been anyone, I guess."

"Stop being boring!" Felix yelled. "Let's dance!"

As if in answer to his call, the music changed to a peppy number and the friends all began jumping around. Athena stayed vigilant, continuing to check the crowd in case her suspicions were correct, but she didn't see anyone resembling Lamorna.

It was so much fun, just to be out, dancing with friends. She pushed her worries away and relaxed.

The music changed again, to a slow, romantic tune.

Elise pulled Athena into a slow dance.

She felt butterflies in her stomach as she leaned into Elise's embrace.

"I have a question," said Athena.

"Is it whether I can see Lamorna?"

"No!" Athena laughed. She'd almost forgotten about her possibly paranoid thoughts. "I'm not thinking about Lamorna at all."

She looked into Elise's eyes and tried to find the right words, but before she could ask, Elise spoke first. "Will you be my girlfriend...officially?"

"Hey," said Athena with a mock frown. "That was *my* question!"

"We can share," said Elise, beaming.

"Then yes," said Athena, pulling Elise into a kiss.

"Gross! You two!" cried Felix. "Break it up! Kissing is for dweebs!"

CHAPTER
TWENTY-TWO

Rosemary was exhausted after a whole day of classes and prepping for the final exams. At five-thirty, she finally had said goodbye to Papa Jack and then headed towards her hotel room to collapse.

As she lay there, glaring at the pure white of the ceiling, she realised her heart was beating abnormally fast. At first, she wondered whether she was having some kind of health episode, but everything other than her rapid pulse rate seemed to be fairly normal. So instead of calling a doctor, she followed the advice that a wise elder had once given her — look within.

Laughter.

Athena.

She could see her daughter glammed up to the nines in her bright golden ball gown.

A tense feeling broke through — the risk of danger.

Rosemary opened her eyes.

Of course! It's the night of the ball. How could I forget something like that?

She'd previously wondered whether she'd be able to sneak away and surprise Athena, or perhaps even just stand somewhere in the background to watch, hiding from the teens, making sure everything went well without embarrassing her daughter. When she'd gotten to London and become immersed in her course, she'd thought less and less about the ball. Now she knew something was not right.

Her intuition was telling her she had to go. She didn't much like the thought of driving in rush-hour traffic. At this time of day she reasoned she'd be better off catching the train. She ran down to the nearby station and boarded the next train to Glastonbury.

Rosemary nodded off on the train, but she'd had the fore-thought to set an alarm. So it was just before the time when the train was due to arrive in Glastonbury village that she was startled awake by her phone vibrating and chiming out an annoying song that Athena liked to set as her ringtone sometimes.

Rosemary had chosen it deliberately as an alarm as it was such an obnoxious sound she was sure it would wake her up. And she was right.

Rosemary got off the train in Glastonbury, feeling a little bleary-eyed and worse-for-wear. As she walked across the platform at the station she realised she was still wearing a chocolate-stained black long-sleeve t-shirt and jeans under her summer coat. She did her best to comb out her hair with her fingers so that it didn't look too matted if Athena spotted her.

As she made her way to Glastonbury Hall, Rosemary tried to reassure her beating heart that everything would be fine and that her fears were probably just her mind playing tricks on her.

Rosemary crept around to the side of the grand old building and peeped through a window. The room was crowded with teens all dressed in charming and exquisite evening wear, smiling, looking nervous, and laughing.

Rosemary sighed with relief as she caught sight of her daughter, dancing with a group of friends to the music played by a band on the stage, dressed as if they were old-fashioned vampires, and perhaps they were, though the only old-fashioned vampire Rosemary knew wouldn't be caught dead in a ruffled collar.

It did look like a lot of fun and Rosemary wondered if she'd come all this way for nothing now that she could see Athena was clearly not in danger. But she kept watch, just in case, as the teens pranced around the room.

She saw Marjie and Elise's mum, Fleur, standing on the opposite side of the hall from the group of teens, keeping a safe distance, no doubt.

Athena was practically glowing.

Rosemary was glad she'd made it, even just to see her daughter all dressed up in her sunshine yellow ball gown. She had a momentary pang of regret that she hadn't helped her get ready. Just because balls weren't something Rosemary had ever particularly been interested in, it didn't mean that she should miss her daughter's special evening.

She had been so wrapped up in her course and determinedly trying not to fail that she'd somehow missed an important milestone.

Just then, movement caught her eye.

She looked to the back of the hall to see a familiar big bearded man in a robe.

It's him!

Of course this ball was put on by the druids, but she wasn't expecting it to be the rogue ones who'd attempted to kidnap them. Neve had assured them the Glastonbury druids were trustworthy, but clearly she'd missed something – either that or this man was an impostor.

She scanned the room, taking in the various teens and parents as she searched for the man. He was nowhere in sight. Rosemary hung back, hoping Athena didn't see her there, looking rough and uninvited.

The song changed to a faster dancing beat and the teens began jumping around.

Rosemary caught a glimpse of the tan robe and red bushy beard as the tall man moved through the crowd, closer to the window where she was standing. And sure enough, the embroidery on the rest of his robe was of holly leaves and berries – it was the same guy who'd tried to abduct them not so long ago.

They're definitely here. And Athena is definitely in danger.

CHAPTER
TWENTY-THREE

Heart racing in her chest, Rosemary ran around to the back entrance of the hall, politely but firmly pushing her way through the collection of fancily and slightly oddly-dressed people who stood around the entrance.

She managed to get inside and found herself in a hallway. It was fairly plain looking in neutral shades. She navigated her way towards the sound of the music, quickly reaching the main hall.

Rosemary tried to stay at the back so that Athena didn't catch her in this state because she did still want to avoid alarming or embarrassing her teen as much as possible.

She scoured the crowd, looking for the rogue druid. Unfortunately, there were so many people in robes, that it was hard to find who she was looking for, tall and bearded though he might be.

Dancers and merrymakers interrupted her view until she finally caught a glimpse of him, just as he turned and laid eyes on her, clearly recognising her as well.

You! she mouthed across the room.

The man's eyes bulged in shock and then he darted back towards the hallway that Rosemary had come through. She followed after him but not before hearing a familiar voice calling "Mum!" behind her.

Athena had seen her, which not only was going to be dreadfully embarrassing for the teen in a way that Rosemary would never stop hearing about, it was also likely to lead her daughter into danger.

Rosemary ran away in the hopes that Athena would ignore her or lose sight of her and she could pretend it was a look-alike.

She followed the man down the passageway into a room near the back that turned out to be a large kitchen and dining area.

Rosemary gulped. The room was populated with a lot of similarly-robed druids. They all turned to stare. Her mouth suddenly felt exceedingly dry. She cleared her throat and coughed a little. "Excuse me."

They looked at her with what seemed to be more puzzlement than anything vicious. Rosemary felt a wave of relief that she wasn't about to be attacked.

"What's going on?" asked a voice from the back.

Rosemary kept her eyes locked on the tall bearded redhead she'd followed.

"You!" she said, pointing at him. "You tried to abduct me. And my daughter as well. What do you have to say for yourself?"

"Uhh...Well," the man stuttered, then began muttering incoherently.

"Told you it was a daft idea," said a dark-haired woman to the left of the room that Rosemary recognised as one of the other people accompanying the redheaded man at the spa.

"What do you mean?" Rosemary asked.

"Mayon over here had the bright idea that to protect the Thorn witches we should take them into our care."

"You're joking!" called somebody else from across the room.

"No, not a joke. Serious, I'm afraid."

"You can't prove it!" said Mayon.

The dark-haired woman laughed.

"Catriona, stop that." Mayon glared at her.

"Mayon, I was there. I don't need to prove it. Admit it was a stupid idea."

Rosemary stood, her mouth hanging wide open. "You were trying to protect us?! And you didn't think of calling first? Maybe sending us a letter? An invitation?"

Mayon looked sheepish. "I...I didn't."

"She's right," said a man with dark long hair. "I was there too. It was a daft idea. If we'd known that was his plan we wouldn't have gone along with him."

"And then you just disappeared," said Rosemary, waving her hands wildly in the air.

"Mum, what's going on?" Athena's voice said from behind Rosemary.

She looked back to see her daughter and a collection of her school friends.

"I'm just clearing a few things up with the druids. Apparently this one over here, got it into his head that in order to protect us, he should chase us down."

"Oh, so that explains it!" said Elise next to Athena. She pointed to Mayon. "I'm sure I saw him slinking around town, looking shady."

"You've been bloody stalking us!" Rosemary thundered, anger boiling in her veins as her fear had well and truly subsided.

The druids all seemed to be peaceful, if slightly puzzled by the situation.

"I told you the Holly Grove was no good," said a man with oak-embroidered robes.

"I'll shut it, Malloy, seriously!"

Malloy laughed. "You can't really even have a proper grove of holly can you? It's a little bush. Oak on the other hand..."

"This is not a competition of greenery!" said Catriona. "I'm sorry, Rosemary and Athena Thorn. It wasn't the right thing to do and we should have cleared things up afterwards. Only, to be quite frank, I was too embarrassed."

Rosemary didn't feel any particular ire against the woman but was still trapped in a stubbornly determined rage at Mayon. "Where do I file a complaint?" she asked.

"Complaint?" said Athena. "You look like you're about to burn down the whole building. Look at your fingers!"

Rosemary looked down to see sparks flying from the tops of her hands. She cupped them together, so as to avoid an accident.

"Mayon will be punished. Won't he?" Athena asked, wringing her hands together nervously.

The druids all looked around at each other. There was a rumbling to the side of the room. The back wall — all of a sudden — looked like it was made of liquid.

Rosemary watched, her rage momentarily forgotten, as a forest landscape appeared, looking suspiciously three dimensional, where previously there had been just beige wallpaper.

The druids all turned in unison towards the foresty wall, though they didn't look surprised, just interested.

There was a glimmer of movement. A woman stepped through the trees towards them, stopping at the threshold of the room.

"Oh...oh no!" said Mayon, his voice almost a whimper. "Not the Elder Priestess."

Rosemary eyed the woman in the forest wall who actually looked rather young. "She doesn't look like an elder," she muttered to Athena.

"I think they mean the tree," Athena whispered back.

"The tree?"

"The elder tree...you know, because they're all kind of tree-themed around here, holly and oak and all that."

"Of course," said Rosemary, rolling her eyes. "So obvious..."

"Mayon," said the Elder Priestess, her voice both soft and deep. And Rosemary realised that she wasn't young, at all. Nor did she show any signs of age. Her clothing looked so forest-like that she could have easily blended into the trees, clad as she was in different fabrics and furs, greens and browns woven beautifully, delicately into some kind of flowing dress and cloak. However, as delicate as she seemed, she clearly held sway over all the druids here, regardless of the particular Grove.

"Mayon, you've been acting out of turn," said the Elder Priestess.

Mayon stuttered. "I'm s-s-s-sorry," he said eventually. And Rosemary could tell that an apology was uncommon, coming from him.

"You should have thought this through with an action so great. You should have examined the Triads and come to us, come to the Elders. Never mount such vigilante action without thinking. You've caused more harm than good."

Rosemary nodded in agreement.

"We are peaceful people," the Priestess continued, turning back to Rosemary. "Mayon acted on what he thought was the right thing to do. I sense no ill-will in his heart, although he was out of line and acted in the wrong."

"Dreadfully wrong," said Rosemary. "We thought we were being attacked by some sort of evil cult. It wouldn't be the first time."

The woman nodded slightly. "Indeed it was wrong. I offer you our profound apologies, Rosemary Thorn, for the stress and emotional harm caused to you by a member of one of our groves."

"That's all very well and good," said Rosemary. "Everyone's sorry…" She still felt a little frustration, though she found herself more and more soothed by the presence of the Elder Priestess.

"I also offer our protection where we can give it," the priestess continued.

"Thanks, I guess," said Rosemary. "Miss priestess…"

"You may call me Elspeth."

There was a hush around the room, as though the rest of those present weren't on a first-name basis with the priestess.

"Thank you," said Rosemary. "Err…"

Elspeth smiled. "It is indeed a blessing to meet a hereditary witch as powerful as yourself and also kin to the druids."

"Kin?" Athena asked. "What's she talking about?"

Rosemary shook her head. "I don't know."

"Your ancestor, Elzarie Thorn, was druid-born."

Rosemary clutched at her emerald necklace.

Elspeth nodded. "Yes, that was her necklace. You know of her?"

"Just the name, really," said Rosemary.

"Then I offer you this counsel, if you wish to take it. Learn about your history, Rosemary Thorn. For in our history, we find true strength and understanding. The power that runs through your veins can be better known through knowing as those who came before. Elzarie was a dear friend."

"You knew her?" Rosemary gaped in astonishment. This druid priestess was obviously several hundred years old at least.

Elspeth nodded. "Our druids can keep watch of your house. We know there are threats that lurk."

"The Bloodstones? That's what caused all of your concerns? That's why that bloody oaf came to try to abduct us for our protection?" Rosemary asked.

Mayon frowned.

There was a general murmur of agreement from around the room.

"They are problematic," said Catriona.

"You're telling me!" said Rosemary. "Do you think they have anything to do with the disappearances? You know people have gone missing – their memories being wiped?"

"We know of no connection," said Elspeth. "But with your permission, we can watch over you. We'll keep ourselves at a distance. We'll be invisible, largely."

She glared at Mayon and he nodded rigorously.

"You'll have no trouble from us," Elspeth continued. "As much as it is in my power to guarantee."

"Thank you. I guess," said Rosemary. "Just keep Mayon away from us and...also be aware that we like our privacy."

Athena shot her mother a look impressing that she'd prefer more privacy in her life in general. Rosemary grimaced, aware that Athena would have questions about why Rosemary had gate-crashed the ball.

"But why us?" said Athena. "Why did Mayon bother to try to...err...protect us?"

"You are more integral to the unfolding of fate than you know," said Elspeth. "The druids have felt the energy building for a while. There are disturbing currents in the air. Planetary alignments have been concerning us. Our Ovates have scried using a variety of methods and they've pointed us to the Thorn family. You must surely be pivotal in protecting the magical world from the threats that are soon to come. That is why I must offer our protection in the most discreet way possible."

Rosemary glared at Mayon.

Athena sighed. "This is one thread of destiny I'd rather not be entangled in."

"Come, Mayon," said Elspeth. The man groaned. He followed Elspeth out into the forest.

Several moments passed before the wall returned to normal as the forest sounds faded away.

"Well, that was interesting," said Athena.

"A little too interesting!"

CHAPTER
TWENTY-FOUR

I t was the morning of Rosemary's exams. She'd been nervous enough before she realised her bain-marie had gone missing again! The younger students must have stolen it again, though whether it was out of resentment or a simple prank, she wasn't sure.

Rosemary sighed as she paced back and forth in front of her kitchen work bench. She felt like a total impostor. An almost forty-year-old with no formal qualifications. The fact that she'd gotten into this relatively exclusive confectionary school had been a stroke of luck. *Or maybe a mistake.* She'd only been sent the invitation after some other student had pulled out at the last minute. They were bound to realise the error and throw her out at any minute. She couldn't risk raising her missing item and rousing suspicion that she might secretly be a total impostor, especially not just before the final exam. She was almost free.

I'm not giving up.

She really needed the certificate so that she could have some sort of claim to being a professional chocolatier with the business she was trying to start.

She felt her chest tighten as the other students lined up their benches with everything they needed to have in front of them.

She looked behind her to see Papa Jack at his station. He gave her an encouraging smile. She had the sudden urge to ask him for help, but it was too late. They were about to start, and she knew she would lose points if she was to ask the instructors for equipment at this stage. They were supposed to be responsible for their own preparations for the duration of the course.

She glared around at the other benches, wondering which of the mean-spirited students had taken her bain-marie to play a trick on her, or sabotage her.

They'd made it clear enough that they didn't think she should be there.

The clock started and Rosemary's chest felt more like a vice around her heart. She looked around the class. The students were all busy focusing on their own work. When she was sure none of the instructors were watching, she got out her chocolate stock, popped it into a bowl, and then held her hands on the sides, allowing it to warm just gently, doing the job of the equipment that she didn't have.

The chocolate melted perfectly. Relieved, she carried on with the exercise. Though unable to follow instructions to save herself, Rosemary tried her best. She couldn't help but add in a few tweaks to the recipe.

Just a smidge of chilli oil, and a sprinkle of cinnamon to bring up the passionfruit flavour in the elaborate truffles. There were three different layers of chocolate that they'd had to make. Each with a slightly different texture and flavour. The recipes were elaborate and Rosemary had struggled to read all the details, let along follow them, but she'd done her best. She only hoped it was enough.

When it came time for tasting, Rosemary brought hers up to the front of the class, just like the other students, thinking about how funny this whole situation was, how much it reminded her of cooking shows on the television.

The other truffles all looked identical, but there was something odd about Rosemary's. It seemed to sparkle, just a little.

The head chef went to hers first, his bushy white moustache twisting upwards in a sneer.

Rosemary gritted her teeth, wondering if she'd accidentally used magic in the truffle, not just to heat the chocolate. This could go terribly wrong.

"Ms Thorn," the head chef said, picking up Rosemary's truffle and examining it. "Something about this is different. You didn't follow my recipe exactly, did you?"

Rosemary bowed her head. "No, sorry. I had to make a few tweaks."

"You made a few tweaks to my award-winning recipe?"

"Err. Yes, sir," said Rosemary uncertainly.

"What did you do!" he demanded.

"I just added in a few little twists."

"Twists or tweaks?" he asked. "What were they? Tell me."

"A very tiny amount of chilli, and just a sprinkle of cinnamon," said Rosemary. "Just very, very, very small amounts."

"Enough!"

Rosemary held her breath. This was not going to be good. She'd been told off several times already for not following instructions. Although this was the first time that the head chef, himself, had actually tried any of her chocolates. Rosemary was hoping he'd understand that she'd made good choices. Although it could go either way.

He took the most dainty nibble at the side of the chocolate.

Rosemary waited, her breath still held, as time seemed to slow unbearably.

The head chef closed his eyes and scrunched up his face.

Oh no...it's all over. What a waste!

Rosemary stole herself for her ultimate disappointment and embarrassment.

She bowed her head but felt a hand tap her shoulder. She glanced across at Papa Jack, who nodded towards the head chef.

Rosemary looked back towards him as he put the whole truffle into his mouth and his eyes lit up with joy. "Oh my! You simply must tell me what you did. This is brilliant!"

Rosemary beamed as many of the students in the class glared at her.

"It was nothing, really," said Rosemary. "Just a couple of little things that I thought would bring out the flavour."

"Oh, this is genius! I had half a mind to dock your grade for not following instructions, but why would you, when you can create such a masterpiece with pure intuition? You've passed with flying colours!" he announced to the whole class, even before he'd finished any of the other grading.

Rosemary continued to beam as she left the room. She didn't care that most of the other students were scowling at her, having all received much more mediocre reactions from the head chef, if he deigned to try theirs at all. Many he just left up to the other instructors to grade, though Rosemary shared a satisfied smile with Papa Jack when he elicited a groan of delight from the head chef and another instant pass.

She didn't think twice about the haters. After all, she was never going to see any of these people again probably. What did she care if they detested her?

She went to her hotel room to rest and then returned to the school to pick up her things, thinking she'd better make sure she said goodbye to Papa Jack, only to find him standing right by her work table.

They were the only ones left in the room and he had an unusual look on his face.

"What is it?" Rosemary asked.

"So you are a witch, after all."

Rosemary froze.

Papa Jack had an unreadable expression. He raised a finger and Rosemary ducked, her heart racing. If he knew about witches, what did that mean about him?

"No, no. Don't worry." His voice was gentle and reassuring. "I did wonder. You have a magical air about you."

"Was it you who took my bain-marie?"

"Of course not, Rosemary. I'd never do a thing like that. It was probably one of the young kids here playing tricks."

His voice sounded genuine but Rosemary narrowed her eyes in suspicion.

"Who are you?" Multiple people were after her and Athena. As much as she hated to think it, the man who had been her only friend in London these past three weeks could well be a spy, planted here to attack her. But if so, wouldn't he have already known exactly who she was?

Papa Jack smiled. "I'm exactly as I've always said, although, like you, I've held a few things back. You could say, I once fancied myself a bit of a magic-user of one kind or another. My son was even better. Then they took him."

"Who took him?" Rosemary asked. "You told me he went missing."

"That's what I don't know. It was three years ago in the

summer. He went for a walk one day and went missing. His wife, too. I was sure it was magical, but of course the police thought that was nonsense. Police around here don't believe any of that kind of stuff."

Rosemary breathed a sigh of relief. Papa Jack spoke with such genuine sadness that she had to believe him. "You should come to Myrtlewood if you want magical authorities. Not that the police are unnecessarily much better, especially not Constable Perkins. Neve's good though. At least she tries."

"Myrtlewood. That's where you said you've lived," Papa Jack said.

"It's a magical village," said Rosemary.

"I thought so. I vaguely recall that my son used to talk about it. That was the first clue I had that you might be what you are."

His eyes were downcast and Rosemary's heart went out to him. She wanted to comfort him, but she didn't really know what to say. To lose a child...she'd lost Athena for weeks to the fae realm, but three years! It was unfathomable. And not knowing what had happened to him and his wife was surely even worse.

"You could come to visit Myrtlewood sometime," she offered.

"If I did that maybe I'd never want to leave," said Papa Jack, his eyes lighting up through the sadness. "A whole magical town!"

"Why not see how it goes?" said Rosemary. "I could hire you to work in my shop when I've actually set it up. Although I shouldn't be making any promises just yet. It might be a total disaster."

"You know," said Papa Jack, "if that offer's still standing, once you've set up, I might just take you up on it. I'm sure whatever disaster Rosemary Thorn creates will be a wonder to be part of."

Rosemary smiled at him. "Thank you for being such a good friend to me. And I trust that you won't say anything about what I am to anyone else."

"Of course not. I wouldn't dream of it. Especially not when you might be a prospective employer. Also, I'm sure you're a powerful witch and I don't want to make an enemy of you!" He grinned at her.

"I hope I see you again soon," she said, giving him a big hug.

"Count on it, boss lady."

CHAPTER
TWENTY-FIVE

"This is ridiculous," said Athena. "I thought you said you were going to borrow camping gear."

"I did," Rosemary replied.

"And I thought you said you'd pack the car."

Rosemary shrugged. "I did. Let's just hope that Marjie's magic teapot is all it's cracked up to be."

"You're serious," said Athena flatly. "Are you really implying we're going to stay *inside* a teapot?!"

"No. Don't be ridiculous."

"Then what?"

"Err...that's where the camping gear is?" Rosemary mumbled.

"Okay then," Athena said, clearly unconvinced. "Why does it feel like we're heading for a total disaster of a weekend?"

"I'm sure it'll be fine," said Rosemary. "Besides, now there's plenty more room for my chocolates."

Athena begrudgingly helped to load up the car with the various boxes of confectionery that Rosemary had spent the last week making since returning from her chocolate course.

They had a quick cup of tea and finished packing before driving the ten minutes to the location of the festival.

A man in long flowing pink robes met them at the gate.

"The gates don't open until tomorrow."

"We have a stall," Rosemary explained.

"Oh, yes," said the man. "Have you got your pass?"

Rosemary waved the glittering pass she'd picked up from Juniper at the town hall offices the day before.

It was a warm and humid summer day. They stepped out of the air conditioned vehicle at the site that the eccentric pink-robed gentleman had directed them to.

"Alright, here goes," said Rosemary. She held up the teapot, tapped the side, and said the little enchantment that Marjie had given her.

The teapot began to rumble loudly. Rosemary's hands trembled. She put the teapot down and pulled Athena several feet back.

They watched as the teapot began to rise into the air. Yellow light shot out of the spout straight upwards. The beam of light solidified into a big brass pole. Ropes flew out from it, before being shrouded in silky blue-and-white-striped fabric, rolling right down to the ground on all sides in a tent shape. Little pegs appeared, hammering themselves into place.

"It's almost like a circus tent," said Athena, astonished.

"It reminds me of a children's toy," said Rosemary. "Or maybe an iced cake."

Athena laughed. "You're making me hungry."

"Do you think it's safe to go in?" Rosemary asked.

"Wait till it finishes rattling."

It was indeed rattling and ringing, a bit like the sound of bells. Rosemary and Athena watched and waited, noticing little golden sparks emitting from the tent.

A few moments later the noises subsided and there was only silence.

"All right. Let's check it out," said Rosemary. She took a few tentative steps forward. When nothing unusual happened she gingerly lifted up a flap at the front entrance of the tent. "Oh, this is nice!"

She wandered inside, with Athena following close behind.

"Lovely!" said Athena.

Inside the tent were several rooms. The main one was furnished with soft-toned Persian rugs and silk cushions and even a few sofas. A table sat in the middle of the room, on which perched the stunningly magical teapot.

To the side of the large room was a kitchen area complete with stove, a kettle, and various other important amenities.

"I could quite happily live here," said Athena as they explored the other rooms, including a full bathroom with a clawfoot tub. There were three good-sized bedrooms with double beds, dressed in silky bedspreads, striped to match the outside of the tent, complete with about a dozen over-stuffed matching cushions on each.

"Talk about glamping," said Rosemary.

"I'll never doubt Marjie again!" said Athena, lying back on one of the couches, putting her feet up on an ottoman. "Do I have to help with the stall? I could quite happily stay here and have a little holiday."

Rosemary sighed. "It'll be fun. I promise."

"Knock, knock!" said a slightly nasal voice from outside the tent.

Rosemary and Athena both jumped. A hand reached through the tent entrance flap, followed by a curly head of chestnut hair. A woman's face smiled towards them.

"Don't mind me, dearies!"

"Who are you?" Athena asked.

Rosemary shot her a warning look. *Don't be rude,* she thought, hoping Athena would pick it up.

"Why, I'm Hyacinth Eldridge, dear," she said. "Just popping by with some complimentary platters!"

"Platters?" Rosemary furrowed her brow in confusion.

"I run the best cheese and preserves stall around and I wanted everyone to sample our delicious food. So I thought, what better way to do it then to offer some platters of snacks to the newcomers?"

Rosemary took a closer look at their uninvited guest. Hyacinth was wearing a floral apron that reminded Rosemary a lot of Marjie. "Okay, sure. Thank you. That's very kind."

"It's mostly just stallholders here tonight," said Hyacinth with an un-called-for wink. "May I cheekily inquire as to what your stall is?"

"Just chocolates." Rosemary smiled. "Nothing else. You won't have to worry about competition from us."

"Very well, dear."

"In fact, you should stop by the store tomorrow," Rosemary said. "I'd like to repay you for your generosity and give you a few treats."

"I'd love to! Alright, I'll be on my way." She slid a cheese board topped with charcuterie onto the table and then toddled off.

"That was odd," said Athena.

"Do you think she's suspicious?" Rosemary asked.

"I don't know. She seems nice enough," said Athena, taking a step towards the table. "But I feel like we should check to make sure the food's safe."

"It'll probably be fine," said Rosemary, though as she uttered the words she wondered whether she believed them.

"We'd better not eat it just in case," said Athena. "Even though I'm starving."

"That sounds like a sensible approach. It's a shame, because after all our hard work it would be quite nice to relax and eat a snack I don't have to prepare and maybe have a cool refreshing beverage."

"After all our hard work?! What are you talking about? Five minutes of putting up tents?" Athena scoffed.

"Plus all the packing and preparing – and the weeks building up to this. I'm ready for a break. Besides, you're hungry too and I haven't eaten since breakfast."

They stepped outside the tent and looked around at some of the sounds to see what was happening and were surprised to find that they were no longer in a mostly-empty paddock. Dozens of tents had been put up in the space of just a few minutes as more and more campers had arrived.

"It's going to be quite some transformation," said Rosemary, watching a large vibrant monstrosity of a tent erect itself nearby.

"I thought you said non-magical people came to the festival, too," said Athena. "What are they going to think about all this?"

"Oh don't worry about that," said a slightly-familiar voice. Rosemary turned to see a woman standing there. The purple streaks in her dark hair complemented the purple and white pinstripe summer suit she was wearing.

"Juniper!" said Rosemary. "Nice to see you. Have you met my daughter, Athena?"

"Yes." Juniper smiled.

"We had that awkward dinner party, remember?" Athena whispered.

"Oh, yes. Of course." So much had happened in the elapsed time, Rosemary could hardly believe it.

"Are you still..." Athena started and then turned bright red.

"Seeing your father?" Juniper asked.

Athena nodded.

Juniper shrugged. "Who really knows what's happening at this point in time? Everything's in flux. There's too much going on."

"Tell me about it!" said Rosemary. "Anyway, what was it you were saying before?"

"Don't worry about the non-magical people," said Juniper. "The mundane folk don't arrive until at least tomorrow, and by then most of the things will already be set up."

"Do you have to tell people to keep the magic to a minimum during the festivities?" Rosemary asked.

Juniper smirked. "To be quite frank, most of them are off their faces, high as kites, so we don't need to worry too much. We've only had a few instances over the years where people have needed bits of their memories wiped. Mostly they just put it down to some good gear."

"Oh," said Rosemary. "How convenient...but is it safe for young people to be around with all the drugs?"

Juniper shrugged. "I wouldn't worry too much. The kind of substances people take at festivals tend to just make them a little bit more creative and playful than usual. They're having a good time. It's not like heavy drinking which brings out the violence."

"They do say alcohol is much more dangerous than many other drugs," said Athena in a slightly superior voice, as if to suggest that by not drinking she was somehow better than her mother.

Rosemary narrowed her eyes. "It's okay in small to medium quantities, surely. Anyway, I'm relieved drug use at these things isn't a problem for safety. So what kind of numbers are we expecting? A couple thousand people?"

"Ten thousand at least," said Juniper.

Athena coughed. "That's a lot! What if I can't find the tent?"

"I have just the thing!" Juniper said, reaching into her handbag and pulling out a small bright green egg-shaped object. She split it in half and gave one half to Rosemary and the other to Athena. She placed a matching green disk onto the side of the tent.

"We use these to help locate other festival organisers and key locations, but this one's a spare. You'll be able to locate each other and your tent."

"How do we get it to work?" said Athena.

"Just hold it and focus on the other half of the egg, or the flat disk that belongs with it, and it'll send out a little signal and lead you that way."

"Sounds great. Thank you," said Rosemary.

"That's brilliant." Athena beamed.

Juniper smiled. "I better be off. I've got a lot of work to do."

"I bet," said Rosemary. "I hope you have some fun too."

"Oh, don't worry about that." Juniper smiled and disappeared.

"Wow. That trick is cool. I want to be able to teleport!" said Athena. "But...are you sure we can trust her? She just put some kind of tracking device on us."

"I'd be more worried if she tried to do that secretly," said Rosemary. "You're the one who insists you have such good instincts about people – except a certain someone who we do not name. What do you think?"

"I don't get a bad feeling," Athena admitted. "It's more just cautiousness...I feel like we need to be careful."

"We do!" said Rosemary. "And I'm glad to hear you say so. Too many strange things have happened lately. We can't be letting our guard down too much."

Athena's stomach growled. "It's too bad, because I would have quite liked to eat that food brought in by that slightly nosy and friendly woman, before. What was her name? Hyacinth?"

"Hyacinth! Bah humbug," said a voice.

They turned to see Marjie emerging from around the side of the tent. "Don't you listen to that old biddy! She'll tell you her food is much better than mine."

Rosemary smiled. "What are you doing all the way out here?"

"I came to help, of course. Unless I'm not wanted, in which case I'll take my picnic basket full of delicious food and my pitchers of lemonade and I'll be gone."

"Don't be ridiculous!" said Rosemary, laughing and hugging her friend. "You're always wanted."

Marjie gave her a satisfied grin. "That's better. Also, I wanted to check out how the tent was going."

"It's fantastic," said Athena. "I must admit I was a little sceptical when I saw the teapot."

Marjie chuckled. "You should know better than to doubt me!"

"Indeed," Rosemary said, watching as Marjie laid out the spread she'd brought on a little outdoor table with matching loungers that had been found folded up just inside the beautiful tent.

THEY TOOK the opportunity on that nice, peaceful afternoon to have a glorious time, as a gentle breeze rustled the air and the sun shone down, eating delicious food and drinking lemonade – Rosemary's happened to be topped up with a little gin – and relaxing.

"It feels like a culmination of all our hard work," said Rosemary. "If that makes sense. Now we get to relax and enjoy."

Marjie poured them more lemonade. "You've worked so hard with your studies, both of you. And your chocolate shop is almost ready!"

"I can hardly believe it," Rosemary said. "The renovations will be finished in a few weeks."

"It's definitely time to relax and celebrate," said Marjie.

"If only I could believe that," said Rosemary. "You know as well as I do that celebrations around Myrtlewood tend to become extreme disasters of one sort or another."

"Well, you're not quite in Myrtlewood, now," said Marjie. "Let's hope this is peaceful! I'll leave you both now and pop out to help you with the stall from time to time during the festival."

"What about your own business?" Rosemary asked.

"I'll close for the weekend. Town's quiet anyway once everyone comes out here. I think I'm due for a holiday, don't you?"

Rosemary laughed. "A holiday while you help me with my store?"

"Exactly," said Marjie. "What else am I going to do? I've got to entertain myself somehow."

"All right," said Rosemary. "I should know better than to disagree with you."

Marjie said her goodbyes and left Rosemary and Athena relaxing under the shade of a large sun umbrella.

"I could get used to this," said Athena. "Wait, where's the sun gone?"

Rosemary lifted her sunglasses and looked around to see they had indeed been shaded out. She got up to examine the monstrous structure that had suddenly appeared to the west of the tent.

"It looks like a castle!" said Athena.

The structure loomed over the smaller tents scattered across the field. "I wonder what kind of teapot that came out of."

"Should we go have a look?"

Rosemary sighed. "Oh fine. I'm starting to doubt the location of our tent."

"Do you think we should move?" Athena asked as they strolled towards the abnormal structure. It was black and silver and castle-shaped. It even seemed to have a drawbridge and a little moat.

A familiar looking Rolls Royce was sitting to one side.

"Oh no," said Rosemary as an elegant sandaled foot emerged from the side of the car. "I can't believe this."

Elamina Bracewell-Thorn stepped out of the Rolls Royce and snapped her fingers and the drawbridge began to be let down.

"Oh...Rosemary," said Elamina as if she was commenting on a speck of dust on her shoe. "I didn't mean to block your shade. Is that your tiny tent over there?"

"Of course it is," said Rosemary flatly. "And of course you did."

"Apologies, my dear cousin." Elamina pouted. "I'm afraid I won't be able to move this old thing now that I've put it up. It takes significant skill and effort to get the chest to open and to pop everything back in and I'm afraid Derse is a little worn-out." She gestured to the side of the car where Derse seemed to be floating in a large paddling pool, sipping a pink cocktail.

"Yes. Looks like he's having a really rough day," said Rosemary dryly.

Elamina gave her a pointed look. "It's always important to rest after one exerts oneself. Wouldn't you agree?"

Rosemary just smiled, refusing to lose any ground to her cousin.

Elamina turned her attention to Athena. "You're looking stunning as usual!" she cooed, giving the teen air kisses on both cheeks. "You really must come and visit us again. We do appreciate you being at the house. Such gorgeous company."

Athena grinned in amusement. Though she clearly wasn't a huge fan of their cousins either, she did find it entertaining the way they treated her compared to her mother.

"I suppose you'll have to move your little tent if you want some sunlight," said Elamina.

"Actually, I think shade in the afternoon is quite good for the constitution," Rosemary replied, shooting Athena an amused grin.

"It was getting awfully hot," Athena added, clearly trying not to laugh. "So we should be thanking you, really. Our tent won't get all hot and stuffy in the afternoons."

Elamina smiled tightly.

"What are you even doing here?" Rosemary asked. "I thought you'd be too posh for something like this, cousin."

Elamina gave a little laugh. "Oh dear. This is not just a little fair or a party. It is singularly the most important event in the calendar year or at least one of them. I know you think your little Myrtlewood celebrations are important, but in the real magical world some of us have responsibilities."

"Such as?" Rosemary asked.

"For your information," said Elamina, "I have the most important sacred ceremonial role. I couldn't imagine you would be interested in such a thing or even pretend to understand. But alas, it has passed to me because our parents have accepted their permanent diplomatic posting in Bermuda."

"What's in Bermuda?" Athena asked. "I think that's where Beryl's parents go all the time. She keeps skiting about it as if it's fancy. Only, I haven't got a clue what that means."

Elamina's eyes gleamed. "Oh, you sweet naïve little cherub!"

Athena was definitely not grinning this time. In fact, her expression looked more like a glare now.

"Bermuda is the magical headquarters for witches all around the world, the powerhouse, and where our witching parliament sits. And, even better, there are no vampires in sight. They don't like the tropics, you see. Too humid and too much sun for them. Nasty little creatures."

Rosemary felt as if she was being baited and wondered how much Elamina knew about her relationship with Burk. Surely, being so sneaky she could have spies everywhere.

Rosemary herself was unsure of the state of her relationship with Burk. They'd had one date. And then she'd gone to study and he'd gone off on very important and apparently secret business. As far as she knew, he hadn't returned and there'd been no contact between them except for a few brief messages here and there of the friendly sort.

At first, Rosemary had been pleased about the lack of pressure, or any kind of commitment. But now she wondered whether it was a lack of anything at all.

Despite that lovely evening they'd spent together, perhaps Burk had gotten distracted with bigger and brighter things. Who knew if he even planned to return to Myrtlewood at all?

"What's the matter?" Elamina asked. "Have I said something wrong?" She feigned a look of concern.

"No. All is well," said Rosemary, adjusting her sunglasses. "Go off and do your sacred ceremony or whatever it is. Thank you for the shade and don't go summoning any old gods or anything."

Elamina's nostrils flared in anger.

"What? Did I say something wrong?" Rosemary asked. "I'm so sorry. Anyway, we best be off." She grabbed Athena by the arm and they ran back to the tent, giggling.

"She's a real piece of work, isn't she?" said Athena. "Every time I meet her, she seems to get worse and worse."

"That's right. Just when you think she couldn't get any more snobby or snarky or precious, she hits a new low."

"I hope she enjoys it," said Athena. "I hope it's fun for her...to be like that."

"Why's that?" Rosemary asked. "I don't really hope for anything good about my cousins in particular, considering how much pain they've caused us."

"Oh, I don't know. It seems like such a waste of energy otherwise," said Athena.

"You sound very wise," said Rosemary, refilling their glasses of lemonade. She handed one to Athena and raised hers to clink. "A toast."

"To what?"

"To having a bloody wonderful time, despite everything," said Rosemary and took a long refreshing swig.

CHAPTER
TWENTY-SIX

The sun was shining the next morning and Rosemary was up bright and early. To her surprise, so was her teenager.

"So this is where the fun begins," said Rosemary, peeking out of the tent.

"My friends are out there somewhere."

"Remember you said you'd help me."

"I also want some social time today. It's Friday, right? And then tomorrow's the big day – the solstice, with the druid ritual and everything."

"There will be music the whole time. Dancing!" said Rosemary. "That's what I need." She could hear the sound of a beat in the distance, as music had already started up somewhere on the site.

Athena grimaced. "I'm not sure my social life can survive your dancing, so I'll be sure to steer well clear of the main dance floor."

"So the big party night is tomorrow," said Rosemary. "And then Sunday we all go home."

"So quick, though they do seem to pack a lot into the schedule."

"I think on Sunday we'll close the stall and take naps."

"Sounds good to me," said Athena. She already had her sunglasses on and was wearing a very summery striped halter top in teal and lavender with denim shorts.

"I've got a top like that," said Rosemary. "But I expect it would be terribly embarrassing for you if I wore it."

"Actually, it would be quite cute," said Athena. "Especially when we're on the stall together. They'll be like matching outfits."

Rosemary beamed at her. "You never fail to surprise me." She quickly got dressed. "Right. Ready to go?"

They carried various boxes and bags over to the space they'd booked for the chocolate stall, Athena navigating using the map they'd been given on arrival.

Several other shops had already set up.

"Look, there's Mervyn!" said Athena, gesturing to the large bearded purveyor of ice cream in his pastel striped apron. He stood next to a cart with a sun umbrella that matched his outfit. "I wonder if we'll still see him once the other stalls are all set up?"

"I doubt it," said Rosemary. "It's early in the morning right now, but by nine when things officially start this place will be packed with stalls."

"So where's your little table?" Athena asked, looking around at some of the fancier setups nearby.

"Actually, I had it commissioned especially," said Rosemary. "Marjie knows someone..."

"Marjie knows an awful lot," said Athena. "But where is it?"

"In this case, apparently," Rosemary said, holding up what looked like a slightly fat briefcase. "I don't expect it will be anything flashy."

"After that teapot situation?" said Athena. "Never underestimate Marjie!"

Rosemary set the case down in the centre of the plot marked for their stall. She flipped open the latch.

"Stand back," said a disembodied voice.

"Alright," said Rosemary, nudging the case with her boot so it was along the front of the market stall.

"I said stand back," said the case and began to rumble.

"Right!" said Rosemary, jumping back.

"Do you think it's sentient?" Athena asked.

There was a whistling noise and they watched as the stall assembled itself right in front of their eyes.

"It's exactly the size of the plot," said Athena suspiciously.

"Well, I did order it to the specifications," said Rosemary.

"It's gorgeous!" Athena admired the sage green and lavender striped awning, which matched the one that was going to be on Rosemary's permanent chocolate shop.

"This is just a miniature version of what's to come!" said Rosemary, delightedly rubbing her hands together. "Oh, I can't wait to get started."

They set out the chocolates in the display cabinet, enjoying how cool the inside of the little shop was in comparison to outside with the hot sun already beaming down.

"I don't remember it being this hot before," said Athena.

Rosemary shrugged. "Nobody ever remembers the weather, so they always complain about it being hot in summer and cold in winter."

"Things are not always as they seem," said Athena as she placed the last chocolates in the cabinet.

Rosemary felt a well of satisfaction as she surveyed the marketplace, which by this time was filled with hundreds of stores. Customers started arriving, though they were only just trickling in since it was still fairly early.

Rosemary enjoyed the elated feeling that arose – the sense of abundance of her hens coming home to roost.

As the crowd grew bigger, Rosemary kept an eye out. At one

point she was sure she caught a glimpse of Lamorna, but on closer inspection, it was an older woman with large dark glasses.

She served a relaxing lavender cream to a slightly harried-looking mother towing twin toddlers, followed by a mango truffle served to a young woman who looked like she was ready to lounge around by the beach.

The woman they'd met the previous afternoon, Hyacinth, stopped by. Rosemary may have been slightly too enthusiastic in her appreciation of the secretly untouched charcuterie board. Hyacinth didn't entirely seem to believe her, but left with a batch of complimentary truffles, somewhat mollified.

They could barely see the ocean from where the stalls were, but when they'd walked past earlier, sun umbrellas and loungers had been set up along the beach with various refreshment stations.

Rosemary looked in that direction, feeling a slight chill.

Athena nattered away to the customers.

"How's it all going?" a voice said.

Rosemary jumped. "Oh, Juniper! We're all fine here. Everything's going swimmingly."

"Funny you should say that," said Juniper.

Rosemary realised that her normally very smooth and calm demeanour seemed slightly ruffled.

"What's wrong?"

"Three more people have gone missing. Can you believe it?" Juniper said.

Rosemary nodded. "I'm afraid I can. I'm a bit surprised it's taken this long."

"The funny thing is that the other man who went missing showed up at about the same time - alive."

"I'm glad he survived," said Athena. "Do they know who he is?"

Juniper nodded. "He's been identified as a mechanic from Kent, though he might have a magical connection somewhere in his family line. His cousin is local."

"How is his memory?" Rosemary asked.

"Exactly the same as that first woman we found. And they all had little pink shells in their pockets."

"How bizarre," said Athena. "What does it mean?"

"I hope this doesn't mean that the festival gets shut down after everyone's hard work," said Rosemary. "Haven't you been working on this for months?"

Juniper shrugged. "It's just my job at the moment. Anyway, I'm also the one who they call to sort out magical messes, so theoretically this other situation could well be my job too."

"Magical messes sound like Mum's forte," said Athena.

Rosemary gave her a gentle nudge with her elbow. "Not my fault!"

"Actually, have you asked Mervyn?" said Athena.

"Who's that?" Juniper asked.

"I forget you're not really local to Myrtlewood anymore," said Rosemary. "Mervyn's the ice cream guy. Makes an amazing raspberry crème brûlée gelato."

"Sounds delicious," said Juniper. "But?"

Athena laughed. "Oh, and he's also a mer...person."

"Interesting," said Juniper, narrowing her eyes. "Well, if you see him, tell him to come my way."

"He's over there somewhere," said Athena, gesturing in the general direction they'd seen him earlier. "Though I'm not exactly sure where now that everything's all set up. I'll go and find him later and see if he knows anything."

"That would be brilliant," said Juniper. "Right. I'd better go and see what else I can do." She popped away, leaving empty air in front of them.

CHAPTER

TWENTY-SEVEN

Athena stood at the back of the chocolate stall putting on sun lotion while listening to Stellium on her headphones. She was particularly enjoying their Saturn album, especially when she was busy getting work done.

She was preparing to go and visit Mervyn if she could find him to ask if he knew anything about the disappearances. She was just finishing with the lotion when a familiar head of blue hair emerged over the counter.

"There you are!" said Elise. She was dressed in a little blue sundress.

Athena beamed at her and ran around the counter to give her girlfriend a hug.

"Settle down, you two!" said Felix.

"The whole group's here," said Athena, smiling around at Sam, Deron, and Ash. "What are you up to?"

"We just came to find you and then we were gonna relax," said Felix. "Maybe have some snacks. Go to the beach."

"Sounds brilliant," said Athena. "Do you mind, Mum?"

"I don't know..." said Rosemary, cautiously. "What if it's not safe."

"Oh come on. There's loads of people around and I'm sure it'll be safe with all the magical people here, keeping watch."

"Oh, go on then. Go have fun. I'm all sorted here," said Rosemary. "Marjie is going to pop in later."

"Excellent!" Athena gave her mother a little hug over the counter and then turned her attention to her friends. "Do you mind if we stop in at Mervyn's cart, if we can find him?"

"A little early for ice cream, don't you think?" said Sam.

"Are you on a special sweet only diet?" Felix joked.

Deron looked interested. "I could go for some ice cream."

"Me too," said Elise. "Any time of day, to tell the truth!"

Athena laughed. "I wasn't specifically wanting ice cream, but I wouldn't say no to some blackberry sorbet."

"What were you wanting, then?" Sam asked, always the perceptive one.

"I just have some questions to ask him, relating to magical sea creatures."

"I think he's back over that way," Ash said. "I saw him earlier."

"Yeah, that sounds right," said Athena. "Alright, let's go."

They began to wander past stalls of wind chimes and crystal pendants, flags and t-shirts, and even a post office that promised to deliver mail to anyone at the festival.

They were headed in the direction of where they thought Mervyn's ice cream cart ought to be.

Ash suspected it was closer to the sea. Athena thought it was slightly more to the east. Eventually they found Mervyn somewhere in the middle.

"This is a nice surprise!" He grinned at them. He was wearing a short sleeved striped shirt with a matching bow tie and a mint green apron that wouldn't have looked amiss behind Rosemary's little counter.

"To what do I owe this pleasure? After an early morning treat?" He gestured to his array of mouth-watering ice creams.

"Maybe," said Athena. "I actually had a couple of questions."

"Ask away!"

"Well, have you heard about the disappearances near Myrtle-wood and up the coast?"

Mervyn nodded, his expression becoming more serious. "I've just heard that a couple of people went missing. There wasn't much about it in the papers. And quite frankly, I never read the paper anyway. Full of nonsense."

"Mervyn is not one for town gossip, either," said Elise with a smile. "That's why we like his shop so much. Safe from all those prying eyes!"

Mervyn shrugged. "What can I say? I'm a simple man with simple but delicious needs." He picked up a little wooden spoon and scooped some strawberry ripple into his mouth. "Mmm. Perfect breakfast food."

Athena couldn't help but giggle at the eccentric merman, or merrow as they were sometimes called traditionally. "So anyway, apparently the other man turned up on the beach, and now three more have gone missing."

"On the beach?" said Mervyn, twirling his rather bushy moustache. "That's interesting. Nobody told me he turned up on the beach, though I suppose it makes sense given they wandered into the sea. Can you tell me anything else? I might be able to help."

"Uhh...there were shells in his pockets, just like the body of the other man they found..."

"Any other details? What kinds of shells?"

"Pink shells," Athena said tentatively. She was unsure if she'd recalled the right details from the previous conversation with Juniper.

Mervyn's eyes went wide. He straightened up with a faraway look on his face. "I've got to go," he said in a more serious tone than Athena had ever heard him use.

"Uhhh..." said Elise.

"What about the shop?" said Sam.

"You can close up or...or run it yourselves if you like," he said, taking off his apron and thrusting it towards Athena. Then he disappeared into the crowd.

They stood there, surprised.

Felix laughed. "Brilliant! I love that man."

"So what will it be? Should we close up or shall we be ice cream sellers for the day?" Sam asked.

"But aren't we going to the beach?" Ash asked.

"Why not both?" said Felix.

"It's a moveable cart," Deron said, giving it a push. The wheels began to rotate. "I don't think he'd mind if we just took it to the beach."

"I don't know," said Athena. "He might not be happy with us."

Elise smiled and patted Athena's shoulder. "I'm sure he won't mind."

After some further deliberation, Athena agreed to her friends' hare-brained scheme. After all, hanging out with ice cream on the beach sounded like far too much fun to pass up.

They pushed the cart, complete with its enormous matching pastel sun umbrella, down the little market lane, towards the sea. They set it up there, just above the high tide line. None of them had any particular experience with running a shop, except for Athena's very brief chocolate stall assistance, and they possibly didn't get the money side of things perfect.

It was quite fun playing shop, and taking turns swimming in the beautiful ocean on such a calm and sunny day.

Athena was pleased she'd had the foresight to wear her bathing suit under her outfit. There could hardly be a safer time.

Being in the water was so soothing and refreshing. She played about, splashing Sam and Deron who were also on this swim break at the same time, and of course, they'd splashed her first.

Athena emerged from the water, drying herself off with Elise's towel.

"Such a babe," said Felix. He gave her a slow smile.

Athena squinted at him, unsure how to react.

"Hey," said Elise, coming over to stand by Athena and wrapping her arm round her girlfriend.

"Sorry, Felix," said Athena. "I'm only interested in fae."

Elise shot her a hurt look.

"Can't blame a guy for trying," said Felix, raising his hands in the air. "My turn for a swim!"

He dashed off towards the water, leaving the two girls alone.

"What's wrong?" Athena asked.

Elise furrowed her brow, the tips of her hair turning red, along with her eyebrows. "Do you think you're only attracted to me because of what I am?"

"Of course not," said Athena. "That was just a silly remark."

"Was it though?"

Athena shrugged. "I've got no idea. But I know that I like you for who you are."

"And what about *him?*" Elise didn't speak his name, but Athena could tell she wasn't talking about Felix anymore. She was talking about Finnigan.

"He's more like you. Part high fae, part human."

"I'm not part of anything," said Athena bitterly. "Please don't bring him up. I was having a nice time. You know I can't stand Finnigan."

She felt grumpy all of a sudden, and cold despite the heat of the sun.

Elise eyed her sceptically. "You liked him first. I know it's stupid, but I can't help thinking that maybe you liked him more. And I'm just a substitute."

Athena shook her head. "No way." She wrapped her arms around Elise, pulling her close. "You're better in every way."

She felt the gentle intimacy of their embrace like a lovely summery cloud descending around them, almost like being in the fae realm... as if Athena could just slip away as their lips met in a mind-melting kiss. And though her feelings for Elise were pure and genuine, and overpowering, in that moment, Athena couldn't help but sense that something was not right.

TWENTY-EIGHT

"Well, that's a great big pile of rocks," said Athena as they made their way up to the stone circle atop the hill where the Summer Solstice ritual had been carried out for generations. As they neared the top, the large standing stones stood prominently against the clear blue sky.

"A great big pile of sacred rocks, I'll have you know," said Rosemary. She smiled at her daughter. Athena had been in an uncharacteristically good and stable mood recently. She'd even helped to pack down the chocolate stall that afternoon, having returned from a surprise beach ice cream adventure that she'd excitedly told Rosemary about.

"Very nice sacred rocks," Athena said, giggling as they joined the large circle of people at the top of the hill for the opening ceremony of the festival.

"It doesn't seem like ten thousand people," said Rosemary.

Athena shrugged. "Not everyone wants to go to the formal opening, I guess. Not even my friends. They said they'd rather hang out back at their camp. Speaking of…Do you think I could stay with them tonight?"

"Unchaperoned?" Rosemary asked, sounding slightly outraged.

"No. Fleur will be there. And same with Deron's dad."

"I suppose so," said Rosemary. "As long as you're sensible."

"I'm infinitely sensible," said Athena, crossing her arms with a grin.

Rosemary nudged her with her elbow. "My little girl's all grown up and is far more sensible than her mother half the time."

"Don't you forget it."

Just then, the sound of a bell rang out and the people around them stilled. Around the circle, druids in different coloured robes stepped forward, creating an inner circle, slightly away from the gathering crowd that surrounded them.

They held up their hands in the air and began to chant. It was a peaceful sound, soothing, and Rosemary was glad she'd made the trek up the hill just for the experience.

"It's nice," Athena whispered. "Do you think they really have been looking out for us all this time?"

"Well, we've had surprisingly less mischief and drama than usual," said Rosemary quietly. "At least for the last week or so."

"Do you think they're only helping us out because we're somehow related?"

Rosemary shrugged. "Pay attention. Something's happening."

Silence descended and one of the druids began to recite a druid's prayer for peace, then he thanked the spirits of the forest, land, sea, and sky for the blessings. The four directions were called in a similar way to the Myrtlewood rituals.

"We stand here," said one of the druids, wearing a dark blue robe, "on this eve of the Summer Solstice, to open the festival and welcome in good energies for the harvest ahead. I speak not only of the harvest of food from our fields and gardens, but of the harvest in our lives as we approach the longest day and shortest night of the year. We stand at the pinnacle of the year and we celebrate all we have achieved so far and much more yet to come. Now it is time to light the sacred torch in honour of Lugh, the sun god."

A woman in an emerald green cloak stepped forward. There was something familiar about her posture, and her light blonde hair.

It took Rosemary a moment to realise it was her cousin Elamina. The hooded cloak she wore seemed rather plain, as were the ceremonial robes underneath. Not her usual style. Her hair was also loose in soft white waves that flowed down to her chest.

"I don't think I've ever seen her with her hair down before," whispered Athena.

"Neither have I, and I've known her pretty much all my life," said Rosemary. "I don't think she's even wearing makeup. Maybe it's part of the gig."

They watched as Elamina reached the centre of the circle. Raising the torch that she carried high in the air, she began to chant some words that sounded like they might be ancient Irish, or even Cornish perhaps.

She lowered the torch down towards the waiting firepit in the centre. It caught alight instantly and the stones around the circle seemed to hum in response.

"Very sacred rocks," Rosemary whispered.

Athena giggled again. "Stop it," she hissed, swatting at her mother.

The sky darkened just then, as if in eclipse. Rosemary looked up to see a flash of blinding light. She felt a chill in her bones.

Hooded figures in dark robes stepped into the circle and more chanting rose through the air around them.

"This doesn't seem right," Rosemary whispered, grabbing Athena's arm just in case as a surge of fear rocked through her.

There was a loud bang.

Rosemary felt herself being flung back through the air but she didn't let go of her daughter.

They landed on the ground. They looked around to see that the other bystanders too had been blown back. The figures in dark robes were nowhere in sight.

"What in Brigid's name was that?" Rosemary asked.

"Good question," said Athena.

"Did you see anything? I was looking up to see what had happened to the light."

Athena gave her a strange look.

One of the druid women stepped forward. "Don't worry folks, just a bit of a pyrotechnic glitch. Everything's fine now, you're perfectly safe." She caught Rosemary's eye and gave her a wink.

"Maybe she knows something," said Athena.

"More than I do," said Rosemary. "Tell me. What did you see?"

Athena looked around as if checking for eavesdroppers. "You're not gonna believe this. I barely do, myself."

"What?"

"Just before the explosion I could have sworn I saw a little box, right in the centre of the circle, kind of hovering in mid-air."

"A box?" said Rosemary, a sense of dread building like a lead weight in her chest.

"Yes. *The* box. At least, that's what it looked like." Athena's voice was almost apologetic.

"Bloodstones," said Rosemary. She glared across the circle at her cousin, who looked unperturbed by the disarray that surrounded them. "I bet Elamina was in on this all along."

"But she made herself look so innocent," said Athena.

"Yes, she did, didn't she? I could have sworn she had nothing at all to do with any of the weird things that happened when we first arrived in Myrtlewood. Besides...you know all about Beltane."

"I thought that little Geneviève was to blame for most of it, aside from the fire sprites," said Athena. "Thank the gods you banished her."

"Banished her to where?" said Rosemary. "They've been so obsessed with that box."

"You don't think...?"

Rosemary shrugged. "I don't know. I couldn't tell you for sure. But I know that's what the Bloodstones think. That must be why they bothered to steal the box from our house in the first place."

"What a rollicking start to our lovely festival," said Athena. "I bet you're going to go all over-protective now and stop me from hanging out with my friends."

Rosemary could tell her daughter was stealing herself for a fight. "No," she said defiantly.

"No?" Athena sounded surprised.

"You go off with your friends," said Rosemary. "Have a nice time and be very careful. And let me know the instant anything terrible happens."

"We should have tested my telepathy more to see how far it can work across distances," said Athena.

"We could have if you hadn't been so resistant about using it. We could still test it. Plus, we've got those little locater things from Juniper. We'll be fine."

Athena stood up and her expression became more serious. "Oh, Mum!"

"What?" Rosemary asked, getting up and brushing herself off from the grass.

"She's coming over."

ROSEMARY LOOKED up to see her cousin strolling towards them, looking glamorous despite her lack of makeup and her plain robes.

"There you are, cousins," said Elamina with a tone of mock concern.

"You came over here after that?" Rosemary asked. "Are you gloating or something?"

"Well, that wasn't the way I'd intended it to go, but you must admit it was quite a spectacular scene. People will remember that for a long time."

"It was you, wasn't it?" said Rosemary. "You've been behind all of this Bloodstone stuff."

"Oh, stop with your incoherent rambling, Rosemary. All I did was carry a torch and say a chant for the ritual."

"Are you okay?" Athena asked, clearly trying to play nice. "I mean, you weren't hurt by the explosion or anything?"

"How sweet of you to ask, little Athena," she said, only slightly patronisingly. "I'm absolutely fine. It didn't seem to affect me. I suppose I am rather powerful, if I do say so myself. Magic on both sides...a little bit like you actually." She gave Athena a knowing smile. "Actually, that was what I was coming across to ask you about."

Elamina was looking only at Athena.

"What?" said Rosemary.

"Despite your mother's somewhat rude outburst, always wanting to accuse me of everything, I wanted to ask *you* to a cocktail party I'm having tonight. There'll be plenty of fancy canapés."

"Where?" Athena asked.

"Over at my little temporary abode."

"Oh," said Athena. "I'll think about it."

"Lovely. And feel free to invite as many friends as you'd like."

Elamina said goodbye, giving Athena air kisses, before turning on her sensible heels and striding off.

"What on earth was that about?" Athena asked.

"I don't know. You and your best friend, Elamina, seemed to be having a wonderful time."

"Don't be silly, Mum. I was just – you know – trying the good-cop thing."

Rosemary smiled. "So you're going to go?"

"Where?"

"To the cocktail party."

"Don't you think that'll be a silly idea given how suspicious you are of her?"

"I suppose you've probably got better things to do anyway..."

"Actually, it might be a chance," Athena said. "I could spy on her using my magical brain powers."

"You'd do that?" Rosemary asked. It was the first time Athena had willingly offered to use telepathy in a long time, aside from mentioning testing its range in case of emergencies.

Athena shrugged. "It's worth a shot, isn't it? We're no closer to discovering what's going on. I need to know if she is somehow connected to the Bloodstones and all the disappearances and every-thing else. Would you let me go?"

"If you do, take friends," said Rosemary. "I don't want you left alone with that lot. Stay together and I'll be close enough, back at our tent, if anything weird happens."

"Don't just hang about on my accord," said Athena. "You should go off dancing. You deserve it. Besides, you need some fun in your life."

"We'll see," said Rosemary. The sound of the bass in the distance was already calling her.

CHAPTER
TWENTY-NINE

Athena linked arms with Elise for moral support as they made their way towards Elamina's rather grand castle of a camping set up. Ash, Deron, Felix, and Sam followed close behind them.

"I'm not sure this was such a great idea after all," said Athena. "It could be some kind of trap."

"Do you really suspect your cousin?" Elise asked.

"Honestly, I don't want to," said Athena. "I mean, she's a total snob and she's quite...odd, but nobody likes to think they're related to some kind of supervillain, do they?"

Elise gave her arm a fortifying squeeze as they reached the drawbridge.

"Halt! Who goes there?" a guard dressed in a suit of armour called out.

"This is so elaborate!" said Ash. "I didn't know you were related to fancy people."

"It's not all it's cracked up to be," Athena muttered.

She gave the guard her name. He checked the clipboard he was holding and then tapped the side of the wall next to him. The draw-bridge lowered over the little moat.

The friends gave each other slightly uncomfortable looks as they stepped across.

"Talk about a trap," said Felix. "Are we going to be sealed inside the dungeons forever?"

They heard smooth laughter up ahead.

Elamina was standing near the entrance, resplendent in the most elaborate ruby and silver ball gown Athena had ever laid eyes on. Suddenly, she felt woefully under-dressed in her casual violet frock. Her friends were also wearing fairly relaxed festival clothes.

"Were we supposed to dress up?" Ash whispered.

"I don't think I brought anything to the festival worth dressing up in," muttered Sam. "We should have brought our ball outfits."

"It'll be fine," said Athena.

"How marvellous, you came!" said Elamina. "And yes, don't worry. There's no strict dress code. Although I did tell the guests that it was medieval-themed. You know, the ones that knew in advance." She gave another laugh. "Never mind!" she said with a wave of her hand. "So pleased you could make it."

Elamina gave Athena her customary air-kisses and then nodded at each of her friends as Athena introduced them, which seemed like the polite thing to do, although she wondered whether it was wise to use everyone's real names. Not for the first time, Athena wondered what her cousin's astrology was like. *Something cold and beautiful and calculating. Maybe a strong Pluto-Venus alignment in Libra with a Capricorn Moon.*

She giggled to herself.

Elise asked, "What?"

"Nothing."

"Would you like refreshments?" Elamina asked.

The friends nodded and Athena wondered again whether they

should be consuming anything here. They followed Elamina over to a fancy bar setup.

Athena took in the big open space, unsure if they were really outdoors or inside. She could see the sky from between sheets of black and purple tulle that stretched above them from a tall pole in the centre, matching the striped walls. The air somehow maintained a perfect temperature, despite the searing heat outside.

The guests were holding glasses of various beverages and Athena reasoned if the others were drinking it couldn't be too bad.

She picked up a tropical pink punch from the non-alcoholic section.

"No wine for you, dear?" Elamina asked. "Is your mother strict?" She had an oddly empathetic tone.

"Not really," said Athena rather curtly. "I just don't like the taste of alcohol."

"Neither do I." She smiled and tapped her nose. "Those of a more ethereal nature mustn't sully themselves. I understand."

"I'll have a wine," said Felix. "Or a beer."

"No you will not," said Elise, pushing him towards the non-alcoholic beverages. "I'm not going to deal with a tiddly fox."

"Good call," said Ash.

"How refreshing! Teenagers who don't drink!" Elamina exclaimed. "Anyway, I best go off and talk to some of the other guests – they're all very distinguished, you know. Do enjoy yourselves, dears, and I'll come and see you later."

"She seems nice," said Deron, looking moon-eyed at the glamorous woman as she walked away.

"Occasionally," said Athena. "You should see how she treats Mum. It's almost like something from a bad comedy."

"So what do we do now?" Felix asked. "Kind of boring just standing around."

"I guess we act normal," said Athena. "You guys can go jump in the pool if you want."

Felix grinned. "Race you!" he said to Ash and Deron, then he ran off and dived – clothes and all – into the swimming pool.

"This is how he destroyed his last three cell phones," said Elise, looking unimpressed. She stayed with Athena while their other friends went to the pool.

Athena fidgeted with her fingernails. "I don't know what I'm doing."

"Can't you use your brain powers to see what they're all thinking?"

"I've never used the telepathy so deliberately to spy on people before. I've been trying not to use it at all."

"Just relax." Elise patted her arm gently. "Take a few slow breaths. Clear your mind."

Athena didn't feel like relaxing, but she recognised the validity of Elise's advice and followed her instructions.

"Maybe try concentrating on Elamina?" Elise suggested.

"Where is she?"

"Over there." Athena glanced towards her cousin who was talking to a short man in a top hat on the other side of the room. She tried to focus, but all she got was buzzing.

"I don't think you're relaxing," said Elise. "You're frowning and your shoulders are tense."

Athena let out a long slow sigh and rolled her shoulders back. "Okay fine. But let's go over to where the others are, close by the pool, so it doesn't look like I'm just standing here and staring at her."

"Try these," said Elise, pulling a pair of dark sunglasses out of her handbag. "She won't be able to see your eyes."

"Thanks," said Athena. "Good thinking."

They wandered over to the pool and sat in the ornate, carved loungers, close enough to their wayward friends, paddling and splashing each other in the pool.

Lying back was a little more relaxing, and with the dark glasses on Athena didn't have to worry too much about looking as if she was staring. She closed her eyes and focused in again.

"Don't watch me," Athena said. "It'll just make me nervous."

"Don't worry," said Elise. "I'll keep an eye on the others. Make sure they don't get up to mischief."

"Thanks. That'll ease more of my worries." She smiled and concentrated on being present.

Athena let her mind drift across the crowd of gathered guests towards her cousin. After a moment, she heard a thought that sounded like Elamina.

All my plans are lining up. Father will be so pleased...

Athena didn't know what this was in response to, but there was no follow up thought either. She sat up and took off her glasses.

Elamina had moved. Maybe that was how she'd lost contact. She'd crossed towards the entrance to greet a man in a pea-green caftan with golden tassels which clashed spectacularly with his pale and blonde features.

Athena gave an involuntary laugh just as Elamina looked over to her and smiled, almost sweetly. Athena smiled anxiously back. Her cousin did seem to genuinely like her. She was sure of that, despite her other personality issues, but what plans were being laid by Elamina and her parents?

Athena quietly relayed what she'd heard to Elise.

"What does it mean?"

Elise looked puzzled. "Who knows? It could be the family Christmas trip to Aspen for all we know."

"You're right." said Athena. "Just because it sounds nefarious doesn't mean it is."

"What about your other cousin? Is he here?"

Athena scanned the room but couldn't see Derse's hulking form anywhere. It took her a moment to recognise him floating on a lilo at the other side of the pool, wearing a pin-striped full body swimsuit. He was holding a cocktail in his hand with a little pink umbrella.

"It's surprising how different people can be at festivals," said Athena.

"He seems like quite the character."

"You wouldn't think so if you'd met him on an average day."

"It looks like he's really relaxing now. Can you get anything from his thoughts?"

Athena put the sunglasses back on and tried to scan Derse, but all she got from him was a thick and beguiling wall of static.

"Maybe I should focus on the other guests," Athena said.

"Just generally?" Elise asked.

"I'll pick a few and see what they're thinking."

Athena tried this but gave up in frustration when her attempts proved futile. All she got were odd snatches of words, though the top-hat man did seem oddly obsessed with the stone circle.

"Well, I suppose that's something," said Elise.

"But we don't know who he is. Do we?"

"Maybe if we go over there he'll introduce himself."

Athena felt a little bit like hiding away but she knew she had to be brave.

Elise stood up and held out her hand to help Athena up. They made their way across to the man in the top hat, who was now talking to a woman in a red silk dress.

"Hello," said Elise warmly.

"Oh!" said the man, his eyes wide as he stared at Athena. "You must be the niece of Lady Bracewell!"

"Ahh, something like that," said Athena.

"Charmed," said the woman, holding out her hand. "My name

is Heather Dupree and this is Reginald Orthorne." She gestured to the man in the top hat.

"Nice to meet you," Athena said. "I'm Athena Thorn."

They shook hands.

"Oh no," Elise whispered. "We've got to go."

"What?" Athena looked at Elise to see her face had paled. She pointed to Felix who was out of the pool, dripping wet, and reaching for champagne from the tray of a passing waiter.

"This is not going to be good," said Elise. "He'll probably guzzle the whole thing if we don't stop him. And believe me when I say you don't want to see the result."

"Excuse me," said Athena, smiling at the slightly stunned adults before she turned and ran with Elise towards the troublemaker.

"Felix!" Elise grabbed his hand and lowered it down slowly, so as to try not to spill the champagne, but Athena was sure he did manage to imbibe at least one large gulp.

"Ugh!" said Felix, spitting it out. "Gross! Is this what mundane peeps drink all the time?"

"Yep, not exactly all the time. But it is considered some kind of delicacy," said Athena as Felix grabbed several canapés from the tray of a waiter passing by to wash it down. Felix swayed a little, and burped.

"I can't believe he'd be tipsy on such a tiny amount," said Athena.

Ash shrugged. "Blame his shifter biology."

"Boring party," he said. "But the canapés aren't bad and I think there's a chocolate fountain in the dining room. Let's go!" He raced off.

Athena and Elise looked at each other and laughed.

"Oh, there you are dear," a woman said from behind her, and Athena turned towards the slightly familiar woman dressed in a hot pink tulle dress. Athena's mind came up blank.

"Hyacinth! Remember me from yesterday?"

"Oh," said Athena.

"I brought you that platter."

"So you did." Athena fidgeted nervously, not wanting to give away that she hadn't tried any of Hyacinth's food in case it was poisoned.

"Anyway, just thought I'd introduce myself." She grinned.

"Nice to see you," said Athena. "This is my friend Elise."

Hyacinth looked out of place, even among the other strangely-dressed guests. "And how did you get invited to such an elite gathering? Pardon me for asking."

Hyacinth was clearly taking in the way Athena and Elise were dressed. She herself looked as though she was about to go for a day at the races with an elaborate matching hot pink hat pinned to her head.

"Err..." Athena was slightly stunned at the snobbish question.

Elise laughed. "Oh, you know," she said. "It's hard to get out of family obligations." She grinned at Athena and then pulled her away from the rather stunned looking woman, towards the promise of a chocolate fountain.

THIRTY

The sound of the beat was intoxicating, as was the Celtic instrumental music weaving around it.

Rosemary danced, not caring what anyone thought.

For the first time in a long time she felt free. Her hair was down and flowing wildly around her. She was wearing a silver sequined top that sparkled under the elaborate lighting. It lit up the dance floor with patterns reminding Rosemary of the forest. All around, the dancers moved, lost in their own trances.

Rosemary's outfit was one she never would have worn – probably ever in her life – before. But Athena had insisted. The shorts were too short and the top was too revealing. Right now, Rosemary didn't give a care in the world.

She lost herself in the movement and the sounds around. From time to time, when she could be bothered looking, she caught glimpses of some of the faces of the Myrtlewood townsfolk around her.

Ferg was wearing a saucy red lacy number, despite the fact that Saturday was the day he normally always wore brown. Even

Constable Perkins was there in a 70s paisley shirt and brown corduroy flares. He seemed to be having a great time, swaying around the front of the dance floor with his arms in the air.

Rosemary had run into several friends with warm hellos and then carried on dancing, but as she continued to sway and whirl around the dance floor, something prickled her spine.

She snapped around, sure that something was wrong, but all she could see were the dancers.

Then she caught a glimpse of a very unwelcome face.

"Geneviève," she said under her breath and began storming across to the girl who looked no more than twelve but was really an ancient vampire.

"Not on my bloody watch, you don't!" said Rosemary. She watched the girl shoot off running through the crowd.

Rosemary chased her, fury burning in her veins. "Little bloodsucker's caused enough havoc," she muttered to herself. She burst through various groups of people in the crowd, trying to find the enemy. She lost sight of her but continued on through the crowd of dancing, costumed people, determined not to lose the brat.

Just then, she saw a small frame and curly hair. Rosemary started running again. She reached forward as she gained on the little girl and managed to grip her shoulder, only to be blown back by the sheer force of the child's scream.

"What is it, little one?" said an older woman in a bright orange kaftan.

Several people rushed over to the wailing child.

"I'm lost and that scary woman's chasing me!" the girl cried.

"Geneviève." Rosemary was sure it was her.

The girl shook her head. "I can't find my parents. Can you help me?" she asked the other woman.

"What was all that about?" said Constable Perkins, grabbing hold of Rosemary's shoulder and spinning her around.

"That was my arch nemesis," said Rosemary. "Or one of them, at any rate. Elamina is probably worse in some regards."

"What are you talking about?" Constable Perkins scoffed. "That there's a little girl!"

"That little girl was the vampire who attacked our house! You remember? The one that you completely and utterly failed to find? The one who killed my grandmother!" Rosemary rambled on.

"Don't be daft," said Constable Perkins. "You vanquished her. You said so yourself."

"So I thought," said Rosemary. "But it looks like her little cult has brought her back to life."

Constable Perkins wiggled his bushy eyebrows. "Are you sure?" He sounded oddly rational for a change.

"Of course I'm sure!" said Rosemary. "I hardly go around harassing children for fun. It was her." Though as she spoke, doubts began to swirl in her mind.

"Isn't it possible there could be another little girl who looks remarkably similar to Geneviève? Perhaps even a descendant or someone with the same heritage?"

Rosemary glared at the police officer. "I think it's too much of a coincidence. The events earlier..."

"Never mind!" said Constable Perkins. "This is police business. Leave it to me."

Rosemary raised her eyebrows incredulously. "You really expect me to settle for that?"

A strange sound flowed through the air. Constable Perkins' face split into a serene smile. "Such a pleasant evening. So good for dancing," he said and drifted away back into the crowd.

Rosemary shook herself, feeling like she ought to be doing something. The little girl seemed to have vanished from where she was before. And the sound permeating the air did seem to give her an odd dream-like feeling.

I should find Athena...but the rational part of her mind seemed so tiresome, so tired. Maybe it needed to go to sleep.

Maybe she needed to let go and relax. After all, she deserved this, didn't she? She deserved one night of pure surrender and joy.

She began to move to the beat without even thinking about it, swaying back onto the dance floor where she bumped almost fluidly into the other people, who moved as if they were one being, like a body of water. Rosemary recalled something Athena had said about the planet Neptune, it's association with dreams and the ocean. *It's like a spell*...Athena had said. Only, that didn't sound so bad.

She felt a slight yearning for the handsome vampire who she hadn't seen in some weeks, wishing he was here.

The dance floor reminded her so much of her dreams of Burk.

Just then, another person collided with her. A muscular body, his arms wrapped around her to steady them both. She looked at his face.

"Liam," she said.

"Rosey..." said Liam, pausing as if struggling to find words. "You're here!"

"What are you doing?"

"Dancing!" said Liam, sounding child-like and excited.

"Shall we dance?"

They moved about together, dancing like little kids, twirling like dervishes. Rosemary was having more fun than she'd had...perhaps ever in her life before. It was glorious. She didn't have a thought or care or worry in her mind, just joyful sensation. Liam spun her around and she noticed another pair dancing. Juniper was there with Dain. They all danced together for a while, simply and playfully. It was all so much like a dream.

Until Rosemary woke.

She was bleary-eyed, looking up at the blue stripes on the ceiling of the tent.

"I have a right headache," she groaned. Then she realised there was another sound coming from the bed next to her. She turned to see Liam, snoring.

CHAPTER
THIRTY-ONE

"Liam, Liam!" Rosemary shook his shoulder.

Liam grunted.

She gave him a little push. "Liam!"

He groaned and rolled over. "Ow. What time is it?"

"I have bigger questions," said Rosemary.

Liam opened his eyes. "What? Rosemary? What are you doing in my bed?"

"This is most certainly not your bed!" Rosemary grumbled.

"Wait, did we—"

"Thankfully, we are both fully clothed," said Rosemary. "If you can call it that." Liam was shirtless, wearing only his jeans, and Rosemary's short shorts and sparkly top didn't leave too much to the imagination.

"Phew!" said Liam. "What a relief."

"Hey!" Rosemary frowned at him.

"No, I just mean...it would be awful if something had happened and I didn't remember it. Wait...what are you wearing?"

"This is how we were both dressed last night when we were dancing, remember?"

"Dancing? Yeah, that was great."

Rosemary shot him an unimpressed look.

"What? It was great fun."

"At the time, sure. But this is not the kind of situation I should be in."

"Hey, I don't know how we got here, either." Liam raised his hands in innocence. "But I'm sorry, I guess."

Rosemary squinted into the light that was shining through the tent's window. "It was...there was something going on with that music. But I don't know what it was."

"Some sort of spell? Magic of the night?" said Liam.

"Really?"

"I don't know, just riffing."

"Look, you've got to get out of here," said Rosemary. "Before Athena comes back from her friend's tent. I don't want to have to explain this situation."

"Fair enough," said Liam. He sounded slightly disappointed. He sighed in resignation and got out of the bed.

"Oh," he said, pausing at the door of Rosemary's temporary bedroom. "I feel like I'm supposed to say something."

"Just goodbye," said Rosemary.

"See you later, I guess," said Liam.

"Bye, Liam."

Rosemary waited until he'd left the tent and then headed towards the bathroom for a shower. On second thought, hearing the sound of ocean waves in the distance, she decided this would be a good time for swim – something a little more refreshing to really wake up her groggy brain. The thought of potential danger did cross her mind, but she reassured herself that she was a powerful witch who stared danger in the face. If anyone was up to mischief she wanted to know about it.

She threw on her bathing suit and grabbed a towel. She still had an hour until the market officially opened and the ocean was calling to her.

It didn't take long to get to the beach, which was blissfully quiet at this time of the morning.

The sea was cold to begin with, but as she waded in and her body adjusted to the temperature she embraced the feeling of walking into the cold water. It was calming, soothing...she let go her need for security, the urge to cling to dry land, and dove into the water, immersing herself in the refreshing feeling.

She swam out a little and then floated on her back, feeling the stress and embarrassment of that morning melting away. She even laughed about it. The look on Liam's face was hilarious.

It was certainly something she wasn't going to tell Athena about.

She made her way back towards the shore, but her eyes were drawn to the horizon. Suddenly, there was an eerie aura to the water.

It shimmered, majestic in the morning light. Something clicked in the back of her mind.

"It's so calm. Didn't I hear waves earlier? That can't be right..." she muttered. "I must have imagined it..."

But a cold feeling stayed with her, giving her the urge to run as quickly as she could out of the sea and back to dry land.

By the time she'd gone back to the tent, showered, changed, and arrived at the store, Marjie was already there.

"There you are, my lovely!" she said, giving Rosemary a big hug. "You look like you've gotten a good amount of sun, already."

"I'm not burnt, am I?" Rosemary asked.

"No, just glowing," said Marjie.

"That reminds me. I've got to put some sunscreen on," said Rosemary. "I've been huddling under the shade and I've hardly been out at all in the sun, but I burn so easily with my pale skin."

"How long are you here for?" she asked Marjie.

"I can help all day if you need me."

"I don't want to be any trouble," said Rosemary.

"Nonsense, it'll be fun."

"That's good," said Rosemary. "We might need you. Things have been...odd."

"What's going on, dear? You sound worried."

Rosemary explained about the incidents the night before with the opening ritual and the unusually mesmerising music, noting Marjie's face crinkling with worry.

"We'll sort it out, dear," said Marjie reassuringly. "We always do."

"Thanks, Marjie. Anyway, I thought I might go along to the high noon Summer Solstice ritual today."

"All that pomp and ceremony!" said Marjie. "Count me out. You go along and I'll mind the store. Enough said."

Rosemary smiled warmly. "Thank you."

"There you are!" said Athena, arriving at the store. She also seemed to be glowing. "I was looking for you at the tent. What happened last night? I hardly heard from you."

"I was trying to keep the telepathy to a minimum," said Rosemary.

Athena smirked. "Oh yes, it was good night then?"

"A bit of a mixed bag, I think," said Rosemary.

She filled Athena in on the situation with the child vampire, and Athena gave her the other minor highlights of her evening.

"Nothing happened after you went back to camp with your friends?" Rosemary asked.

"Nothing of note," said Athena. "We just kind of hung out."

"That's something," said Rosemary. "A nice quiet time with friends is notable in my book."

"Well, Felix was there and somehow got tipsy from one gulp of wine, so it was hardly quiet. What about you? What happened after the whole situation with Geneviève?"

"Err— well..." Rosemary felt distinctly awkward. "There was this funny music and everyone seemed to dance. It was a lot of fun, but I can't help thinking it was magically instigated."

"Party magic!" Athena said. "Sounds grand."

"It wasn't quite as good as you'd think," said Rosemary. "It made people a little bit weird."

"But you enjoyed yourself at the time? No regrets, I hope?" There was a slight lilt in Athena's voice.

Rosemary cleared her throat and got busy wiping down the counter. "None to speak of," she muttered.

It was true. She didn't do anything that she regretted, at least not that she could remember.

The night had become a sort of glorious haze.

"You don't think it's messing with your memory?" Athena asked.

"I certainly hope not," said Rosemary. "I've had quite enough of that already, though it's true I don't remember getting back to the tent."

"What do you think it all means?" Athena asked. "The explosion of stones and the disappearances and the weird music..."

"Such an odd collection of occurrences," said Marjie, tutting.

"I think you're right about the box, at least," said Rosemary.

"Great, just what I wanted to be right about," Athena grumbled sarcastically.

"Better to know," said Marjie, carrying a tray of tea and treats she'd somehow whipped up around to the front of the chocolate store and serving some for each of them.

"Thanks," said Rosemary. "Tea is exactly what I need."

"If only we had somewhere more comfy to sit around the stall. I could go back to the tent a fetch a lounger, I suppose."

"Say no more!" Marjie reached into her large orange handbag and pulled out several small boxes. She set them on the ground and a moment later a sun umbrella, several loungers, and a paddling pool appeared.

"Brilliant!" said Athena.

Marjie beamed. "Just what the doctor ordered. Take a seat and let's see how much of this we can figure out."

They spent the bulk of the morning doing exactly that. They took turns at serving customers and spent the rest of the time sitting around and drinking tea and trying to figure out the mystery.

Several clearly mundane people approached the store from time to time, asking for the "special chocolate".

Rosemary had laughed and asked them what kind of special they were after, selecting carefully crafted mood-enhancing confectionery that she thought would best suit their personalities and cause the least chance of negative side effects.

"I feel like some kind of drug dealer," she said.

Athena laughed. "At least if the cops nab you, they won't find any traces of narcotics or anything. And these chocolates are seriously good!"

Marjie chortled.

"Are you sure about that?" said a voice.

They turned to see Detective Neve.

"It's been ages!" Rosemary got up from the lounger to hug her friend.

"I've been keeping busy," said Neve. "Don't you worry."

"That's exactly what worries me," said Rosemary. "The disappearances?"

"I'm afraid so," said Neve with a grim expression. "There have been more."

"Juniper told us yesterday," said Athena.

Neve shot her a strange look. "Oh, did she? Well, I'm afraid that's not the last of it. In two days, half a dozen people have been reported missing along the coastline further north."

"That's awful! Won't the regular authorities start asking questions?" Athena asked.

Neve shrugged. "They think these are all just your standard summer drowning victims. Not that there should be anything standard about that, but it does happen."

"Who's to say they're not?" Athena asked.

"They all have a lot of similar circumstances," said Neve. "That's the alarming thing. They've been seen wandering into the sea with their clothes on, had been acting strange, they wouldn't normally go swimming, that kind of thing."

"It does sound uncomfortably familiar," said Rosemary.

"At least they're not being murdered," said Athena.

Neve sighed. "Well, what it does mean is that the Coast Guard are doing overtime, up and down these beaches all over the region. If there are dangers out there then they're at risk too."

"That doesn't sound good," said Marjie.

Neve nodded. "And while they're not being murdered, they do seem to be kind of missing something when they come back."

"Not just their memories?" Rosemary asked.

"It's hard to say," said Neve. "Losing a great big chunk of your memory is like losing yourself."

"Tell me about it!" said Rosemary.

"But at least you could function, Mum, despite the weird meddlings of the fae."

"And my own grandmother!" said Rosemary glumly. "But yes, you're right. Compared to these people, I was very lucky."

"It might come back though," said Athena.

Rosemary smiled at her daughter. "After this is over, we can see what we can do to help them, magically. Una will have some ideas. Her tonic worked a treat."

"Speaking of Una, have you seen her?" Neve asked.

"No. Why is that?" said Rosemary.

"I was sure she was supposed to be here. The apothecary shut up for the summer..."

"Is this something you wanted to ask her about, dear?" said Marjie.

"I was going to ask her about memory as a matter of fact. And a couple of other matters."

"Well, if we see her we'll tell her to find you," said Athena.

Neve gave a strained smile. "Thanks. I best be off."

"Oh!" Marjie cried, startling them. "This is me!" She raised her hand in the air.

"What's you?" Rosemary asked.

"I hear the music starting time for the Claddagh dancing! I'm off!"

Marjie jumped out of the lounger and pranced around.

Rosemary laughed.

"Reminds me of Galdie!" Marjie crowed. "Are you okay if I take my break now?"

"Of course." Rosemary grinned. "Go and have fun!"

As Marjie skipped away towards the sound of the jaunty music, three familiar druids approached the chocolate store.

"You don't look too happy to see us," said Catriona. "And I don't blame you."

"It's not you I have a problem with," said Rosemary, glaring at Mayon.

"I'm so sorry," he said, hanging his head.

"Maybe we shouldn't have approached," Cat continued. She

was wearing relatively normal clothing for a druid. In fact, they all were.

"I barely recognised you," said Athena.

"Was there something you wanted?" Rosemary asked.

"We were actually just wandering along and the chocolates looked really good..." said the dark haired man named Colla. "And then we saw you and we thought...Oh, well I don't think we had time to think actually."

Cat looked at him, unimpressed. "We'll just be going."

"No, wait," said Athena. "I have some questions."

"Yes, we do have some questions," said Rosemary. "Now that I think about it..."

"What do you want to know?" said Cat. "Ask away."

"What do you know about magical sea creatures?" Athena asked.

"Any kind in particular?" asked Catriona.

"Kind of...sentient ones that can do magic, I think."

"You mean like the merrow?" Colla asked.

"Not necessarily," said Athena. "I mean, like any that would make people wander into the ocean or leave pink shells in their pockets or maybe have a strange effect on people...spellbinding? Isn't that the word you used, Mum?"

"Something like that," said Rosemary.

"Sounds to me like sirens," said Mayon. "But you don't hear much about them these days. They haven't been seen in a long time. My old grandpa used to tell me tales."

"The typical ones?" Rosemary asked. "Sailors at sea?"

"And the like," said Mayon.

"What happened to them then? Why haven't people heard of them for a long time?" Athena asked.

"The witches took care of them," said Catriona. "Forbade them from interfering with people. Sent them away from all land. They keep to themselves now. In the deep."

"I see," said Rosemary. "Well, thanks for the intel."

"We'll be on our way then," said Cat.

Rosemary smiled. "I don't mind selling you some chocolates." They ordered several varieties of truffles, and as Rosemary was packaging them up she had another thought. "What are you actually doing to protect us? If that's going on...I'm curious."

"Just keeping an eye out at your house and the festival in general," said Colla. "But it's not just to do with you. There have been strange happenings."

"Tell me about it," said Rosemary. "Anything you can share?"

Colla shrugged. "People going missing, strange sounds coming from the ocean...You probably know more than we do."

Rosemary shook her head. "Your guess is as good as mine at this point, but keep us updated if anything else happens."

"Very well," Catriona said and off they went.

"Odd kind of people, aren't they?" said Rosemary. "And what's this about strange sounds coming from the ocean?"

"I don't know, but Mervyn might," said Athena. "As for the druids, I kind of like them...aside from that weird abduction thing."

"So what do you think?" Rosemary asked.

Athena's brow furrowed. "Could magic sea creatures be initiating some kind of enchantment? Sorry, that came out garbled. I mean – could it actually be sirens?"

"Maybe getting through whatever magic was put in place," Rosemary suggested.

"Yes. Or maybe somebody is sort of imitating them."

"Those are both clever guesses," said Rosemary.

"I'm afraid all we've got is clever guesses at the moment, isn't it?" said Athena.

"I wish there was more." Rosemary caught a glimpse of Juniper down the other side of the market lane, talking to a man in a fedora and a three piece suit. She wasn't looking their way, so Rosemary pointed her out to Athena.

"Do you think we could ask her? See if she knows anything else?"

"She's *your* friend," Athena said. "But what if she's behind all this?"

"I hope not." Rosemary chuckled. "She may have dragged your father into it."

Athena shuddered. "Heaven forbid. But, seriously! She could be some kind of mastermind."

"Don't be silly," said Rosemary. "Juniper clearly takes her job seriously. She cares about this festival going well. I doubt she'd be cooking up all sorts of mayhem, creating more messes to deal with. Who would do that?"

"But it's a perfect cover," said Athena. "Think about it. She might have been hired by Elamina and the other Bloodstones as well. She's some sort of double or triple agent...or maybe she has other loyalties?"

"Who knows with Juniper," said Rosemary. "Neve said she's always danced to the beat of her own music. But I'd like to think she's not completely evil."

CHAPTER
THIRTY-TWO

The drumming started just before midday. Rosemary and Athena said goodbye to Marjie at the chocolate stall and followed the beat, summoning all who wanted to attend the noon Summer Solstice ritual. They slowly climbed back up the hill. On the way, they watched as dancers in bright coloured drapey dresses and shawls whirled around in some kind of half-synchronised, half-improvised choreography.

"That looks like fun," said Athena, grinning at her mother. "Was that you last night?"

"I was just as graceful."

Athena laughed.

"Where are your friends today?" Rosemary asked.

"They should be coming here, actually," Athena replied. "I said I'd meet them."

"I'll let you know if I see any of them."

"Thanks, Mum."

They continued up the hill. Hundreds of people gathered all

around and it was hard to see what was going on, let alone find Athena's friends.

"I need to get closer," Rosemary said. "How am I supposed to figure out what's going on with my devious cousin and the ancient vampire brat if I can't even see?"

"Come on, then." Athena pulled Rosemary by the hand and they gently pushed their way through the crowd, rousing only a few annoyed glances.

Eventually, they made their way to the standing stone circle where the proceedings were already underway.

"Looks like we missed some of the pomp and ceremony Marjie was complaining about," Athena whispered. "Look, there's Elamina."

This time, their cousin wore a bright flaming red and yellow cloak and a crown that looked as if it were made of fire. The clearly magical flames danced above her head.

"She's no shrinking violet," said Rosemary.

Elamina walked silently into the centre of the circle, raising her arms in the air.

"That should be you," Athena said.

Rosemary laughed. "Yeah, thanks. I think I'll pass the theatrics over to people who care about them, though it is a pretty cool outfit."

They watched as Elamina began a musical chant.

Energy seemed to rise in the centre of the circle, swirling around in the air.

"What do you think she's doing?" Rosemary asked in an urgent whisper. "Is it evil?"

Just then, a loud shout rang through the air. Heads turned towards the voice as a man burst through the circle.

"Stop!" he cried. "This is all wrong."

Elamina did not look impressed and Rosemary couldn't help but enjoy the moment. "This is the second time she's been interrupted while doing her special thing."

"Shhh," Athena said. "Listen. It's Mervyn!"

Rosemary squinted into the bright sunlight to see that the rather tall man in a striped pink shirt was indeed their local ice cream merchant. "What's he doing here?"

Everyone looked around, confused.

"Whatever you're doing," he bellowed, "you've got to stop it! You're calling more of them in, making them anxious, making them more active."

"Who? What are you talking about?" said one of the druids.

Mervyn clenched his fists in frustration. "It's the sirens!"

There was a murmur of laughter. "Someone's off his rocker," muttered the old bearded druid nearest Rosemary. "We haven't seen the likes of sirens in a hundred years or more."

Several of the druids stepped forward to lead Mervyn away.

"Wait!" he cried. "You've got to stop. Cancel the festival! More people will go missing – it could get so much worse!"

There was more laughter. "Was that some kind of skit?" a woman next to Rosemary asked.

"Clearly a mundane visitor off his rocker," said an older man.

"I've got to go after him," said Athena.

They fumbled and pushed their way around to the part of the circle where Mervyn was being led away. He shook off the druids, who left him, satisfied that he was no longer trying to disrupt the proceedings.

"Nobody listens," Mervyn said as they approached. "Athena, you believe me, don't you?"

"I'm afraid so."

"The problem is nobody else seems to," said Rosemary.

"At least I have two witches on my side. I suppose that's something."

"What did you find out?" Athena asked.

"I went out to sea."

"As a merman?" Athena asked.

"In my merrow form, yes. As soon as I get into the sea, I start to transform. It's automatic."

"I'd love to see that!" said Athena.

Mervyn shot her a disapproving glance, as if it was a highly inappropriate thing to say.

"Sorry."

"Never mind that," said Rosemary. "What did you find at sea?"

"Well, I went deep. Found some key contacts of mine. They said things have been strange this summer. They felt calls."

"Calls?"

"Yeah, sort of like sonar – the way whales communicate – I suppose."

"What does that mean?" Rosemary asked.

Mervyn looked grim. "Someone has been awakening the sirens."

"Awakening them?" said Athena. "I thought they were just banished from land and lived deep in the ocean."

"The deepest ocean," said Mervyn. "Slowly going about their lives in a dream-like state, as if they'd forgotten all about humans. That was the powerful magic that the witches used. It sent them away and created much more safety for ships and people along the shorelines."

"But now somebody is calling them back?" Rosemary asked. "Waking them up from their trance."

"It seems so."

"That's what Mayon suggested," Athena muttered. "He's one of the druids."

Mervyn looked hopeful. "Druids are powerful and organised, at least, in a manner of speaking. If you can convince the druids, then we might be able to do something to stop them. I'm not sure who is summoning them, but I know it's connected to whatever's going on at this festival."

Athena gave her mother a meaningful look. "Not Juniper..."

"Possibly Juniper?" Rosemary said. "I don't know. But I wouldn't be surprised if my cousin was involved in this. Especially after that bloody Beltane fiasco."

"What can be done to send them back?" Athena asked.

Mervyn shook his head. "It's not my kind of magic. You witches would have a better idea than me. Maybe the druids too. I suspect they helped with the initial banishment. There's been an accord between the witches and druids for a long time, you see. That's why they celebrate the solstices together."

"If only we had treaties with all magical folk and they stopped being harsh to each other." Rosemary was thinking of the fae, vampires, and werewolves, who were so misunderstood.

"Maybe one day we will," said Mervyn. "But right now people's lives are at stake. Diplomacy can wait."

"Not just their memories?" Rosemary asked.

"I'm afraid," said Mervyn, "if the sirens reach full power they will regain their ability to take a lot more than memories. They can take hopes, dreams...My contacts say they can even take the souls of those they entrap and then leave them to die under the sea when their attention wanes."

"Memory loss is starting to look strangely appealing, in comparison," said Rosemary.

Athena grimaced. "We need to figure out what we can do to stop them."

"Well, my guess is that tonight is when everything's going to get weird," said Rosemary. "And I don't mean that in a derogatory sense. I mean it in the mythic sense."

Mervyn gave her a strange look.

"It's the shortest night of the year," Athena said. "We don't have much time to figure this out."

They said goodbye to Mervyn. He seemed to have calmed down a little at least, with the promises of trying to get the druids on side.

"Where do you think we can find our druid friends?"

"They're watching us all the time, aren't they?" Rosemary said. "A note pinned to our tent might do it."

"Okay, great," said Athena. "But anyone could find it. Even Elamina might deign to stoop that low. Wait a minute. What about the post?"

"Post?" Rosemary said.

"Yes, you know, the Postal Service. "That little office in the market not far from your stall."

"I didn't see that," said Rosemary. "Mind you, I haven't looked at much else at all in the market."

"It's a magical post," Athena continued. "But don't tell that to the mundane folk. You send a letter and the post is delivered to whoever it's for."

"That sounds perfect," said Rosemary. "If it's not corrupt."

"It's worth a try," said Athena. "Plus, we can always be slightly cryptic."

They made their way back to the market, debating over whether it would be better to leave the festival altogether for safety reasons. Rosemary was starting to think so, but Athena was firmly against. Whether out of a strong sense of social responsibility, or too much taste for the excitement of danger, Rosemary wasn't entirely sure.

"Here it is," said Athena, gesturing to what appeared to be a miniature old fashioned post office.

"Do we go inside?" Rosemary asked.

"No. Not unless you've got a parcel. Look, here's the letter writing station on the side." She gestured to a bench stacked with envelopes.

Rosemary stepped forward and picked up a pen and a slightly-crumpled envelope. "Okay. What do we write?"

"We address it to the druids."

"Just the druids?"

Athena picked up another pen and a piece of paper. "We should send it to Catriona."

"Hmmm...Catriona the druid. Do you think that'll be enough? I don't know her last name."

"If it's magical enough," said Athena, "maybe that will work. Maybe put the other one on there too. What's he called? Colla?"

"Alright then, to Catriona and Colla, the druids."

"What should we write inside?" Athena asked.

Rosemary laughed. "Please come and pick up any sirens behaving badly?"

Athena sighed and began writing. "Let's say: urgent message from the Thorns. Your help is required. The creatures we spoke of in our conversation earlier are to blame for the recent disappearances. We have it on good authority. Rally the forces. See what you can do to help."

"Only slightly cryptic," said Rosemary. "Nice. I like it."

Athena sealed the envelope and handed it to Rosemary.

Rosemary raised her eyebrows. "What do we do with it?"

"Put it in the box, of course. Maybe visualise it going to the intended recipients."

"You sound so formal and fancy." Rosemary turned and noticed an old fashioned red post box right next to her. "Was it there the whole time?"

"Yes," said Athena. "Sometimes it's not magic. It's just our brains playing tricks on us."

"Indeed."

CHAPTER
THIRTY-THREE

Athena exited the tent that evening feeling as prepared as she'd ever be for mystical, magical, mayhem.

She was dressed in slightly more clothing than she had been in the last couple of days, if only because it offered more options for hiding the various enchantments and concoctions that she brought up before leaving home, just in case.

She was followed out of the tent by Elise, Felix, Ash, Deron, Sam, and Rosemary. They were all equally prepared to find sirens, however that was done...or whatever else they encountered along the way.

"Where do we go?" Rosemary asked.

"The dancing," said Athena. "That's where the energy is. Didn't you say that's where you heard that entrancing music last night?"

Rosemary gulped and nodded. Athena looked at her mother. It had taken a lot of convincing for Rosemary not to make them leave the festival altogether and not to revert to her old over-protective instincts.

In the end Athena's iron will had prevailed on the one condition that if anything got truly dicey she would steer clear. Athena threatening to run away from home may also have been a contributing factor.

Rosemary was not keen on Athena's friends joining them either. But they'd all been at the tent by the time the Thorns had returned after saying goodbye to Marjie at the chocolate stall. And by the time Rosemary and Athena had filled all the teens and the parents in on the goings on, they were all determined to help if they could.

Fleur had gone off on reconnaissance to try and see what her family might know about sirens, and Deron's dad was staying back at the base camp to be a safe haven if anyone needed to return.

Athena listened to the music as they neared the dance floor...the wavering sound of the fiddle against the deep bass. She felt a lightness come over her. The fear and doom and foreboding seemed to lift a little and she wondered if that was just the ordinary magic of music or if a siren song had already begun.

She looked at Rosemary.

"Is this what you heard last night?"

"No," Rosemary said. "This is like how it was before."

"Okay."

"Let's dance!" said Felix, taking Athena's hand and spinning her around. She looked across to Elise, who waved her away.

"Have fun. I have the next one."

Athena beamed at her. The friends all danced together, taking turns at spinning each other around.

Rosemary seemed to have wandered off, deeper into the dance floor.

Athena was slightly glad she didn't have to watch her mother flail around like a mad hippie. She was spared that embarrassment, at least.

After half an hour of dancing, she felt thirsty and wandered across to a refreshment station for some punch. As she stood there sipping the pink and refreshing drink, another familiar face emerged from the crowd.

It was Finnigan and he was looking right at her.

Athena felt her rage boil up.

Not him again. I can't have him ruining this night.

She looked around for Elise, wondering what her reaction would be. She could see her familiar blue hair off to the side of the dance floor.

Athena quickly gulped down her drink and crossed back towards Elise. "Let's go," she said, grabbing her hand.

"Why? What's going on?" Elise asked. "Are you in danger?"

"Not...exactly," said Athena, trying to pull Elise away.

"Athena, talk to me," said Elise.

"I don't want to ruin your night."

Someone stepped in front of them, blocking their path.

"Fancy seeing you here," said Finnigan.

Athena's heart sank. "This was exactly what I was trying to avoid."

"What's going on?" Elise said. "Why are you even here?"

"Just having fun," said Finnigan. "Dancing, enjoying the festivities."

"Stay away from us," said Athena. "This is harassment. You'll be expelled from school."

"Who needs school when there's a party?"

"Are you on the cream or something?" Athena glared at him.

Elise gave her a tense look. "Let's just go."

They began to walk away. But then a strange sound began to beam through the music. A kind of blissful hum.

Athena felt as if she was melting slightly, but in a pleasant way. A smile split over her face.

"Now why would you want to go?" said Finnigan. "The party's just starting."

CHAPTER
THIRTY-FOUR

"Stay vigilant," Rosemary muttered to herself.

She made a show of dancing while paying close attention to the crowd as people twirled and boogied around her. Everything seemed to be perfectly normal.

The beat picked up and Rosemary danced faster, while still keeping an eye out on the goings on around her. The music sounded familiar, as if she'd heard it in one of the dreams. The ones she'd had leading up to summer.

She felt a pang of yearning for Burk and wondered when he'd come back to Myrtlewood. She pushed those thoughts out of her mind.

"Focus, Rosemary," she said to herself.

She caught a glimpse of Liam across the floor but tried to keep a distance from him this time, at least.

Rosemary raised her arms above her head as she danced and accidentally smacked somebody as she did so.

"Oh, sorry," Rosemary said, then recognised the woman she'd hit. "Una, you're here!"

"Of course. We're having a brilliant time!" Una's long, brown hair was out, flowing around her as she swayed to the music. She wore a paisley purple and green dress that reminded Rosemary of the sixties, though it was a more modern design, not that there was time to think about fashion.

"What's wrong?" Una asked. "You've got quite a serious look on your face."

"Detective Neve was looking for you earlier."

"Me?" said Una. "What have I done?"

"No, nothing," Rosemary assured her. "It's just...you've heard about the disappearances?"

"The people going missing? There's been surprisingly less gossip than usual. I suppose adults aren't as interesting as children. Besides everyone just assumes they've drowned."

Rosemary nodded. "Well, they've come back...some of them anyway, with their memories impaired. I think Neve was wanting to know if you have anything that could help."

"I can try, but I'm a little busy right now." Una smiled and spun around.

"So am I," said Rosemary.

"But from the look on your face it doesn't look like you're busy having fun, which is a little bit tragic."

"Not exactly fun," said Rosemary. "Something's going on at this festival. Do you know anything about sirens?"

"Nothing in particular. Are they causing trouble?"

"I'm afraid so," said Rosemary. "Warn everyone you know to be vigilant. It's not just the sirens though. I'm pretty sure there's some serious organised magical crime going on. Including the same group that attacked our house when we first arrived in Myrtlewood."

"Not the Bloodstones?"

Rosemary nodded. "I think they're trying to get their power back."

"That's not good at all. I'd better go and warn Ashwyn."

"You haven't seen Juniper around at all?"

"Juniper? No, I assume she'd be quite busy."

"You're right," said Rosemary.

Una gave Rosemary a strange, startled look. "You don't think she has anything to do with this?"

"I'm hoping not, but I thought I'd better update her, at any rate...see if she knows anything that we don't."

"I'll let you know if I see her. I'd better go." She gave Rosemary quick hug and disappeared into the crowd.

Just that moment, the most delightful sound rolled across the dance floor.

Rosemary felt her body swaying involuntarily. She felt her fear dissolving. Surely there were no problems here.

Everything was so...delightful.

She danced and swayed with the crowd, enjoying the movement as the lights beamed down in captivating patterns.

There was a feeling almost like a wave washing over her.

The energy spoke to her.

The sea, it seemed to say. *The sea...the sea.*

Everyone turned at once in the direction of the ocean.

Rosemary felt a craving wash over her. The only thing she wanted in that moment was to go for a swim.

It seemed that everyone simultaneously had the same idea. The crowd all began to move, dancing in a liquidous fashion, towards the ocean.

Everyone was moving down the pathways of the festival like rolling waves.

They reached the shore – thousands of people – far more than had just been on the dance floor – all assembled there and stepped slowly into the water.

Rosemary felt the tiny rolling waves as they rushed over her feet. She giggled at the tickling sensation.

Such a beautiful night. Such a beautiful feeling. The experience of a lifetime.

Nothing was holding her back. Nothing was stopping her.

She waded deeper, deeper into the water, but something interrupted her bliss.

Somebody was shaking her.

"Rosemary! Rosemary!"

She turned to see Burk. And it felt as if she was waking up from a beautiful dream into a horrible nightmare.

"Are you...real?" She reached out to touch her face.

"What's going on? Rosemary, you all seem to be sleepwalking into the sea."

"What?" Rosemary came to her senses and realised she'd been enchanted again without even knowing it.

"Athena!" she said.

Burk frowned in concern. "I'll look for her."

"I'll find her," said Rosemary. "I have various means."

She called out to Athena in her mind, but there was no sound. Rosemary started rummaging in her pocket for the half-egg-shaped thing that Juniper had given her, her hoping that it wasn't some kind of elaborate trick.

"Tell me everything I need to know," Burk said. "What's going on here?"

"Sirens!" said Rosemary.

"Of course."

"Wait, why are you immune?"

"I'm hardly a living human," said Burk.

"Well, I'm a witch," said Rosemary.

"Which is probably why you have some immunity. You seem coherent, at least after I snapped you out of it."

"What about everyone else?"

"There'll be various degrees of resistance to the charms."

Rosemary shot Burk a suspicious look. "You seem to take this all rather matter of factly. A lot of people didn't believe that it could be sirens."

"I've been around a long time," said Burk. "And I'd already suspected as much, considering how everyone is acting."

"It doesn't make sense, though," said Rosemary. "Unless..." She looked up towards the hill to see lights flashing. "This must be some kind of distraction from the Bloodstones. They're trying to divert everyone away. Wait, I know where to go."

"Go then!" said Burk. "I'll sort this out."

"How?"

"I'll call in a vampire Code Seventeen."

"What does that mean?"

"Rallying – in case of a disaster – for the sake of the public good."

"I had no idea vampires did that sort of thing."

"I told you we weren't all evil...a number of times actually. Anyway, now's not the time for explanations. You go. Do what you need to do. We will take care of these people."

Burk darted away as quick as lightning, and Rosemary started running back towards the shore.

The egg device Rosemary had managed to retrieve from her pocket felt like it was pulling her in a particular direction, hopefully towards Athena, though her teen hadn't answered her phone or responded to Rosemary's text. She also hadn't responded to her telepathically or tried to reach out.

Rosemary dreaded the silence could mean her daughter wasn't

conscious. But then again, perhaps it was just the siren song inter-rupting the frequencies. Athena must still have had her half of the egg.

In fact, the egg seemed to be leading Rosemary towards the other destination she had in mind.

THIRTY-FIVE

Athena danced and swayed to the vibration of the music. It almost felt like thicker sweeter air which wrapped around her. All her cares had faded, and now she hoped it never ended.

She'd never known such bliss.

She felt someone take her hand and looked up to see a boy.

"Finnigan," she said.

There was something in the back of her mind, an inharmonious note, when she saw him. But he smiled at her. "Spin for me, Athena."

She spun around, enjoying the sensation of her body as she moved around.

A scream rang through the air. She looked towards it to see a girl, a blue haired girl. A familiar, beautiful, wonderful, blue haired girl whose smile had the power to make Athena's heart sing.

Only, instead of smiling, her face looked horrified. "Athena, stop! Snap out of it."

"W—what?"

"What are you doing?"

Athena looked around and started to see clearly.

"Oh my good gracious Bridget. What's happened?" Elise whispered. "The spell of the sirens."

"It's beautiful, isn't it?" said Finnigan.

"Oh, shut up," said Elise.

"Yeah. Get out of here."

"You know," said Finnigan with a faraway look in his eyes, "I think I might just go to the sea. I feel...a wave...pulling me."

All of a sudden, all heads on the dance floor turned abruptly in the direction of the ocean.

A slow, dancing, stampede began to move.

"Here!" Elise said, grabbing Athena's hand and pulling her out of the way, off to the side of the dance floor.

"I think my mother might be in there," said Athena, trying to call out to Rosemary with her mind.

"Where are they going? Wait, why aren't you affected?"

Elise looked slightly guilty. "I didn't want to say anything before. And neither did Mum...Sirens are kind of like nymphs. Our heritage is very similar. I suspect that's why."

"I wouldn't have judged you," said Athena. "I know you're not like that. I mean, I don't know anything else about sirens. So maybe I shouldn't judge them either. But this does not look good."

Elise smiled. "Glad you don't think I'm some kind of evil creature."

"Never," said Athena, pulling Elise into a hug.

Then she closed her eyes and concentrated on Rosemary.

Mum! she called out. *Listen to me. Can you hear me?*

All she got in return was static.

"Crap!" said Athena. "My telepathy isn't working. They must be jamming the airwaves with their alluring tunes."

"What's it like?" Elise asked as the crowd continued to sway and dance as they walked, as if mesmerised.

"What?"

"Being under their spell. You were kind of lost there for a moment."

"It was amazing." Athena's eyes were shining, her voice was soft. "I forgot everything. Even who I was...pretty much."

"That doesn't sound amazing to me," said Elise, looking around at the zoned-out people walking past them in procession. "It sounds terrible. Like you've been dosed with something, against your will."

"Terrible but also kind of joyful, fun...free."

"What are we gonna do?" Elise asked. "Should we could go back to base camp and ask Deron's dad?"

"I don't even know where our other friends are," said Athena. "Probably in this heaving mess."

There was a buzzing in Elise's pocket. She lifted out her phone. "Mum's calling." She wandered away from the music to take the call and Athena followed, only catching snippets of the conversation.

Elise finally hung up.

"I have to go back to camp. Mum's there. Apparently, our wonderful shifter friends weren't affected and they had to carry Sam and Ash, kicking and screaming, all the way back to camp and sober them up."

"Okay," said Athena. She hesitated.

"Are you going to come with me?"

"I've got to find my mother," Athena replied.

"Will you be okay?" Elise asked. "Just a minute ago you were..."

"I'll be fine now," said Athena, feeling sure of herself. "You snapped me out of whatever spell this is. Thank you."

"I thought so...well, go! Be safe!"

"I will," said Athena.

Elise turned in the direction of camp.

"Wait a minute," said Athena. "Elise, before you go, I hope you don't think anything bad about what happened before. I don't even really remember, but I know Finnigan was there, and you screamed and..."

Elise shook her head. "I know you didn't mean it. None of these people meant to do anything that they just did. And Finnigan...he was just trying to take advantage of you. He's at fault. It's just...it wasn't a good experience."

"I'm sorry."

"For what?"

"Sorry you had to go through that."

Elise smiled a sad smile. "Just another opportunity for me to work on my insecurities, isn't it?"

Athena pulled her close and kissed her. "I'll see you soon," she said and then began running in the opposite direction.

At first she thought to go to the sea to seek out her mother, knowing Rosemary had been somewhat susceptible to the siren song from the night before, though she didn't know any of the details of what that might have entailed and probably didn't want to either.

Athena sighed as she waded through the thousands of people. It was hopeless.

Then she heard a humming and a chanting and the sound of drums. Only, it wasn't coming from the dance floor.

It was coming from the hill.

Maybe Rosemary was there, or maybe she wasn't, but something was going down at the sacred stone circle, something bad. Athena could feel it in her gut. Whatever it was, somebody needed to stop it. She began running as quickly as she could.

CHAPTER
THIRTY-SIX

Rosemary was in such a hurry she didn't even see the person coming towards her in the dark until they'd bumped right into each other.

"Watch it!"

"Athena?"

"Mum!"

"Where are you going?"

"There!" said Athena pointing towards the hill. "Where were you going?"

"I was looking for you, actually," said Rosemary. "This egg thing works pretty well."

"That's good to know. I totally forgot about mine."

"I noticed you didn't check your cell phone either," Rosemary grumbled.

"Flat battery. Not much charging around here."

They looked up at the hill where electricity sparked in the sky.

"Except maybe those very sacred rocks," Athena added.

Rosemary giggled. All of a sudden the situation seemed hilarious. Athena joined in as well. Then they both let out a long, slow breath at the same time.

"So the sea thing is a diversion," Rosemary said. "They must be working together. This whole thing is too well planned."

"I figured that," said Athena. "But..."

They looked back towards the ocean to see waves rising up and strange green lights.

"All those people..." said Athena.

"The vampires have some kind of student army style response to a crisis. Burk's rallying the troops right now to try and save all those zombie blissed-out people wandering into the sea."

"That's new, and also excellent," said Athena. "But I don't like their chances."

Rosemary looked back to see the waves rising even higher above the crowd. They were hovering there, defying gravity, but it was a disaster waiting to happen. She had to squint to concentrate and keep her bearings through the intense sound of the captivating music. While at first it had been beautiful, it was now just irritating her.

That's good...cling to the irritation. It's better than getting spellbound!

"You're right," said Rosemary. "Those waves are a disaster waiting to happen. This might be a distraction from whatever is going down on that hill, but it's working. We'd better go!"

They raced back towards the beach. The crowd swayed in the shallow water. Burk was nowhere in sight, but Rosemary could see something else. Within the waves themselves, were glowing beings. Their long hair swayed in the water; seaweed draped around their pale, opalescent bodies; their eyes glowed green.

"That's where the sound's coming from!"

"Sirens!" said Athena. "They're beautiful."

"If pond scum is your cup of tea," said Rosemary, loudly enough that she hoped they could hear.

Silvery laughter seemed to dance around them, echoing across the beach.

A woman appeared atop the highest wave, her long blonde hair perfectly dry, her cloak the colour of the sea.

"Lamorna," said Rosemary. "I knew you were some kind of beastie."

Lamorna laughed. "Well, consider yourself bested by a beastie, then." She rolled her eyes.

"You have five seconds to stop all this before—"

"Before what?" said Lamorna. "I have an entire army of sirens, and that's not all..."

She flicked her wrist and out of the ocean rose a dozen huge greeny-blue creatures. They looked to be covered in fur along with seaweed, and their ears were a lot like– "Sea bears!" said Rosemary.

Athena gasped, though it seemed to be more in excitement than fear. She began whispering excitedly. "I can't believe it – they're real! I just want to hug them!"

Lamorna scowled. Clearly the oceanic teddies were not having the desired effect. "They have sharp claws," she muttered. "And they're fast. They could rip your—"

"Sure, sure," said Rosemary. "But you have to admit, they're cute!"

Lamorna raised her arms and the sea bears growled. The sound rumbled across the beach as they began to approach.

"Okay, maybe not so cute," said Rosemary.

"Still a bit cute," said Athena. "Cute and scary."

What are we going to do? Rosemary attempted to communicate telepathically and to her relief she got a reply.

Blast them! Give them everything we've got.

What about all the people? Rosemary asked.

We can target the magic at the sirens and bears, while taking care to push the water away from the people. Hopefully we can buy enough time before Burk and his vampire friends arrive.

Sounds risky, said Rosemary. *But I can't see a non-risky way out of this situation.*

Take my hand. We can bolster each other's magic.

Rosemary held Athena's hand and they stared down Lamorna and the encroaching sea bears.

The siren smirked. "Think you can take us and still save these—"

Rosemary didn't give her a chance to respond. She blasted golden light towards the siren while Athena sent a wave of purple energy towards the bears.

The creatures stumbled backwards, but Lamorna was unaffected. She laughed. "You think you can fight the powerful magic of sirens, bolstered by Neptune?"

Rosemary was taken aback, but Athena's voice broke through to her mind again.

That's it!

What?

Siren magic is like Neptune. It's all a spell...and it's vibrational. I know what might work. My teacher said celestial magic is all about balancing the forces. Every power has an opposite tension. Saturn is the antidote to Neptune.

Rosemary frowned in confusion. *I thought you said Saturn was bad.*

No – it's just hard – groundedness and structure – it's cold hard reality – the wakeup call everyone needs.

Sounds pretty bad.

Athena let out an exasperated sigh. *Come with me!*

She began pulling Rosemary away as Lamorna cackled maniacally.

"But all those people!" said Rosemary when she was sure they were out of earshot.

"I don't like our chances of saving them when the sirens themselves are immune to our magic."

"Where are we going?"

"Over here." Athena pulled Rosemary into a beach DJ hut. It had been abandoned, probably by people who were now standing in the sea, and was pumping out a slow techno beat. "Give me your phone!"

"Why?" Rosemary asked.

"I told you. Mine's flat."

Rosemary shook her head as she rummaged for her phone. "Only if you tell me what this is all about."

"What did I just tell you? What counteracts Neptune?" Athena asked.

"This is no time for a pop quiz."

"No – Saturn!"

"What are you doing?"

"Jamming their frequency!"

Rosemary watched, baffled, as Athena opened the music app and brought up her favourite band. She frowned in disbelief. "Really?"

Athena selected the Saturn album.

"I don't think we have time for..." Rosemary began to protest, but Athena shushed her. She plugged in the AUX cable and turned up the volume. Corrosive heavy metal music blasted through the speakers.

"We need more Saturn energy. Mum, do you still have that onyx in your handbag?"

Rosemary bit her tongue so as not to protest and rummaged through her bag, looking for the black stone Serpentine had mysteriously brought her one day. Surely, if there was meaning in the universe, a cat-delivered crystal associated with Saturn was a sign. "Here!" She held up the small black rock.

"Hold it and concentrate on the energy," said Athena. "I'm going to draw on your power as you do and boost the Saturn resonance."

Rosemary held the stone and focussed. It was quite a small and light object, but its energy was hard and dark and heavy. A lot like Athena's descriptions of Saturn. She felt Athena drawing on her power, a little bit like the sensation of a magic vacuum.

"It's not loud enough," Athena muttered, looking back towards the sirens. "Block your ears, Mum, and stand away from the speakers."

Rosemary did as she was told.

Athena threw on a pair of headphones lying by the mixer. She closed her eyes and sent a wave of barely-visible magic towards the speakers, amplifying them to excruciating levels.

Rosemary watched in awe as the sirens thrashed about, fighting back the sound of Saturn. The people seemed to wake up and look around, confused and scared.

"Run!" Rosemary yelled, but it was barely audible over the music.

Lamorna screamed, but found herself voiceless. The sea bears began to retreat. The huge waves started to shudder.

"Oh no!" she cried out. "They're going to burst."

But just then, another wave seemed to crash in. It was dark and incredibly fast. When Rosemary squinted she could just see that the new wave was made up of people, clad in black and moving at alarming speeds. The vampires swooped in and dragged the people to safety, just as the waves crashed down, coming three-quarters of the way up the beach, lapping at Rosemary's ankles.

"That was amazing!" she cried, hugging her daughter.

"It was rather excellent," said Athena. "Now what?"

"We head up to the top of the hill," said Rosemary, feeling

strangely invigorated. "And see what they were trying to divert us from. Keep a distance, though."

"I'm surprised you're letting me go at all," said Athena.

"Well, you've survived this long," said Rosemary. "I'm sure you can make it at least until the next seasonal ritual."

Athena laughed. "Do you think it really could be Elamina behind this?"

"I guess we'll find out soon enough."

CHAPTER
THIRTY-SEVEN

They made their way quietly, stealthily, up the hill. Rosemary's heart was racing as they approached. Dozens of hooded figures were gathered, but they all faced inwards, making it possible to approach without being seen.

"They must be really confident that their distraction is keeping us occupied," Athena whispered.

"Hopefully the vampires will keep Lamorna from giving them an update. Come on, over here."

She pulled Athena behind a large rock further back from the stone circle.

Rosemary peeked out from behind the rock, scanning the gathered crowd around the sacred stones. "Typical. They're all wearing hoods."

"Do you recognise any of them?" Athena asked quietly.

"I'm pretty sure that's Elamina on the far side," Rosemary whispered. "I can see a little bit of wavy white hair. Not many people have locks like that."

"If so, then you were right," said Athena, sounding almost forlorn.

"You sound like you're getting a little attached to her, aren't you?"

"She is family, of a sort," said Athena.

"Not all family is good family," Rosemary replied.

"Very true. I'll remember that next time we're fighting."

"Oh no," said Rosemary.

"What?"

"There's Juniper." She'd spotted her would-be friend standing a couple of places away from Elamina.

"Sorry, Mum. I know you didn't want her to be evil."

"You win some, you lose some," said Rosemary. "Hey, there are a bunch of druids in the crowd too! Those double-crossing toads!"

"Shift over. I want to see."

They both squished to the side so that Athena could get a better view. Catriona and Mayon were recognisable towards the back of the crowd, despite wearing much darker robes than usual.

Rosemary sighed and whispered, "We thought we could trust them!"

Athena shrugged. "Maybe we were both wrong."

A small hooded figure, who could only be Geneviève, stood in the centre of the circle, waving a long staff in the air. It began to glow and the stones around them hummed, including the one that Rosemary and Athena were standing behind.

"Something tells me this is not good," Athena hissed. "What do we do?"

"There you are," said a voice behind them

Rosemary turned, shocked see Juniper standing there.

Rosemary held up her hands. "Don't hurt us." Her voice wavered.

"Why on earth would I do that?" Juniper asked.

"Err...aren't you involved in all this?" Rosemary waved her hand in the general direction of the crowd.

"Don't be ridiculous," Juniper hissed. "I'm just trying to figure out how to stop it. The druids have kept me informed. We're all on the same team here – us versus the Bloodstones."

"Oh..." said Rosemary, though she was somewhat relieved that the druids might not have been terrible double-crossing toads after all.

"How do we know we can trust you?" Athena squinted at Juniper.

"Suit yourself," said Juniper.

"Alright. What's going on, then?" Rosemary asked. She risked a glance back towards the circle, hoping that Juniper was indeed on their side. "It's not looking good, there's a lot of light and glowing and stuff. I bet that little creature is about to harness some ancient power for her own purposes."

"Sounds about right," said Juniper. "They've been doing a lot of chanting, and it's building up to something, but I'm not sure what. I assume they're harnessing the ancient magic here from the ley lines, along with the energy of the festival and the astrological alignment."

"I hate to say I told you so," Athena whispered, crossing her arms.

"Yes, fine. You were right. I was wrong. But more importantly, what do we do?" Rosemary asked. "Should we just charge in there and blast them?"

"Honestly? That's as good an idea as any," Juniper replied. "Running in and blasting them might at least disperse the magic. They've managed to draw a lot of energy already – not to mention how potent it must be to have brought their leader back in the first place. I thought you'd dusted her."

Rosemary sighed. "So did I...Okay, you wait here, Athena. Juniper, care to join me?"

Juniper gave her a slightly frightened smile. "This is not going to be pretty."

Rosemary held her breath as they began running towards the gathered hooded figures. Rosemary felt slightly reassured that at least her new friend didn't appear to be evil, and that some of the crowd were apparently on her side.

They pushed their way through the assembled group. Just as she reached the inner perimeter there was a blast of purple light. Rosemary watched in horror as Elamina stood forward.

"You!" Rosemary pointed at her cousin.

She was both shocked and also simultaneously vindicated. She'd never trusted Elamina.

"Rosemary?" said Elamina, with a sour expression.

"I knew you were a bad seed, but to team up with the Bloodstones must be a new low. You said they were beneath you! Wait a minute..."

Rosemary looked around the circle for a certain tiny vampire only to see her sprawled out on her back, arms and legs flailing in the air.

"Nice of you to join us, dear cousin," said Elamina.

"But...what's going on?" Rosemary asked.

Elamina looked bored. "We are trying to stop the Bloodstone Society from drawing on ancient power and the celestial alignment, or course."

"But..."

Elamina raised her index finger. "I believe I have this under control." She turned back to the crowd, some of whom were gathering around their tiny leader. "You're all under arrest. Especially you." She pointed at Geneviève.

"How dare you!" Geneviève cried, with a furious expression. "You said you wanted to join us."

Some of the crowd began to disperse, running away into the darkness, though the druids seemed to be going after some of them. Rosemary's heart leapt watching them escape, but others remained, and the druids were doing a good job of keeping them restrained.

Elamina laughed. "How dare I, indeed! How about by the powers in Bermuda, the witching parliament, and I don't know... the Magical Investigations Bureau!"

"Oh, not MIB," somebody near Rosemary groaned.

Elamina clapped her hands and a bunch of black clad figures appeared behind the remaining figures. They held out their hands. Spider webs of light emerged from them, magically wrapping everyone standing there in cocoons of what Rosemary assumed was some kind of magical restraint.

"This one, ma'am?" one of the black clad figures said, gesturing to Rosemary.

"I suppose you can spare her," said Elamina. "Although I do wonder whether there's some kind of charge for interrupting a secret undercover investigation. Obstructing the course of justice or something? Do we have a magical equivalent to that?" she asked the man standing next to her, who happened to be wearing a black top hat and had a twirly moustache.

He shook his head. "Afraid not."

Elamina shrugged. "I suppose it wouldn't look that great for the family anyway. Best we keep this under wraps."

Rosemary coughed. "So you're saying you're now some sort of FBI agent in the magical world?"

Elamina smirked. "Such an imagination you have. No, I was simply helping out the global witching authorities. After all, Mama and Papa do work so hard for them." She pouted.

Athena joined the circle next to Rosemary. "That was unexpected."

They watched as the MIB agents began to teleport the attending crowd, one by one, out of the circle.

"Wait!" Athena called.

"What's that, dear cousin?" Elamina asked.

"Wouldn't it be good to know their identities?"

"All in due course," said Elamina. "But I suppose it wouldn't hurt to remove one or two masks."

Rosemary was sure her palms were itching before the pastel pink mask was pulled down, revealing Despina's sour face.

"I'm not going to speak," she said. "Not even one word."

Rosemary laughed. "That's already nine too many."

One of the MIB officers took off another mask and Rosemary recognised Hyacinth of the charcuterie platter.

"I knew it," Athena muttered. "Glad we didn't eat your food."

Hyacinth smirked. "I wish you did. Losing you meddling witches would make the world a better place."

Rosemary raised her eyebrows. "For evil, maybe."

Athena gasped and Rosemary looked around to see that both Perkins and Ferg were among the group. "You!"

Perkins stuttered. "I...Unhand me! I'm undercover."

Rosemary shook her head in disbelief as Detective Neve made her way into the circle. "It's true," she said. "Perkins thought he might have a chance of catching the bad guys if he was in disguise. Of course, he was sure you were to blame." She looked at Rosemary.

"She's here, isn't she?" Perkins grumbled. "Clearly suspicious."

"And Ferg?" said Athena, her voice strained.

"He was here with me," said Juniper.

"And so am I," said a familiar voice, wrestling free of a druid and removing his own mask.

"Dain?" said Rosemary. "So how many Bloodstones have you

actually caught? I can't believe none of you thought to tell us about your undercover sting! This is appalling. Why didn't you ask us for help? I thought the Thorn magic was supposed to be useful."

Elamina cleared her throat. "It is, and you may recall that I, too am a Thorn. I didn't want to messing everything up as usual!" She laughed coldly. "What's appalling is how you managed to bungle the whole operation anyway. Many of the culprits have escaped."

Rosemary's shoulders slumped and she felt the weight of exhaustion finally catching up with her. "This is not how I expected my evening to go."

CHAPTER
THIRTY-EIGHT

Rosemary and Athena lounged on the couches in the living room of Thorn Manor, with their feet up and a pot of tea between them.

They'd just returned from the festival and brought their things in from the car.

"You're all unpacked, then?" Rosemary asked.

"Sort of," said Athena. "I'll do the rest tomorrow. Partying really takes it out of you."

"I must admit I'm feeling kind of deflated, myself," said Rosemary.

Athena laughed. "You can't be the one to save the day every time."

Rosemary sighed. "I don't like the fact that Elamina was."

"And me," Athena protested. "It was my music that disrupted the siren magic."

"That was clever and impressive." Rosemary smiled "I'm not grumpy about that part at all."

"At least the chocolate stall went well."

"True. I've got a bunch of orders to fill too," Rosemary rubbed her temples to ease the tension. "I just don't like how Elamina came across as so cool and had organised a secret sting operation behind our backs."

"Dad didn't even know she was involved," said Athena. "And neither did Neve, I asked. They were all just pulled in by their magical superiors to help without knowing the details."

Rosemary sighed. "That makes me feel slightly better about being left out of the loop," said Rosemary. "But it still stings that it was all my cousin's doing. Hey, you don't suppose she was the "Thorn" that the druid oracles were meaning, not us? Maybe they should have been protecting Elamina the whole time."

"You might be right," said Athena. "But their called 'ovates' not 'oracles'."

"Whatever..." said Rosemary. "I've had enough divination to last a lifetime, though I must admit, you did a brilliant job on that celestial magic stuff. Who knew astrology could be so useful."

Athena laughed. "And so were you, little Serpentine." She reached down and scratched the kitten behind the ears. "I wonder what Elamina's chart is like. She's so *interesting*."

"Blast her," Rosemary muttered. "If it wasn't for our conniving cousin our summer would have been so much more pleasant."

"Family issues," Athena joked. "You should probably see a counsellor about that. You need a professional."

Rosemary threw a cushion at her. "Maybe you're right."

"I do admit Elamina was pretty awful to you, though."

"As usual," said Rosemary. "Who wouldn't have family issues in these circumstances?"

"Fair enough," said Athena. "She's always so nice to me."

Rosemary groaned. "It was embarrassing, rushing in there like that. I'm going to have a vulnerability hangover for a week at least."

"It's okay, Mum," said Athena reassuringly. "Hardly anyone was there to see it. And many of the ones who were have more important things on their minds while they face some sort of witching trial."

"Thanks for the empathy," said Rosemary, and she meant it.

Her phone buzzed and she checked it. "Finally some good news!"

"What is it?"

"Neve said the new tests came back. Not only is the baby healthy, but it has both her and Nesta's DNA! How cool is that?"

"That's awesome," said Athena. "Isn't magic amazing? I do remember reading something in the folklore about enhancing the fertility with one's beloved."

Rosemary smiled. "That's what Nesta said too, in a rather too cute way, but I didn't think it was possible."

"Our whole lives are somewhat impossible," said Athena, returning the smile. "So what now?"

"We go about our lives in a wonderful, harmonious way. I run my chocolate shop. You go to school, grow up, and have a stable life?"

"Sounds blissfully boring."

"Hey! Don't you go getting an appetite for danger," Rosemary grumbled.

Just then, little Serpentine sprang up onto the couch and nuzzled at Rosemary, who patted her back affectionately.

"Aren't I supposed to be getting a familiar sometime?" Athena asked. "That's what Granny said."

"When you've mastered your powers, or something," said Rosemary.

"I'm sort of learning how to use them," said Athena. "We've been doing a lot of practice. I can even use my telepathy deliberately. What's the hold up?"

"We can share this one," said Rosemary, patting the cat. "Can't we, little Serpentine Fuzzball Thorn?"

"I think she already likes me more than you anyway," said Athena, reaching back over towards the cat, who immediately lost interest in Rosemary and climbed onto Athena's lap instead.

"She seems like a perfectly ordinary cat," said Rosemary, slightly offended.

"You mean aside from bringing us the crystal we needed? Maybe she'll get more interesting as our powers grow," Athena suggested. "But it's not fair. When do I get one?"

The doorbell rang. Rosemary and Athena looked at each other.

They opened the front door to see a short man in a top hat standing there wearing black robes.

"Madam and Mademoiselle Thorn." He bowed.

"Err," said Rosemary. "You're the man from the stone circle, aren't you?"

"Reginald?" said Athena.

Rosemary gave her questioning look.

Athena shrugged. "What? He was at Elamina's cocktail party."

"You didn't tell me that," said Rosemary.

"I didn't recognise him in the dark."

Reginald cleared his throat. "I have something for you."

He held out what appeared to be a parchment scroll bearing a rather old fashioned looking red wax seal. Rosemary eyed him suspiciously. The scroll reminded her of a letter Granny had received from the Bloodstone society at some point back in history.

"A summons," the man said.

Rosemary raised her eyebrows. "A what?"

"From Bermuda," he explained as if this should be obvious.

Rosemary and Athena looked at each other.

"Ahem, hem," Reginald said, clearing his throat. "Excuse me, I forget that you are new to the world of magic. Have you not heard of Bermuda?"

"Something about it," said Rosemary, wracking her brain, but all she could recall was some vague mention of diplomatic postings for snobby people.

"The witching parliament," Reginald explained, furrowing his brow when they did not look impressed. "Most witches would be honoured to receive an invitation of such importance."

He seemed rather miffed.

"Oh," said Rosemary, reaching out and taking it. "Well, thank you..." But before she could decline, he bowed and disappeared in a puff of smoke.

Rosemary coughed and groaned.

"Just what we need," she said. "Something tells me things are about to get *interesting* again!"

EPILOGUE

Detective Constantine Neve yawned as she finished typing up her report on the Summer Festival. It was dark outside the police station and Constable Perkins had gone home hours earlier, leaving her with the bulk of his paperwork.

It was well and truly time for her to be getting home to Nesta who was keen to celebrate their news about the baby. She felt warm and even excited when she recalled the phone call they'd received earlier. The baby was fine, healthy, human... and *hers!*

A smile spread across her face just as her phone started to ring again.

She answered it casually, assuming Nesta was calling.

"Detective Neve?" said the rather stiff voice on the other end.

Neve shook herself and responded in a serious tone. "Yes. How can I help you?"

"This is Chief Leopold from the MIB. We've finished our work at the festival site and wanted to inform you of the situation here."

Neve suppressed a sigh. "Yes, Sir. I assume this is too important to wait until morning."

She steeled herself for bad news.

"You're going to want to hear this, Detective."

"How many casualties were there?" Neve asked. The sirens had led so many people into the water, she was dreading the result.

"Actually," said Leopold, his voice becoming less serious and more excited. "There were none. In fact, the opposite."

"What?"

"All the festival attendees are accounted for."

"Amazing," said Neve, beaming. This was turning into a great news day. "Excellent work, Sir."

"Put that down to your witch friends and the vampire volunteers," said Leopold. "We're simply the cleanup crew."

"But what did you mean by the opposite of casualties?" Neve asked with a curious lilt to her voice.

"That's the puzzling thing," he replied. "We've accounted for two extra people."

"*Extra* people?"

"They weren't festival attendees and aren't from around here at. As far as we know, they shouldn't have been on site."

"That's...well, that's unusual, but surely not a bad thing," said Neve.

"Perhaps not," said Leopold, his voice stilted. "Only...there's something strange about them."

Order Myrtlewood Mysteries book five!

A NOTE FROM THE AUTHOR

THANK you so much for reading this book! I so much fun writing it. I love Myrtlewood with all it's quirky characters and cozy magical atmosphere.

If you have a moment, please leave a review or even just a star rating. This helps new readers to know what kind of book they're getting themselves into, and hopefully builds some trust that it's worth reading!

You can also join my reader list or follow me on social media. Links are on the next page.

ABOUT THE AUTHOR

Iris Beaglehole

Iris Beaglehole is many peculiar things, a writer, researcher, analyst, druid, witch, parent, and would-be astrologer. She loves tea, cats, herbs, and writing quirky characters.

facebook.com/IrisBeaglehole

twitter.com/IrisBeaglehole

instagram.com/irisbeaglehole